CH01464543

MY CHRISTMAS BILLIONAIRE

S J CRABB

MY CHRISTMAS BILLIONAIRE

Can two people who hate Christmas save it?

When billionaire Robert Harvey received several threatening Christmas cards, he called in the professionals to solve the mystery.

However, he never expected Detective Constable Jessica Taylor to be the answer to his prayers.

Like him, she is career driven, abrupt and focused and desires no friends or life outside of her occupation.

They say opposites attract, but kindred spirits are a force to be reckoned with, and Robert is immediately drawn to the feisty detective.

To avoid suspicion, they devise a fake relationship as a cover story, but living in close proximity will prove extremely challenging.

As Jessica delves deeper into Robert's life to find the 'Post-man' she soon discovers that he, or she, is the least of her problems.

Family life is about to collide with their professional one and for two people who hate the festive season, they must step up and make it the most magical one ever before the Postman delivers his promise and makes it their last Christmas.

PROLOGUE

JESSICA

The dark mornings don't help my mood and as I drag my body with a superhuman effort from the warm cosy bed, I curse Winter. My teeth chatter despite the central heating because I turned it down in a vain attempt to economise due to the rising fuel costs. Some call it a crisis. I think it's the end of my world as I know it because to me hell is looking like a place I'm keen to book a flight to because at least it will be hot there.

Grabbing my dressing gown, I head to the shower and hope the water's hot despite this ungodly hour.

I'm not a morning person. In fact, some people say I'm not an afternoon or evening person either, but I'm unconcerned about that. I'm not worried about anything other than striving for excellence and proving that I'm better than everyone else.

As the steam from the shower chases the chill away, I relax a little as my mind powers up and reminds me how important today is. A small tingle of excitement builds inside me as I contemplate what it will bring because, finally, against all the odds, I'm about to step away from the shadows and take on my first solo mission.

1

The vibration from my Apple Watch signifies the allotted two minutes is up and reluctantly I step from the shower and curse my frugality as I wrap the cold towel around my heated skin.

I should be grateful for the cool environment because it makes my regime easier to stick to and ten minutes and three notifications later, I am in my small kitchen, flicking the switch for the kettle, suited and booted as my mother would say and ready to take on the world.

The steam from the kettle is most welcome as I toss the green tea bag into the mug and reach for the jar of vegan muesli that I've grown a liking for. A splash of soya milk makes it edible and as I stir in some natural low-fat yoghurt, I anticipate the next notification in two minutes' time.

Two minutes to eat and fuel my body with just enough to operate without clogging my arteries and diminishing my energy levels before I've even made it to the office.

The excitement that's been building for several days now threatens to play havoc with my mind set because I have programmed myself to stay focused on the only thing that matters to me. My job.

I've worked my way through police training college, endured the horrors of life on the beat and scaled my way through every department to reach the one that was the reason I joined in the first place.

Detective constable Jessica Taylor. A role I have coveted ever since I became addicted to Miss Marple, and Murder She Wrote as a child.

How I longed to solve the crimes of murder most foul and I joined up as soon as I could and the rest is history.

Another vibration tells me to put down my spoon and take up my toothbrush and after a cursory glimpse at my reflection, I am as ready as I'll ever be.

Yes, Jessica Taylor is about to make a name for herself

because today I am going undercover, at least I hope I am because Detective Inspector Ranauld told me I was.

* * *

I DON'T EVEN NOTICE the nip of frost in the air as I stride along the frozen pavements towards the tube station. I don't even see the homeless man cowering in the shop doorway as I pass in a euphoric haze. The fact I see several misdemeanours from a passing cyclist doesn't even register as I consider what the job could be.

Will it be drugs? I wonder how I feel about that. Am I required to infiltrate a drug's ring and be responsible for a haul of millions, saving the streets of London from even more misery and wasted lives? It could be a sex trafficking ring or a heist. Images of the glory I will bask in when I deliver the criminals bang to rights heats my heart as I plod through the commuters on their way to a much less worthwhile job than mine.

Sometimes I wonder if they would gaze at me in awe and nod their heads with respect if they knew who walked among them. I certainly would because I don't do mundane. I don't do the ordinary and my job matters. It's life or death, well death mainly because when you work as a detective, death is just a by-product of a file that opened from nowhere, allowing us to peer inside a dark chasm of pure evil.

Feeling smug, I hang from the metal pole of the tube as it careers through the darkened tunnels, the slightly noxious smell causing me to pull my woollen scarf a little higher to cover my nose. I never make eye contact with anyone on my journey because I have no interest in making friends and actually passing the time of day with the general public. I have only one thing on my mind and that's focusing on my career and making a difference to the cruel, miserable world we inhabit and destroy without thinking of the consequences.

My watch vibrates, and I notice I have achieved the desired number of steps to finalise my morning routine and I breathe a sigh of relief. There will be no falling behind today. Not on the most important day of my life because this is the day all my learning and patience will pay off.

As I push through the revolving door of the station, I keep my eyes lowered because making friends with my colleagues has never been an option. I have no friends, a family I rarely see and only one love in my life. Work!

"Jessica."

Detective Inspector Ranauld greets me as I hover nervously at his office door and the weary look in his eyes tells me that the job is important. I expect he needs my help with an unsolved crime, having tried and failed with my predecessors before me.

He nods towards the seat in front of his desk, and I perch on the edge and look him steadfastly in the eye, waiting for him to deliver my assignment. Part of me hopes it involves some kind of gadget. Something that James Bond would use. A hidden microphone perhaps, or a cleverly disguised stun gun secreted in the body of a fountain pen. Could it be the keys to a super car? I could live with that.

He clears his throat and sighs wearily.

"I have an assignment for you."

My heart starts racing as I struggle to keep my excitement from showing.

His finger taps on a sheaf of papers that I'm guessing are top secret and will test the resilience of my oath of attestation.

"Have you heard of Harvey's?"

"The department store?"

I'm a little surprised because that's not far. In fact, it's a short walk away from where I'm sitting now and he nods, leaning back in his chair as he fixes me with a grim expression.

"What do you know of the owner?"

"Nothing."

I'm blunt because why on earth would I know anything about the person who owns a shop I never set foot in?

He nods and pushes a sheet of paper towards me, and I see the photograph of a man who I've never seen before in my life.

"Robert Harvey. Grandson of Jefferson Harvey, the chairman of Harvey's department store."

"What about him?"

I study the photograph with interest because this man doesn't look like a super villain. In fact, he is rather easy on the eye and I'm guessing it's just another occasion when the suspect turns out to be a big disappointment to the rest of mankind.

"Robert Harvey is the current CEO of the store and has reported several threats made against him."

"What threats?"

"He's been receiving Christmas cards that he's not at all happy about."

"Why? Doesn't he approve of stripping nature's resources to make disposable forms of greeting that relegates nature to tomorrow's trash?"

Inspector Ranauld arches his brow and peers over his glasses, causing me to squirm in my seat.

"Do we have a problem, detective?"

His glare reminds me of his golden rule not to bring personal beliefs into the workplace.

"No sir."

I grace him with a hard stare of my own and he nods, apparently satisfied.

"Good. I need you to be on board with this."

Basking in my own self-importance, I face him with a steely resolve.

"How can I help?"

"You will need to go undercover at the store and try to find out any gossip about him. Who hates him, past relationships, any scandal, that kind of thing?"

"And then?"

"Report back and between us, we'll discover who hates him enough to send those cards."

I'm a little confused because surely this isn't worthy of an actual file in Detective Inspector Ranauld's already bulging filing cabinet. Then, as if he reads minds as well as be the best detective I have ever had the pleasure of working under, he leans forward and lowers his voice.

"We are treating this seriously because Robert Harvey is a powerful man."

"In what way?" I'm confused because as far as I can see, he's just a shop owner.

My superior shakes his head. "We think it may be the start of blackmail, possibly a kidnapping. When you target as man as rich as Robert Harvey, you can be sure money is involved somewhere down the line."

"But sir, there are many rich men in London. I fail to see why a man with one store is considered such a target worthy of the taxpayer's money."

"Because Robert Harvey isn't just rich, detective, he's a billionaire, and that's a whole lot of reasons to ruin his Christmas."

As I glance down at the photograph, I wonder about the personality behind the man staring rather superciliously into the camera and shrug mentally as I consider my mission. My thoughts turn to my instructions and Detective Inspector Ranauld says gravely, "You start today. Report to the staff entrance at Harvey's. The instructions are in the folder. If I were you, I'd grab a coffee and study the file because I have arranged your induction in one hour's time."

His phone rings, causing him to say curtly, "I have faith in you, Jessica. If anyone can discover what's going on inside Harvey's, you can."

As I head out of my superior officer's office, it's with a great deal of self-importance as I wander towards my desk. A few pairs of curious eyes turn in my direction, but I catch none of them. I am close with no one for a very good reason. I don't have time to forge friendships and get dragged down in office politics. They are my colleagues who stopped trying to include me in their alcohol induced circle months ago and I'm guessing none of them are that interested in what went on in the office, anyway.

CHAPTER 1

JESSICA

*T*he woman staring at me with a worried frown makes me wonder what she's hiding. As instructed, I read the file and discovered that Robert Harvey is much like me. A man after my own heart and not somebody with a wide circle of friends. His entire life appears to be work and more work and I admire him for that.

Clearing her throat, the woman who introduced herself as Hazel Armstrong says with a slight quiver to her voice,

"Um, well, if you've finished, I'll show you to your locker."

She stands and as I rise to follow her, she casts a strange look in my direction, and I wonder if I've found my man already. Then again, I have been known to intimidate people with the arrogance I wear like a second skin. She is probably wondering why an obviously successful woman like me was hired for mere shop work, and I can't blame her. I would come to the same conclusion and so I smile superciliously and say somewhat sharply, "How long have you worked here, Miss Armstrong?"

"Oh, it's Mrs and um, seven years."

I make a mental note that she's married, which means I'll

need to research her husband as well and I say conversationally, "What does your husband do for a living?"

"He's a taxi driver for Cabtex."

My ears prick up because it has been well documented that particular company doesn't reward its staff well and I wonder if they are struggling.

"Do you live in London, Mrs Armstrong?"

"Cheam."

"I see."

If she thinks my questions are strange, she doesn't show it and just scurries beside me like a dog on the end of its master's lead.

We pass through corridors into an older part of the store, and I note the rather crumbling walls and lack of paint, which is the antithesis of the rest of the smartly styled store. In fact, Harvey's is radiating wealth due to its marble floors and fashionable styling. It appears that Mr Harvey likes the finer things in life and hasn't held back on making this store a prestigious place to shop in.

She pushes open a huge fire door and says, slightly breathlessly, "Here we are. You should find everything you need in the locker."

"Like what?"

I'm a little confused, and she says brightly, "If the, um, uniform doesn't fit, you know where to find me. Once you've changed, head to the fourth floor and ask for Dusty Bennett. He's the department manager and will show you the ropes."

I am mildly interested in what this position will involve and whatever it is, Detective Ranauld obviously feels this is the best possible start to my investigation and I nod, mentally dismissing Mrs Armstrong already.

"Thank you."

She seems grateful to leave and as I swing open the door to

the locker provided, I blink in disbelief at the layers of tulle and sequins winking back at me.

Reaching out, I grab hold of the material and draw out what appears to be a fairy costume.

"Mrs Armstrong!" I call out, but the silence tells me she's out of earshot, so I race to the door and shout at her retreating figure as she almost sprints down the corridor.

"Mrs Armstrong!" I call louder and only the slamming fire door tells me she never heard or has decided to ignore me.

"What's up, love?"

A kind voice comes from behind and I see a man pushing a floor cleaner towards me.

"And you are?"

"Albert, Miss, been here twenty-five years, so I can probably answer your question if you have one."

He grins and I stop for a moment and say with interest.

"So you know how things work around here?"

"If I don't by now, I guess I never will."

He flashes me a toothless grin and I point to the costume in my hand. "Do you know what this is?"

He appears slightly surprised because, of course, it's obvious what it is and I say hurriedly, "I mean, why would this be considered my uniform?"

"Why not? You get fairies in fairyland, don't you?"

"Fairyland?"

"On the fourth floor. From the first of November the house of horror is transformed into all things Christmas and fairyland is our theme this year. Obviously, you're one of the inhabitants of that, which could be worse, I suppose."

"It could?"

I'm seriously doubting that right now and he shrugs. "The girl before you was a zombie. Quite an ugly one at that, and she hated every minute of it."

"I'm not surprised."

I regard my outfit suspiciously, and Albert smiles through the gaps in his teeth.

"I think you'll make a pretty fairy, miss…"

"Taylor."

He glances around him and lowers his voice. "Word of advice, don't trust anyone. This lot would stick a knife in your back if their life depended on it."

"Why do you say that?"

"Because they're ambitious. They all want a piece of the pie and they're hungry."

He whispers, "It's why people don't last long at Harvey's. They see the pretty things and head home to poverty every night. They can't afford the lifestyle they sell and resent it."

Albert is now my new best friend because he could be the wealth of information that I need right now, and I edge a little closer.

"I'm guessing you have some intriguing stories about this place. What can you tell me about our illustrious leader, Mr Harvey?"

"Not a lot." Albert shrugs.

"I've seen him a few times, but he doesn't mix with the staff. He rules over us like a king, and only the chosen ones ever get to speak to him."

"Then he's a fool."

I curl my lip in disgust. "What sort of man employs hundreds, if not thousands of staff and doesn't even bother to interact with any of them? He sounds like a complete loser."

Albert cackles, which slightly unnerves me, and then winks, a toothless grin accompanying his words.

"Keep on telling yourself that, love, and you may still be here next year."

"What makes you say that?"

"Because a young pretty girl like you is just the sort to get

MY CHRISTMAS BILLIONAIRE

ideas above her station and try for the pot of gold at the end of the rainbow."

He grins as he heads off, leaving me to stare at the costume in my hand, and I sigh heavily. I never expected my first under-cover operation to be in fairyland, but I guess as disguises go, this will be the perfect one. Seasonal work will explain my appointment and it's as good a place to start as any, I suppose.

13

CHAPTER 2

JESSICA

I feel like a fool and as I studiously try to ignore the interested looks thrown my way, I hold my head high and stride though the department, looking as if I have every right to be here.

In fact, as grottos go, this one is fantastic. Like the rest of the store, no expense has been spared and if I had any interest in fantasy land, I would be in heaven right now.

It's like an explosion in a glitter factory and the entire place shines like the brightest star in heaven. Sparkling Christmas trees in pink, white and silver, contrast with the more masculine theme of a dark glittering forest, where it appears the boys like to hang out.

The girls' department is stereotypical pink frills and fanciful nonsense, and I can't fail to be impressed with the displays of fairy castles and snow-covered grottos that would be any little girl's dream. Pretty pink dressed dolls and fluffy toys are stuffed everywhere and even the air smells of candy floss with its slightly sickly aroma of excess and sugar overload.

In direct contrast, the boy's area is pure fantasy with its

dark glittering trees filled with weapons and soldiers that guard the royal palace next door. Clockwork trains and bubbling cauldrons sit alongside smart electric toy cars and toys from the galactic.

I approach a woman dressed as a fairy, grateful I'm not the only one and as she smiles at me in a friendly manner, it strikes me that she is probably as grateful as I am that she's not the only idiot in the room.

"I'm here to see…"

"Oh, you must be Crystal's replacement. That was such a sad story."

"Really."

My ears prick up because this could be just what I'm looking for. "Yes. She found her boyfriend cheating on her when she returned home, and they had a huge fight."

"They had a fight."

My mouth drops to the floor, and she giggles. "Not literally. Anyway, he told her to leave and as it was his name on the rental agreement, she had no choice and was homeless overnight."

"Where did she go?" I am horrified on her behalf, and she says sadly, "What we all do I suppose, when we have no other option. Go home to our parents."

"That's not so bad." I'm lying through my teeth because if I had to return to the mother ship, I would consider I had failed at life.

"In Edinburgh."

"I see." Now I know why there's a vacancy because I'm guessing the wages don't allow a person to commute from the other end of the country and she sighs. "She's working in Poundland now. Such a tragedy."

I'm not sure I agree with her because wearing a costume like this is most definitely a tragedy and I say quickly, "So, Mr…"

She points to a smartly dressed man wearing a black suit that makes him stick out like a sore thumb.

"Over there. Good luck."

Dusty Bennett is nothing like his name suggests. He has the look of a lord, and his clipped British accent tells me he didn't go to the local comprehensive. He appears almost bored as he casts a cursory gaze the length of me, causing me to bristle in indignation wrapped in feminism.

"Miss Taylor, I presume. I have you assisting Santa today."

"Really."

I can't think of anything worse as I gaze at the line of excited children waiting patiently for their turn in Santa's grotto.

"Yes, just act like this is the most exciting day of your life and show the next ones in after two minutes."

His eyes narrow as he says fiercely, "Every two minutes, Miss Taylor, or we'll have a problem."

He waves his hand towards what appears to be a wooden cabin in the North Pole and says quickly, "You can swap with Sonia. She's not the best fairy there is and has scared more children than she's charmed. I expect you to be better."

"I am the best, Mr Bennett. You have my word on that."

He seems doubtful of that and turns away with a deep, "You need to be. Good luck."

As I smooth down my insanely large skirt, I hate the fact it pops right back up again, and I don't miss the appreciative gaze of a father holding his daughter's hand nearby.

Furious at his blatant interest, I pity whoever married that creep and turn away with a despairing huff.

Men. Flash them a pair of legs and the promise of what lies at the end of them, and they act like a dog on heat.

I pointedly ignore him as I stomp past and only when I get

to the front of the line do I whisper to Sonia, "The cavalry's arrived."

The relief on her face speaks volumes, and she says gratefully, "Thank God. I'll head back at lunchtime to relieve you. Enjoy."

As she scurries away, I take a deep breath and glance down at the expectant face of a small girl who appears to be around four years old, dancing on the spot, appearing to need the toilet.

"Perhaps your daughter needs a bathroom break?"

Her mother throws me a worried glance. "She's fine. Just excited."

I'm not convinced, but as the door opens to the grotto, I take that as my cue to get the child in and away before she wets herself.

Opening the door with a flourish, I say grandly, "Santa's waiting, make sure you're good and whatever happens, don't sit on his knee."

The mother looks worried as I fix her with my best safeguarding expression and say sternly, "Rule number one. Never sit on a strange man's knee."

Her child appears worried and looks as if she's about to cry and her mother says with a nervous laugh, "Santa's not a man, darling, he's magical. You can trust him."

I roll my eyes and wonder when common sense was abolished and turn my attention to the child instead. "Word of advice from a fairy. Trust nobody until they have earned that trust, no matter who they say they are."

The line is now impatiently shifting behind us and the mother glares at me as if she wants to drive my fairy wand through my heart. Sighing, I fling the door open and see the red suited Santa residing on a velvet throne and say loudly, "Here he is. Santa is waiting, so hurry up, he doesn't have long."

They edge inside the room, and I hear a loud, "Ho. Ho. Ho. Who do we have here?"

The little girl starts to cry and with a sigh, I close the door and stare into the startled eyes of his next victim.

After ten minutes of what appears to be a repeat performance every time, Dusty Bennett arrives by my side and says quickly, "Gloria will take over from you. Perhaps you would be happier refilling the shelves."

If anything, I'm grateful about that because the sound of crying children is seriously beginning to grate on my nerves and as I follow him to the storage room out the back, he says with a sigh. "Remember you're in fairyland, Jessica. Normal rules don't apply here and it's your job to keep the fantasy alive, not crush it to dust underneath your golden shoe."

"What do you mean?"

I'm incensed at his criticism, and he sighs, "Just stock the shelves and observe how things work around here, for all our sakes."

As I push a silver cart laden with boxes of beautifully dressed china dolls, I wonder about the decadence all around me. These dolls alone cost over one hundred pounds each and I'm guessing the recipient would be just as happy, even more so, with a much cheaper version.

I locate their shelves and start filling them and wonder how I can possibly find anything out working like a servant disguised as the Trojan horse.

By the end of the day, I'm so frustrated I could cry. I've come up with absolutely zero. All I've discovered is that retail is not a career option, for me, anyway. It's seriously hard work dealing with disgruntled mums who never planned ahead and left their child's Christmas to the last minute. Angry voices fill the department as their desperate pleas go unanswered and I even had to tackle one mother to the ground after she entered into a tug of war with a woman who grabbed the last toy off a shelf. Apparently, it was the 'must have' of the season and she saw it first. A police record shouldn't be on anyone's Christmas list, and this department should pay danger money to its staff.

Dusty was suitably impressed with my quick action, and I even got a pat on my back for my trouble.

"Well done, Jessica, although a quiet but stern word may have traumatised the watching children a little less when they experienced a fist fight in the sparkle kingdom."

"If you say so, Mr Bennett, but quite frankly, you should never shield children from the realities of life. They won't thank you for it in the long run."

As the department empties and the lights dim, I make my way to the exit sensing I just experienced a challenge I will never recover from. I am exhausted and mentally drained, which causes me to make a decision that is completely alien to my usual calm and rational thinking. The fact I was too exhausted to even change my outfit shows how scrambled my mind is because now in the cold winter's night, I'm aware how ridiculous I look, and the journey home could be an extremely mortifying one.

I shiver and pull my coat as far around me as possible but due to the insanely padded skirt, I only succeed in covering half of my body and a sudden gust of wind lifts the front of my skirt so high I'm glad it's dark out here. Apparently, streetlights do a good job though, because the hoots from the passing traffic and the jeers from a crowd of guys heading out for the evening cause my cheeks to flame.

"How much, darlin'? I've got a twenty with your name on it."

As I resist the urge to draw out my warrant card, I merely resort to sign language in one last act of defiance.

Headlights approach and, feeling desperate, I step into the road and hold up my hand with a firmness that has always served me well until now and, as the tyres squeal and the brakes scream, I wonder if that was a step too far.

"What the hell?"

The car door slams as the disgruntled driver exits and stares at me in utter amazement as I say firmly, "I need a cab."

"Do I look like an Uber?"

I squint into the darkness and must admit this car is a little grander than the usual taxi around these parts and I shrug? "How was I to know?"

"So, you thought just flagging down any car would do?" He rolls his eyes. "What's the matter? Do you believe in your own magic and think if you wished hard enough, you could magic a cab out of thin air?"

"I'm sorry, ok but there was a fifty-fifty chance you would be a cab."

"And you were willing to gamble your life on a fifty-fifty chance." He shakes his head despairingly. "I could be a murderer, you know, or worse."

"Worse than a murderer, I doubt it."

The traffic behind him starts a concerto of the loudest kind and with an irritated grumble he says roughly, "Get in. I'll drop you to the nearest cab company."

Spying the group of guys filming me on their phone, I say eagerly, "Thanks but word of warning, if you try anything, you will be wishing I *was* a murderer–got it?"

Before he can answer me, I jump into the back of his car and sigh with pleasure when the warm air reaches out and wraps me in a loving embrace.

The driver's door slams and as he puts the car into gear, it rolls away from the scene of my humiliation and he says angrily, "You are the most stupid woman I have ever met. What possessed you to dress up like a pantomime fairy and walk the streets of London at night? You're certifiably insane."

"For your information, I am working, and this costume was

probably thought up by the arrogant idiot who rules over the rest of us in his ivory tower while making decisions that ruin lives."

"Wait, what did you say?"

"Oh please, do you need a hearing aid for Christmas? Don't pretend you never heard me."

"Are you talking about fairyland at Harvey's?"

"Of course I am. Do you honestly think I'd dress up in this monstrosity willingly?"

"You seem stupid enough." He snarls. "I mean, what sane person steps in front of the moving traffic?"

"A desperate one, perhaps. Someone so keen to get home and try to forget the day from hell lining another man's pocket just so he can spend Christmas in the Caribbean or on his own private island, more likely."

"Wow, you have a huge chip on your shoulder."

"I don't."

"You do. Come to think of it, people like you rub me up the wrong way."

"People like me. I take it you're referring to the hard-working masses who endure hardship and humiliation just to pay inflated rents to landlords who capitalise on people's misery."

"I take it back."

"What back?"

"You don't have a chip on your shoulder. You're staggering under a boulder."

"Says you."

"Yes, says me."

I glance around and note the plush leather interior of a car that definitely wasn't bought from second hand Jim's car lot and realise my cab driver is one of them, making me snort derisively.

"So, what do you do for a living?"

"That's none of your business."

"Someone's touchy."

"Someone's wondering how he ended up with an obnoxious fairy in his car."

"Then stop and I'll leave you to your soulless life."

"You're judgmental too. Don't you ever give it a rest?"

"No."

As I lean back, I savour the luxurious surroundings and his voice wafts out of the dim light towards me.

"So, you work at Harvey's. How long have you been there?"

"Today is my first day and let me tell you this, that place is hell on earth."

"You didn't enjoy it then."

"Do I look as if I enjoyed it?" I feel extremely disgruntled and snap. "Pretending to be a fairy to a pretend Santa is not my idea of pleasure, if you must know."

"What is then?"

"Excuse me."

"Your idea of pleasure. I mean, what would you rather be doing?"

As I remember what I live and breathe for, I say with a sigh, "I would rather be pulling out my fingernails one by one before plucking every hair from my body with tweezers. Whoever invented retail is a sadist and don't even get me started on Christmas."

"Not a fan?"

"Waste of time for anyone over the age of ten."

"Then we agree on something."

"You're not a fan either?"

"Of the holiday, no. It merely disrupts life and costs me money."

"It appears you have a lot of that if this car is anything to go by."

"I do."

"Lucky you." I yawn loudly.

"You can drop me here. I'll grab the tube. It's only a few stops away and you are now officially off the hook, knowing you have done a good deed for the day."

"It's fine. I'll drop you to your door. I would worry about you on the tube at this time of night."

"Then you would know where I lived. No thank you. For all I know, you could stalk me and ruin my life. I'll take my chance surrounded by the masses, clinging to a pole on the underground."

The amusement in his voice makes me smile as he says in a softer voice.

"Then allow me to do as I promised and drop you to a cab company. Pole dancing on the tube could be considered an offence."

"The tube is fine, but thanks for your concern."

He pulls over and as I open the door and a gust of icy air hits me, I'm almost tempted to take him up on his offer but with a deep sigh instead, I say over my shoulder.

"Thanks for the ride. Enjoy the rest of your life."

I'm met with silence and as I slam the door, I'm just grateful that I'll soon be home and to hell with cost cutting. I'm cranking the heating up and sending the bill to Detective Inspector Ranauld.

CHAPTER 3

❧

ROBERT

*T*he encounter stays with me for the entire journey home. It was unexpected, interesting, annoying and informative. To be honest, meeting one of my employees is unusual, especially one as far down the command chain as a Christmas temp with an attitude problem. Despite everything though, it was the first time in a very long time that I felt alive.

Perhaps it was because she didn't know who I was. Her honesty was refreshing, if not unwelcome, and yet it changes nothing. I'm in business, and everything is done with the maximum profit level in mind. I am trying not to remember the way our conversation became a game to win points and I like to believe I won the most, but if I'm honest, it was probably a draw. However, sparring with the hired help is strangely addictive and I'm almost disappointed she didn't take me up on my offer to complete her journey. Then again, it was probably for the best because it's unlikely I will ever see her again, and what happened tonight will become a conversation over a dinner table one evening at one of the soulless parties I am forced to endure.

I try to relegate the encounter to the past and flood the car with the usual classical music that calms my weary spirit away from another day of problems, spreadsheets and people trying to become my new best friend. All except one, that is, and for some reason, my heart feels a little lighter than it did when I started this journey. I almost wear a smile on my face when I push through the door of my insanely large mansion in Kensington and fling my keys to the hall table with disdain.

As I rip the tie from my neck and shrug out of my jacket, I distance myself from my corporate identity to relax in my empty home and recharge my soul. Silence. Pure and unadulterated pleasure that calms my spirit and wraps me in comfort.

Solitude. Just what I like. Alone with the trappings of my wealth and shielded from a world that just wants to take all the time. Nobody is interested in the man in sweatpants and a tight t-shirt, watching football on the seventy-inch screen in his private sitting room, surrounded by takeout that was dispatched on the doorstep courtesy of Deliveroo. This is my life and I'm happy with it. My own company is more than good enough and always will be.

My spirits are high when I retreat to my study, knowing that my team remains at the top of the premier league for another week at least. As I pour myself a celebratory brandy, I take up my position behind my desk and reach for the post, kindly organised by my housekeeper, Mrs Grant. As I think of the elderly lady who has served me well over the years, I congratulate myself on an extremely satisfying appointment. We never meet. It's always best that way and while I work during the day, she manages my home and ensures I have a stocked refrigerator and my affairs are organised.

Following a swig of brandy, I reach for the first letter and, using my silver letter opener I slice it open, relishing the crispness of the paper as I make a clean cut.

A cursory glance tells me it's not important and I place it in my assistant's tray to deal with tomorrow when I return to the office. My life runs like clockwork with every eventuality catered for and I deposit my personal post in Sylvia's tray as I step past her desk in the early hours of the morning, knowing it will get the attention it deserves. Invitations are politely declined and birthdays acknowledged with a card and flowers or a generous bottle of wine.

I sift through the usual junk mail, cards from acquaintances and family, along with the usual bills, and then as my letter opener slices through the final envelope, my heart sinks.

Another one.

The cheap flimsy card with a robin on the front is different to the usual ones I receive and as I open it the stark letters of hate make my eyes bleed.

Men like you don't deserve to see another Christmas. Enjoy this one, it will be your last.

If I feel anything, it's anger at the person who believes they have the right to spoil my day and my fist balls as I imagine meeting whoever is sending them one day. I will show no mercy because the kind of person who sends a threat disguised as a greeting is the lowest form of life.

Sighing, I add it to a pile of similar cards and wonder why the police aren't treating my complaint seriously. It's been over a week since I first made it and I've heard nothing. If it wasn't for the late hour, I would be straight on the phone to the local station because I am fast running out of patience with this. A man in my position can't afford to be complacent when it comes to threats, and the fact I live alone is not a blessing in cases like this. The house feels eerie and the silence echoes around me like the demons circling because there is something deep inside me telling me I can't afford to ignore these cards. One was easily dismissed, two was annoying. However, looking at the pile that is growing by the day, I expect there to be around twenty of them by now.

I push back my seat and head off to check the security is in place because the last thing I need is an intruder intent on a misguided vendetta to make me pay for their own hang ups.

As I check the windows, doors and empty rooms, of which I have many in this ten bedroomed mansion, in one of the most desirable addresses in London, I curse myself for not staying at the waterfront penthouse I usually reserve for any guests visiting town. If anything, that would be a safer option because, as its name suggests, it's the topmost apartment with security that is so tight, they could store the crown jewels in there and give the Beefeaters the day off.

As I walk, I try to work out who could be doing this. I don't know many people and I'm not sure I've caused anyone to hate me this much personally. The fact I'm a public figure always brings with it a closer scrutiny and I have known of many people in my position to hire a full-time security team because of stalkers and threats just like this. I'm almost considering it but the fact I hate people so much makes that option even worse than opening a threatening letter because then I would have to actually talk to someone. All I want to do is shut myself away and clear my mind of problems at the end of the day.

Once I am reassured that everything is normal, I head to my home gym and start my workout, trying to drive any fear from my mind and concentrate on keeping fit.

However, there is one conversation that just won't go away and one image of a rather belligerent fairy scowling at me through my rear-view mirror that stays in my mind.

The image of her shapely legs crossing and uncrossing as she berated me, makes my interest grow and the way she rolled her eyes when I spoke makes me smile. For some reason the petite blonde who looked like candy floss with a centre of the sourest lemon, makes me laugh to myself as I picture her let loose on the tube, scowling at anyone who dared cast an amused look in her direction as she hurtled through the tunnels dressed like Tinkerbell. Such a surprising end to a mundane day and the fact I know where she'll be tomorrow is making me consider breaking my own rule and heading down to reacquaint myself with the vitriolic bad fairy.

The harder I try to distance her from my thoughts, the closer she gets until I can think of nothing else. Even the card pales into the background over my desire to see the fairy again one more time. Perhaps it's just to banish the image that is growing more fanciful by the minute. Remind myself how irritating people are to me most of the time.

As I shower and get ready for bed, I hope I wake up without this curious need to see her again and yet when I close my eyes, there she is standing behind them, glowering at me and looking as if she would rather be anywhere else.

CHAPTER 4

JESSICA

*A*s soon as I open my eyes, I'm angry. It's probably because the first thing I see is the hated fairy dress that I tossed on the bedroom chair when I returned after the most toe-curling commute of my life. The looks, the comments and the sheer number of phones pointed in my direction probably mean I am now a TikTok sensation. Especially because I glowered at anyone who dared stare at me, and I overheard a man introducing me to his video feed as one of Santa's naughty fairies who was obviously tossed out of fairyland. The fact I showed him my middle finger merely demonstrated that I need anger management classes and fast.

As I follow my usual routine, I grab the dress and stuff it into an oversized bag and head off to the scene of my worst day ever. I vow to wrap this job up as quickly as possible before my sanity explodes in a torrent of anger, directed at the very man I have been sent to protect.

Throughout the journey, I try to remember my meditating skills and take several deep breaths to regain control of my senses. I need to be emotionless, practical and retain an open mind and so, as soon as I enter the staff entrance at Harvey's, I nod to the security man and sign in with a flourish.

Rather than going straight to fairyland, I head in the opposite direction to personnel and Mrs Armstrong blinks in disbelief when I slam the costume down on her clean and tidy desk and say imperiously, "To retain the excellent reputation of your store and ensure that no child's Christmas spirit is damaged forever, I suggest you relocate my services to a more suitable department for my skills. I might suggest security if you need some ideas."

"B-b-but…" She stammers as she peers at me in confusion and I fix her with my most imperious expression that usually has them cowering away in fear.

I hand her my warrant card and say steadily, "As you can see, I am more than capable of carrying out the most basic security duties and my skills would be best utilised in patrolling the store. If you need a reference, you can call Detective Inspector Ranauld at Scotland Yard, who will give you everything you need."

She stares with her mouth wide open, and I briefly wonder if I should have blown my cover so soon and I lean forward and whisper, "This stays between us. I am officially warning you not to breathe a word of my true identity to anyone—whoever asks and failure is rewarded with a night in the cells. Do I make myself clear?"

She nods, apparently dazed, and I say firmly, "So, we are agreed. I will patrol the store as extra eyes brought in for the Christmas period, and I expect you to clear it with your head of security. I will be undercover as a store detective and so must not be approached by any member of staff in case they blow my cover. Make sure your departments know the score and fabricate whatever excuse you need to keep them off my back." I turn to leave, and she says hesitantly, "Miss Taylor…"

"Yes."

"Is there something we should know? It's just, well, um, why are you here?"

I fix her with a steely gaze. "Classified information, Mrs Armstrong. You will know when my job is done."

She appears nervous and any normal person would feel bad for her, but normal hasn't been part of my life for a while now and so I nod in her direction and head off to do what I was sent here for. Find out who is targeting their billionaire boss.

* * *

As decisions go, this was one of my best because now I am left alone to pry into this store in glorious solitude, just the way I like it. As I cover ground, I glance around with disdain because the price tags on most items here would feed a small family for a week. One handbag alone cost over one thousand pounds, and I imagine that even if I had more money than their owner, I would never spend it so frivolously.

Despite my disapproval though, I gaze longingly at the rows of beautiful dresses and cashmere jumpers when I find myself in womenswear. I let my fingers sift through the finest silk lingerie, imagining how it would slide against my skin and the smell of leather in the shoe department is as intoxicating as the finest perfume in the rather noxious perfumery downstairs.

My fellow workers are smart, polite, well-mannered, and attentive to the customers and I wonder if they feel the same way I do as they watch others more fortunate flash their credit cards and leave with bags full of luxuries to toss into their designer closets when they get home.

It is undoubtedly another world and one that I have no place in.

I reach for the cocktail dresses and as I sift through the

rails, I wonder which one I would choose when a conversation nearby captures my attention.

"I heard he's looking for a wife."

"Isn't every man."

The woman sighs and says wistfully, "I caught a glimpse of him last week. He is so handsome. I wish he would glance in my direction only once."

"The trouble is, he would probably fire you on the spot. He has a reputation for that."

"So I heard. Why is it that men like him are lacking in personality? Gerald from menswear told me that Mr Harvey fired Jerome from men's watches because he was late in one day because his child was sick."

"Disgusting." The other woman agrees. "Did Jerome find another job?"

"No, he got such a bad reference from Mr Harvey that no one will hire him. He's claiming benefits and his poor children won't be getting much from Santa this year."

"I still wouldn't say no if he asked me, though." The other woman giggles and her colleague grunts in reply. "That's your problem. You never do."

They erupt into peals of laughter and are only silenced when the department manager stops by and says tersely, "Girls, there is no time for conversation between staff in Harvey's. Remember, you are here to do a job and those rails need straightening."

She moves off as the women scurry to opposite ends of the department and I make a mental note to check out Jerome with my accomplice in personnel.

As I move through the store, I eavesdrop on many conversations concerning their boss, and none of them are good. Names drop from their lips of fellow staff members, all with sorry tales of their own and I make surreptitious notes to check out every one of them. In fact, by morning break, I consider adding my own name to the list because the picture that's emerging is one of a very undesirable human being that I would hate to meet, let alone work for.

"Hey, is this seat taken?" I glance up from my chair in the staff canteen and nod with disinterest at the smiling man, who drops into the seat beside me.

"No, it's free."

I turn my attention back to my Americano, shifting away from him slightly, giving him no encouragement to talk to me.

"You must be new here. I'm Rory, I work in men's gifts."

I nod and stare at him with a considered expression.

He takes a sip of his coffee before smiling. "You must be new."

"Must I."

I really don't want to encourage conversation with him, but he doesn't get the message.

"I know everyone who works here."

"That quite a statement."

"I've worked here for years and seen them come and go. To be frank, a lot go. They can't hack it."

"Why is that?" I lean forward, more interested now because he could be just the man I need.

"Conditions aren't that great." He shrugs. "Don't let the surroundings fool you. This place runs on goodwill and fear most of the time."

"Fear! I find that hard to believe," I scoff, and he shrugs. "You're new. You'll soon learn."

"So, enlighten me."

He leans forward and whispers, "The owner is a... well, let's say I don't swear in front of a lady."

"Mr Harvey?"

"Yes." He shrugs. "It's a shame because his father was completely different. Mr Harvey senior was a kind man who treated his staff well."

"Was?"

"He retired two years ago, which is a shame because his son is all about the business and nothing about the staff."

"He must have made a few enemies."

"If you count the entire staff, then yes, that's quite a few."

"Have you met him?" I ask because it appears that not many do, and he shakes his head. "I've seen him in the distance, but not to speak to. He surrounds himself with his team, who never stray from his side. The only people he apparently speaks to are his immediate staff and board members. Once a week he hosts a meeting of floor managers and that's about it."

"So, he never mingles with his staff."

Rory is wearing a knowing smirk that instantly rubs me up the wrong way. "What?"

"If you're thinking of catching his eye, I would reconsider."

"I'm not thinking of any such thing." I huff indignantly and he shrugs. "You wouldn't be the first pretty girl to fantasise about our elusive leader. Some guys too."

Drawing myself up to a straight-backed sitting position, I scowl. "I'm here to work and nothing else. Not every woman is hoping to catch the attention of a man."

The salacious glance he throws me makes me bristle with anger and he says with a low hiss, "Shame. Anyway, if you fancy meeting some of the other workers, we all head across the road to The Viking after work."

I raise my eyes and he grins. "To drown our sorrows and moan about our jobs. If you like, I'll buy you a drink later and tell you anything you need to learn about Harvey's."

"Maybe." I shrug and stand, cutting off this conversation with an abrupt, "Anyway, for your information, I'm here to do a job and I'd thank you for ignoring me if you see me around the store. I work for the security team undercover and would appreciate your discretion."

He nods. "Of course. Your secret is safe with me…"

I ignore his obvious attempt to learn my name and turn my back on him, walking away with a deep sigh. At least I know what pub to avoid in the future. It was obvious the invitation was for much more than a drink, and the last thing I need in my life is a man complicating it.

CHAPTER 5

ROBERT

Sylvia regards me as if I've grown two heads overnight as she stands in front of my desk for our early morning briefing.

"I'm sorry, sir, you want to schedule a walkabout?"

"Is that a problem, Sylvia?"

I fix her with my usual autocratic look, and she says quickly, "Of course not, sir. May I ask who you need to accompany you?"

"I can walk around my own store unaccompanied, Sylvia. Just let me know when I don't have meetings so I can plan it."

She colours up and says quickly. "You have two thirty to three thirty put aside for paperwork. Prior to that, there is the usual monthly meeting with the department managers and following it, Mr Saracen wants a word."

I groan inwardly. Mr Saracen is a pompous bore and head of the third floor. He's always attempting to bend my ear about mundane matters just to inflate his own self-importance among the staff. He likes to proclaim that he has the ear of the CEO, which gives him kudos among the staff when he sweeps past them. He's the last man I want to spend time with today, so I say irritably, "Cancel it."

Sylvia's eyes are wide. "But…"

"Cancel it, Sylvia. Reschedule it for after closing time if he insists."

I bite back a grin because it's well known he is one of the first managers out of the door come closing time because he prefers to make the early train home. He lives one hour away, and the next train is the slow one, which takes one and a half hours to do a journey that the fast train achieves in thirty minutes. It's little pieces of information like this that I use to my advantage to get what I want, and I doubt I'll be seeing him when the doors close for the night.

Sylvia tries to disguise her eye roll but fails and when she receives my scowl in return she says hastily, "Of course, sir, consider it done."

She exits the office in haste, and I smile to myself. Despite appearances, I have a fondness for Sylvia that she will never know about. She is a mother of three who dotes on her family but spends many hours past her official one's trying to do her best job. She relies on it because her husband is out of work and her children are growing up fast. As the main breadwinner, she can't afford to lose her position and so works diligently just to keep the wolf from the door. It's just a shame she works with a particular brand of wolf and yet I allow her to get away with more than most.

I know what the staff think of me. Not a lot, I guess, but I'm not my father who was loved by everyone. Generous, convivial and the worst businessman because of it. My grandfather was more like me and under my father's rule, Harvey's suffered, and it was touch and go if we would survive at all. The profits were squandered on staff parties and bonuses and in his mission to be popular and create a fun working environment, he nearly caused the doors to close for good.

When he stepped down, it was at the request of my grand-father. Jefferson Harvey was appalled at how far the profits had sunk and as the chairman he had the power to hire and fire at will. He wasted no time in 'retiring' my father and installing me at the helm under instruction to pull the business up from the gutter back to the dizzying heights it enjoyed under his rule.

As it turned out, my father was more than happy to oblige and spends his pension travelling the world with my mother, who always enjoys spending the profits, anyway.

So, I brought a new era along with me and have earned my reputation as the cold unfeeling beast who looks down on his subjects with a scowl and the promise of unemployment if they displease me.

Now I'm alone, my thoughts turn to my passenger again for probably the thousandth time since she vacated my car. My scowling fairy. A woman who interested me more than any other because, like me, she doesn't appear to suffer fools gladly.

The whole purpose of my walkabout is to stride into fairy-land and antagonise her some more and it's been a scenario that has gained in momentum ever since I decided it would shake her image from my head. I just need to burst the bubble she has created and see her for what she is. Another employee who will irritate me and send me back to the comfort of my office with normal business resumed.

Somehow, I get through the morning, hating the fact she occupies my mind for most of it. In fact, I have never met a woman who does before, which is why she intrigues me so much. Maybe it was the disinterest she showed towards me, or perhaps it was the way she reminded me of myself. We appeared to share things in common and I have never met a woman who challenged me as much as she did during that brief encounter.

I suppose it has been magnified in my mind and the reality will disappoint me when I see her again. Part of me sincerely hopes it will because the last thing I need to develop is an unhealthy fascination for a woman who is sure to be nothing but trouble, anyway.

* * *

As I walk through the store, I'm accustomed to the incredulous looks thrown my way. It never bothers me and for the most part, I ignore every tentative smile and every attempt to engage my attention. I only stare at the things that interest me the most. The tidiness of the displays, the general housekeeping of the store and the lines at the service points. If I see items out of place or low stock, I want to know why and I have earned my reputation as a beast and wouldn't want it any other way. It's important that standards are withheld and the store shines at every opportunity and I don't hesitate to reward incompetence with a P45 and a bad reference.

My diligence has paid off because our reputation is soaring. Magazine interviews and press evenings have elevated our standing among the general public. A few paid visits from well-known celebrities have earned us gossip column inches and all of it was a contrived plan to make Harvey's the 'must go' place to be seen in London.

I sweep through the store like an ill wind and glower at anyone who appears to be slacking. By the time I reach fairy-land though my attention is no longer on the condition of my store, it's searching for the one person who has unknowingly captured my attention.

A brief glimpse of tulle and sparkle flashes past me and I turn in that direction, following the fairy into the grotto that has been named the best one in London, ensuring our lines are long and anticipation high. The fairy stops short of the grotto and whispers in the ear of another fairy and my heart quickens when they swap places and as the fairy turns and smiles at the nearest child, my heart sinks.

It's not her.

A hesitant cough sounds behind me and I hear, "Mr Harvey, sir, it's an honour."

Turning, I see the rather stiff floor manager, Mr Bennett, almost hyperventilating with excitement and my heart sinks.

I merely nod as he says with a slight stutter. "C… Can I help you, sir?"

"Possibly." His eyes light up and I jerk my thumb in the direction of the grotto. "I understand there's a new fairy who started yesterday. I need a word."

For some reason he sighs and shakes his head with disapproval.

"You must be talking about Miss Taylor. I'm sorry, sir, she never returned."

"Excuse me." This is not what I want to hear, and he sighs, shaking his head in disapproval. "To be honest, I was quite relieved. She wasn't, shall we say, suited for the role."

"Why not?" Picturing the rather angry fairy, I can almost guess what's coming, and he says with a sigh, "She was very abrupt and whatever she said to the children caused them to cry and fear meeting Santa. I had to move her to re-stocking the shelves instead and I suppose it was after she rugby tackled a customer to the ground that I knew it wasn't going to work out."

"She did what?" I'm actually horrified, and he wrinkles his nose in disgust. "Apparently, she broke up a fight between two ladies who wanted the same toy. Most distasteful, if I might add. No, Miss Taylor did well to stay away. She wasn't cut out for fairyland."

Despite the appalling scene he describes my mouth twitches as I picture it and wish I had seen it for myself. However, the fact she's not here is extremely inconvenient because now I want to find her even more.

Turning on my heel, I walk away without explaining my departure to Mr Bennett and head straight to the top floor. There is only one person who can give me the information I seek and if she doesn't have it, I will be looking for a replacement human resources manager before the day is over.

CHAPTER 6

JESSICA

*B*y the time the doors close for the day, I have alerted security to no less than ten shoplifters. Not bad for my first day on the job and bad news for the security team at Harvey's. I can only imagine the loss this store suffers daily and I'm guessing if the tyrant boss at the helm found out about it, he would replace his team with a new one. I certainly would, and yet I'm more annoyed that I haven't discovered any incriminating gossip concerning him and a reason why anyone would send him threatening Christmas cards.

It's well known Mr Harvey is disliked. He's definitely not popular, but that doesn't cause me a moment's thought. He doesn't need to be popular to be in charge and from what I've seen today, he's not strong enough in my opinion. His profits are disappearing faster than the countdown to Christmas and that's just the things I've seen. I can only imagine the true value of loss and wonder if this store will survive another year at this rate.

As I grab my coat from the staff locker they assigned me, I feel like a failure. One day of snooping has given me nothing at all, and now my only chance lies in a pub across the road. It pains me to mix with the likes of Rory, but I have no choice. I need to go deeper undercover in order to solve the mystery of this vendetta against his boss and if a couple of drinks after work don't do the trick, then I'm not sure where to go next.

The chill in the air surrounds me as I step onto the brightly lit streets of London where daylight turned to dusk hours ago courtesy of the long evenings and short dirty days. Nothing looks good in winter. The trees are naked against the frosty air and their only purpose is to house strings of fairy lights to create an atmosphere that leaves me as cold as the temperature outside. Rain drizzles down almost 24/7 and the passing traffic takes great joy at splashing the crowds as they hurry past on the narrow pavements. Shops are brightly lit with windows dressed to entice and loud Christmas music tries to add cheer to the disgruntled passers-by who would rather be anywhere else.

I reach the pub and push in through the shabby door, and the sound of false merriment causes me to shudder. The scent of stale beer and the sticky carpet underfoot makes me wonder if this place deserves its health and safety certificate. It appears that most of Harvey's likes to congregate here because I recognise the uniforms of the various departments from the store.

As I pull my coat tighter around me, I glance around for the man who invited me here.

"Jessica!"

I peer in the direction of the voice and see Rory waving madly at me from his position by the bar. "Over here."

With an irritated sigh, I force my way through the crowd and his cheeky grin greets me as I draw by his side. "What can I get you?"

I fumble in my purse for a ten-pound note and he waves it away. "You can get the next round. What's your poison?"

"Um, a white wine spritzer please with soda, not lemonade, no ice and no lemon?"

He raises his eyes at the preciseness of my request and places my order with the bartender.

"So, you made it then."

"So it would seem."

I don't like the way his eyes are running the length of me with considerable interest, and I pull my coat a little tighter around me.

He hands me the drink and clinks his pint glass to mine. "To another day in hell."

"I'll drink to that." Somebody to his side muscles in and knocks his glass against ours and I stare into two brown eyes that gaze at me with interest.

"Hi, I'm Adam. I work in accounts."

"Jessica."

He waits for my job title, and I say politely. "I'm pleased to meet you, Adam. I started yesterday in fairyland."

Adam raises his eyes. "Wow, a real-life fairy. Can I make a wish?"

Like Rory's, his eyes reveal what he's thinking, and I scowl. "Only if you want to be disappointed."

"Oh, I doubt that. My success rate is quite high. I'll take my chances." He presses closer and Rory laughs out loud. "Back off Adam. Jessica isn't as easy as your usual conquests."

Adam presses even closer and his arm slides around my waist as he leers, "I'll be the judge of that."

Shrugging him off, I glare at him and say icily, "There are laws against sexual harassment in the workplace. I suggest you read up on them before you're calculating your benefit entitlement instead."

Adam laughs out loud. "A feisty one, even better."

Rory appears a little worried and says to his credit. "I mean it, Adam, back off. You know what will happen if someone reports you."

Adam shrugs. "I'm not at work now and if Mr Harvey was

here, there's not a lot he can do anyway outside of office hours."

He grins but to my relief steps away and says slightly angrily, "Anyway, he could try, but I understand every entry on his balance sheet which would be gold for his competitors. If he ever tried to fire me, I would sell that information to the highest bidder and watch with great delight when his beloved grandfather's store crashed and burned."

He raises his glass and chucks down the contents in one greedy gulp and slams it on the bar with a loud, "Another one, Mike, when you're ready."

Rory shakes his head and offers me an apologetic smile.

"Tell me…" I address my question to both men.

"I get the impression the staff hates the owner. Is he really that bad?"

They share a look and Rory nods. "He wouldn't win any popularity competitions. I mean, the turnover of staff is embarrassing, and that's probably because we're just about paid minimum wage and the hours he expects us to work are ridiculous."

"It's not as if he can't afford it either." Adam interrupts. "I've seen the profits, and it's no wonder the man's a billionaire."

"You mean he earns billions from Harvey's?" I'm astonished and Adam laughs out loud. "So, you don't know then?"

"Know what?"

"Mr Harvey didn't become a billionaire at Harvey's. He was one before he came."

"Then why work here? It doesn't make sense?"

"Family loyalty, I suppose." Rory shrugs. "His father was in charge before him and was loved by everyone. Then one day he was replaced with his son and the atmosphere changed overnight."

"In what way?"

Adam scowls. "He started firing almost immediately. Each

department lost a third of their staff and the rest were supposed to be grateful and take up the slack. New contracts were drawn up, holiday entitlement was slashed, and wages reduced."

"How?"

I'm shocked and Rory sighs. "The rate stayed the same, but all bonus schemes were scrapped. Many relied on them to make ends meet and they disappeared overnight."

Adam nods. "Suppliers were called in and expected to offer huge discounts if they wanted their products in the store. Christmas parties were banned alongside anything outside of the hourly rate. Overnight, Harvey's went from being a great place to work to the workhouse and it was because of one man. The billionaire who decided to play shop."

The bitterness in their eyes gives me two possible suspects but somehow, I doubt they would stoop to sending the CEO a threatening Christmas card but it's obvious somebody has a huge grudge against the man in charge and now I know where I need to focus my efforts.

I excuse myself and despite the calls to stay, I head back through the crowds with more purpose than when I came in.

First thing tomorrow, I'm heading back to personnel and my new role will be assisting Mrs Armstrong because I need to trawl through the employee records as a matter of urgency.

CHAPTER 7

ROBERT

*M*rs Armstrong shrinks into her seat, trying to make herself as small as possible under the frown that I'm directing her way. "What do you mean, you can't help me?"

The frustration is threatening to unleash my inner beast, and she says in a whisper, "I'm sorry, sir. Miss Taylor no longer works in fairyland. She has been redeployed to another department and I'm afraid I must refer any enquiries to a Detective Inspector Ranauld at Scotland Yard.

I blink in the hope this is just an inconvenient dream and I will wake up back at home ready to start my day. However, when I open my eyes, Mrs Armstrong is looking distinctly uncomfortable and I count to ten and say in a measured tone, "Just so I'm clear. My personnel manager is unwilling to give me, the CEO of the company, a simple explanation concerning the employment of one of my staff. *My staff*, Mrs Armstrong. Not Detective Inspector Ranauld and so, as your boss and the man in the charge, you had better give me the information I need, or you will be pleading for a job with the man who apparently pulls your strings now."

She pales and stutters, "P… please, sir. I don't want to do the wrong thing, but Miss Taylor swore me to secrecy."

I am holding onto my last nerve and prepare to fire her on the spot, but then something occurs to me that causes me to back down in an instant.

Without another word, I spin on my heels and leave the terrified personnel manager cowering in her chair and head to the sanctuary of my office with a small smile on my face.

It appears that I no longer need to find my fairy because if I'm right, she will find me and when she does, I'll be waiting and this time I'll be the one demanding answers and I can't wait to see the expression on her face when she discovers who's in charge around here.

* * *

I WORK LATE to make up for my impromptu walkabout and just before she heads home, Sylvia heads into my office.

"Will there be anything else, sir?"

I note how tired she looks and feel responsible for that. Due to the Christmas rush and the endless meetings that are lined up, she has stayed late every night this week for no reward other than keeping her job.

She even works through her lunch, taking bites of the sandwiches she brings from home and if I were human, I would give her a break.

She blinks wearily as I tap my finger lightly on the desk and say abruptly, "Did you take a look at the pile of cards I brought in?"

She nods, looking worried. "I documented them as you asked and emailed the detective who has been assigned to your case."

"Remind me of his name."

"Detective Inspector Ranauld, I think. I could double check if you give me a minute."

"No need. The name seems familiar." I say as an aside, "Have you heard from him?"

She shakes her head. "Just once when he said he would be in touch. I'm sorry, sir. Would you like me to chase it up again before I go home?"

"No."

I lean back in my chair and nod dismissively. "|You may go."

She turns to leave, and I say without looking up from my computer."

"Oh, and Sylvia…"

She replies anxiously, "Yes, sir."

"I don't want to see you here tomorrow."

For a moment I think she's gone and then she says in an anxious voice, "Have I done something wrong sir, it's just…"

"Sylvia." I fix her with a frown, causing her lower lip to tremble and her skin to turn as white as the winter snow. "I've calculated that you've worked more than your contracted hours for the past few months. You are here early and leave late and never take your allotted breaks. Tomorrow you will enjoy a day of rest knowing that you've earned it. I may be a hard taskmaster, but I am human, despite popular opinion, and so I expect you to enjoy your day and come in refreshed and ready to carry on the excellent job I've grown accustomed to from you."

I'm not sure if it's my imagination or not, but her lip quivers and her eyes fill with tears as she says gratefully, "Thank you, sir. I appreciate it."

"Then leave before I change my mind."

Once again, I lower my gaze and hear the office door close softly behind her. If anything, I feel bad that I haven't stepped up before this. She looks so weary, and I take full responsibility for that. The trouble is, now I'm minus an assistant tomorrow which should be ok, but there are back-to-back meetings all day and nobody to organise them. Perhaps I should have planned this more carefully, but for some reason something hit me hard when she stood before me.

I know I'm cold and unfeeling. I always have been but lately it's not sitting well with me. When my fairy stopped my car, I was ready to tell her what I thought of her and send her on her way. However, something stopped me and an unusual act of kindness on my part awakened something in me that I liked. It felt good to help somebody in need. Even a surly fairy who didn't have a good word to say to me. For some reason, it lit something inside me I liked and when I returned home to my empty mansion, I couldn't think of anything else but her.

Now I know who sent her it's lit a spark inside me because one thing's for sure, I haven't seen the last of her and if I'm right, she will find me and for some reason, I'm looking forward to that moment more than anything.

JESSICA

Mrs Armstrong is gawping at me as if I've grown two heads. I know I make her nervous, it's obvious but when I instructed her to allow me full access to the personnel files on the computer, she paled and mumbled something about clearing it with Mr Harvey first, causing me to glare at her and say icily, "May I remind you that I am here on official police business. I am undercover and trust you to assist me. If you are unhappy about that, alert your boss to the fact you employed somebody without going through the usual process and see how long he allows you to keep your job."

I don't care that she looks as if she's about to cry because this is my big chance. My first solo job and whoever is targeting her boss had better watch out because I will stop at nothing to find them and make sure they spend a long and lonely Christmas behind bars.

Against her better judgement, Mrs Armstrong allows me access and I spend most of the day researching the staff, starting with the ones who recently left, were dismissed or resigned.

My notebook is filling up with potential candidates and I am staggered by how many people left his employment in the past month alone.

Once I'm finished, I type a quick email to my department and instruct them to discover what they can about the names I've given them. If there are any suspicious circumstances, I am confident we will uncover them and, for the first time since I arrived, it's as if I'm getting somewhere.

As closing time approaches, I finally have something to go on and so, rather than follow the rest of the staff towards the staff entrance, I take a different path and head up to confront the man himself. It's finally time to meet the most hated man in this building and try to unravel the mystery of the poison postman.

CHAPTER 8

ROBERT

I am already regretting giving Sylvia tomorrow off. I never realised how much she does for me. There will be no endless supply of coffee. No gentle reminders of meetings that are waiting for me. No prompts throughout the day of my diary and nobody to fetch me lunch and organise me. Subsequently, I'm now extremely irritated and so when there's a loud knock on my office door at six pm prompt, I say angrily, "What is it?"

The door flies open, and I blink in amazement as a very confident woman strides inside, looking like every dream I ever had disguised as a nightmare.

For a moment I stare in utter surprise, which is nothing to the look she gives me when she hisses, "I might have known."

I recover fast and smirk, "What's the matter? Do you need a lift home and couldn't bear waiting in the cold this time?"

"You!" she snarls, and it's almost an accusation, causing me to shrug. "Is that the best you can do? You weren't short of words the other evening, if I remember correctly."

"I see." She glares at me, her eyes flashing and leans on the desk, facing me off with a superior smirk on her face. "You coward. You allowed me to rant and rave about this place and didn't even give me the courtesy of revealing who you were."

"Miss Taylor." Her eyes widen as I address her by her name and for the first time since I've met her, she looks a little unsure.

"Firstly, why would I tell you my life story when you crashed into it uninvited? Secondly, your mouth was running quicker than my car so I never got the chance and thirdly, you were so judgmental I'm guessing it would have only stoked your vitriolic fire even more. No, I was happy to help and happy to escape your obvious hatred for anyone who has done better than you."

"How dare you!" She is positively breathing fire and for some strange reason, it ignites my interest even further. In fact, I can't remember the last time I was so attracted to a woman and all I can picture is running my hand around the back of her head and pulling those angry lips to mine while I demonstrate how much I desire her. However, she is obviously having none of those thoughts because she pulls back and starts pacing my office with a rather fetching scowl on her face.

"How did you discover my identity? Was it Mrs Armstrong?"

"Who?" I'm confused, and her derisive laughter irritates me. "Who? Are you kidding me? She's your personnel manager, you moron. The woman who slaves away dealing with your rash decisions to streamline your workforce, causing you to be the most unpopular boss in history since Scrooge."

"Now you're being overdramatic. Calm down."

"Dramatic, you say. If you think this is being dramatic, then I feel sorry for the bland, boring life you must live in your ivory tower." She appears to take a deep breath. "Now, are you going to sling insults at me all night or not because if you take my advice, you will sit back, shut up and listen to what a mess this company is in?"

Now I'm listening because at the mention of my company, I'm all ears.

She perches on the seat opposite my desk and crosses her legs, making my eyes gaze lazily down the length of them despite my better judgement. An irritated, "Eyes on my face, Mr Harvey, if you please." Causes me to glance up and she spits, "Firstly, I am no fairy, just in case you were wondering."

"You've got that right." I snipe back and she sighs as she runs her fingers through her long blonde tresses, causing me to shift slightly in my seat. The fact she's so attractive hasn't escaped me and if anything, the image I had in my mind is nothing to the vision before me. If God moulded my perfect woman, it's Miss Taylor, attitude and all and it's taking all my self-control not to proposition her and take her home for my own amusement.

"Now, I have been deployed here to discover the identity of the poison Christmas cards that you reported to the local station, which I have codenamed the postman."

I bark out a laugh and if looks could kill, I'd be dead by now and she huffs. "Given your prominence in the business world, it was forwarded to the department I work for as a matter of urgency."

I'm a little surprised at that because I've heard absolutely nothing and wait for her to finish before I speak.

"Due to your financial status, I was assigned to your case and went undercover in your store to find out what I could."

"So I heard." I shake my head. "I can't say I'm surprised that it didn't work out for you. You're not really cut out for customer service, are you?"

She sighs and fires back. "I'm not here to trade insults with you, Mr Harvey. I'm here to discover who hates you enough to want you dead, although the list is long, and I am considering adding my own name to it."

Despite her tone, I laugh out loud, which causes her to blink and appear a little surprised. "Did I say something to amuse you, Mr Harvey? Because I can assure you, I am not laughing."

I lean back and smirk, "It's a start, I suppose."

"What is?"

"Your feelings towards me."

"I don't have any."

"Are you sure about that, Miss Taylor, because I believe you are delusional. In fact, I'm of the opinion that you like our conversations a little too much and if I asked you to accompany me to dinner, I'm guessing you would be tempted."

Her mouth drops open and for the first time she doesn't have a quick retort and I watch her eyes narrow and her face flush as she growls, "I'm not here to date you, Mr Harvey. I'm here to protect you."

"That's settled then?"

"What is?"

"You are here to protect me and to do that properly, you will need to stay close to me. I mean, the postman may be out there waiting. My life is possibly in danger, and you would fail in your mission if I was murdered in cold blood as an act of revenge. You would never forgive yourself and neither would your colleagues because you would have let the team down."

"What are you saying?" She appears lost for words for once and so I lean forward and stare her straight in the eye and say firmly, "Until the postman is found, you must remain by my side, and we will work together to discover their identity, even if it takes until the New Year."

The red tinge to her cheeks causes me to groan inwardly because Miss Taylor doesn't even realise how attractive she is. To be honest, today is panning out better than I dared hope for because as soon as she stormed into my office, I knew I couldn't let her leave. There is something so enticing about my detective and as she stares at me through the most astonishing brown eyes, I allow myself to imagine every dirty thought running through my head right now and pray that Santa delivers them to me in one beautiful gift-wrapped package that goes by the name Detective Constable Jessica Taylor.

CHAPTER 9

JESSICA

For the first time in my life, I have no words. The man staring at me from across the desk is undoubtedly the most infuriating one I've ever met. Cocky, self-assured, and yet strangely mesmerising. The fact I've even noticed him is surprising me. I'm not interested in snagging a man, and especially not an arrogant one like him, but there is wisdom in his suggestion and now I think about it, I'm inclined to agree. Working in close proximity with him would take me deeper undercover. It would give me access to the areas of his life that he hides away from everyone else. Detective Inspector Ranauld will applaud my diligence and when I'm victorious, he will reward me with grittier missions, darker criminals, and I will finally realise my dream.

All I must do is get through the day without murdering the very man I'm sworn to protect, and the sooner I find the post-man, the quicker I'll be out of his life.

Reluctantly, I must agree this is the best decision all round, so I nod. "Ok."

He looks surprised. "Ok?"

Rolling my eyes, I fix him with my most 'she means business' expression. "You've got yourself a bodyguard, although for appearances, we need to come up with a cover story."

"Why?"

"Because the postman mustn't know we are onto him. So, let's get to work. Where does he deliver these cards? Here or to your home?"

"My home."

I don't miss the gleam in his eye as he says with a smirk, "Obviously, the threat is there. I'm guessing you should come and check it out,"

"My thoughts exactly." He looks surprised as I reach out and wrestle back control of the situation. "Ok, I will need to relocate to your home. I require my own room with a bathroom and my own space. Hopefully, it won't be for long, but it's a necessary evil I'm afraid when you work undercover."

I don't like the spark in his eye as he nods, looking a little too pleased with himself.

"Consider it done. I have several bedrooms for you to choose from. It won't be difficult giving you your space either, because I enjoy a lot of it."

"There he is again."

"Who?"

"The arrogant jerk who considers he's God's gift to mankind. A little humility would serve you well in life so that not everyone who meets you will consider you an arrogant pain in the rear end."

"Rear end." He laughs out loud, and I feel my eyes flashing as I bark. "Are you making fun of my grammar now? You're insufferable."

"I never said I wasn't." He shrugs. "So, what's our story? This will be interesting."

Thinking on my feet, I say with a shrug, "If anyone asks, I'm a friend who has come to stay."

"A friend." He shakes his head and laughs.

"Firstly, nobody would believe I had a friend and secondly, the fact you have been seen in my store working would raise a few eyebrows."

"So, what's your big plan, then?"

I fold my arms and he leans forward and stares right into my eyes and says huskily, "You're my lover."

"Absolutely not." I feel my skin prickle at the thought and fleetingly wonder why it's not an unpleasant sensation.

"Why not?" He shrugs. "We met in the lift one night after work and got talking and discovered a genuine connection. I took you to dinner and one thing led to another, and we've been inseparable ever since. Think about it, it's more believable than the friend's idea."

I hate that he's right. I detest the fact something like that could really happen and my skin crawls at the definite looks I'll get when people judge me for being a loose woman. They will call me a gold digger and say I always had him in my sights and picturing their knowing smirks and judgemental attitude is making me sweat. However, I can't escape the fact I'm under-cover and sometimes it requires placing myself in situations that are uncomfortable, so I sigh heavily and nod. "Ok. Have it your way, but just so you know, I'm only doing this because it's my job and no other reason. So we both understand, I am not attracted to you in the slightest. I don't like you; you are every-thing I detest in a man, and I am not looking for any attach-ment. Once we find out who the postman is, I'm moving on and you will never see or hear from me again. Have I made myself clear?"

"Perfectly." I don't miss the smirk on his lips and say roughly, "There will be rules, of course."

"Of course." He leans back and grins.

"Fire away."

"Firstly, there will be no touching. I require my personal

space and you must respect my privacy. My bedroom door must have a lock on it, and I would remind you that I am trained to defend myself if you get any ideas about the role we're playing."

"Go on. Anything else?"

"We will work diligently to resolve this unfortunate event and you must cooperate in every way. I will need full access to your life, and that includes details about past and present relationships and acquaintances."

He nods again and says firmly, "Then we have an agreement, Miss Taylor, or may I call you Jessica?"

"You may, Robert."

His name tastes unfamiliar on my tongue and yet not unpleasant and as I stare at the person who has become a twenty-four-hour job, I hate the shiver that passes through me as I study a man who probably never has to try. The dark hair that lies a little longer on top, framing velvet brown eyes that smoulder when he looks at me. The strong jaw shadowed by dark stubble creates a raw masculinity that should be illegal on a businessman. His well-cut suit that is slightly open at the neck, his tie lying loose after a hard day at the office and the well-manicured nails that reveal he doesn't get his hands dirty to enjoy the fruits of his labour.

There is something rather appealing about the man I must shadow and the arrogant glint in his eye tells me he knows the effect he is having on me, so I glower at him with hooded eyes and say through gritted teeth.

"Then it begins tonight. We'll head to my apartment, and I'll pack a few things. After that, we will stop for dinner before heading to your home. Any questions?"

I stare him straight in the eye and he nods, straightening up and flicking his computer off.

"Sounds good to me. After you."

He stands and waves his hand towards the door and with a sigh, I head off, knowing without a doubt that he is checking out my rear end as we go.

CHAPTER 10

ROBERT

*T*hings have worked out perfectly — for me, anyway. As I follow my fairy to the exit, I congratulate myself on a plan well executed. I'm not even sure why I want her with me as much as I do. I hate entertaining, prefer my own company and most people rub me up the wrong way. Except Jessica Taylor, it would seem.

So far, there is nothing about her that I don't like, and I suppose I've been searching for a distraction for a while now. Most of the time I'm happy with my life but increasingly I've begun to wish for something more. Somebody to share my life with whom doesn't irritate the hell out of me. She will certainly do that, but there's something more to her. A spark, a challenge, a delicious distraction, and I'm certain that once I've spent more than twenty-four hours in her company, I'll be showing her the door in every sense of the word.

I don't miss the curious glances thrown our way as we head through security and into the underground car park that not many people know about. Central London is not a place to bring a car unless you have your own parking space and money is no object. Lucky me because I have both and as Jessica stands impatiently by the passenger door, I find myself taking longer than normal to get inside, merely to rub her up the wrong way.

As soon as the door opens, she's inside and wastes no time with conversation, which I like. In fact, I've never met a woman who is so like me. Maybe that's why I'm drawn to her because I recognise a lot of my own qualities in her. I understand them and prefer them and so I don't even try to make her feel at ease because I'm guessing she is already.

We head out into the London traffic and after a while she says scratchily, "You haven't requested my address for the sat nav."

"Who needs a sat nav? I thought you would be more than happy to direct me."

"Then you thought wrong. I mean, why install a sat nav and not use it? You must utilise every opportunity you are presented with."

I grin to myself because that is exactly what I'm doing, and it amuses me when she angrily taps her address into the destination.

As the computer starts to speak, I huff, "Perhaps I prefer not to hear the incessant commentary of a journey I already know by heart."

"I doubt that."

"Doubt what?"

"That you know this particular journey."

"Why not?"

"Because I doubt you've even driven south of Putney in your life."

"You know nothing about me."

"I know enough."

She turns and stares out of the window and says quickly, "Hold back a little, will you?"

"Why?"

"The car beside me needs to get in front."

"And you think I'm happy to let anyone in? Don't you want to get home tonight?"

"Just do it."

"I beg your pardon?"

I can't believe how rude she is, and she says slowly, as if talking to an idiot, "Then let me spell it out for you. The car beside me is driven by a man who looks familiar to me. Don't ask me why, but I think I've seen his face before. I need to grab a picture of his licence plate to forward to my department in case he's off a Photofit somewhere."

"You're kidding."

I am momentarily stunned, and she says quickly, "You may have left work for the night, but I am always on duty. Just because I am concentrating on your predicament, it doesn't mean I close my eyes and ears to other cases. Don't question me because I only request things that are necessary."

I drop back and she takes a picture on her phone and obviously forwards it along with a text and I can't help tormenting her. "You're not allowed to use your phone while driving, it's an offence."

"I'm not driving."

"That doesn't matter. It could be considered a distraction to the driver, and I believe the ban extends to the passenger."

"Not in all cases."

She sighs. "Leave the law to me and do what I say. I wouldn't tell you how to run your business, although I'm tempted."

"Why are you tempted?" I say with amusement, and she shakes her head as if pitying me.

"When I worked undercover, I caught no less than ten shoplifters in one day. They were only the ones I saw, which means you have a serious problem."

Now I'm listening and she carries on, unaware how much her words anger me.

"It's obvious whatever security measures there are in place aren't up to the job, and I'm guessing thousands of pounds of profit leak through your system every day."

I say nothing and she continues. "You enjoy no loyalty from your staff who are using their positions to gain information about your business practices. Without naming names, one individual told me if you fired him, he would sell your secrets to the highest bidder. The only conversation regarding you is how ruthless you are and therefore your staff owe you absolutely nothing at all."

"Except their monthly pay checks, that is."

I am fuming, and she laughs out loud. "For a hard day's work. Have you ever worked in your own store doing what they do, or lived their lives and walked in their shoes? Of course not, because men like you get offered everything on a silver platter and expect the rest of mankind to respect you for it. Honestly, it's men and women like you that make the rest of us angry. Why should we struggle and scrape by working all the hours we can just to look up to people like you who think they are above us?"

"You know nothing about me."

I am already regretting my decision to spend time with this woman, and she says with amusement.

"Ok, tell me I'm wrong. Tell me you suffered to get where you are and everything you own was achieved through hard work and sacrifice."

"It's true." I can almost taste her triumph. "I am fortunate. My family is wealthy, and I've always been surrounded by money. I attended the best private schools and never had to work hard for anything material in my life."

"I knew it."

"But wealth isn't only about money and material things."

"They help."

"What if I admitted I am the poorest person I know for love."

"What's that supposed to mean?"

Her bored response does little to make me feel any better and if anything, I'm surprised I even said what I did but now it's out I ponder on it for a moment and say ruefully, "All of my life I've had something to prove. That I was the best academically, had the best manners, and excelled at everything I put my mind to. Anything that didn't make money or allow you to grow as a person was deemed irrelevant and so family days out to the beach, to watch a movie, or just to eat junk food was forbidden."

"My heart breaks for you."

She sounds bored and yet I can't stop now I've started and for some reason the words begin to flow.

"I spent my youth at museums, cathedrals and chess club. Any friends I had were soon bored because I wasn't allowed sleepovers, to attend parties or enrol in sports after school. During the holidays I had a private tutor, and I worked every day. If we went abroad, the tutor came too, and we would play chess as the only means of relaxation."

She remains silent and I say bitterly, "When it came to exams only A stars were good enough. If I got less, I was forced to study longer and harder and re-take them. Working hard was my life and even television was made up of documentaries to stimulate my brain and I saw none of the popular films that my fellow students would discuss between class."

"That's not a bad thing." I may be mistaken, but her voice has softened a little and I say with interest, "What makes you say that?"

"Well, it obviously worked because you're successful."

"Am I?"

I stop at the traffic lights and glance at her in the dim light of dusk. I'm not sure if I'm right, but she is regarding me with a very different expression now. A little curious, some pity and, if I'm not mistaken, more interest than before.

"You have money, billions, so I understand. How did that happen? Did you win the EuroMillions?"

She grins, and it shocks me so much I forget where we are and it's only the honking of horns behind me that returns my attention to the road. For a moment I don't answer because I am reliving that expression in my mind. If anything, I'm shocked at my reaction to her. In that one second, I saw a different side to the woman who has captured my attention so readily and now I've seen a sliver of who she is behind the mask she wears so fiercely, I am keen to pull the rest off and discover the treasure within.

"So did you?" Her soft voice wafts around my soul, shaking me back to reality and I grip the wheel a little tighter and say dismissively, "Something like that."

Luckily, the sat nav speaks up with a resounding, *"You have arrived at your destination. Your destination is on your right."*

As I pull into a small car park, Jessica says briskly, "Park in the space by the green car. It's the one I've been allocated, although I don't drive."

"You don't drive." I'm astonished and she huffs. "Why drive when I can walk to the station or catch a bus at the end of this road? Cars aren't that necessary, and I watch my money because not all of us have billions to waste on things we don't need or want."

As she slams the car door, I smile to myself. Normal service resumed and I'm more than happy about that because for a moment back there I would almost describe us both as human.

CHAPTER 11

JESSICA

I'm not sure how this has happened, but as soon as I stepped into my flat, I was conscious of another extremely large presence following in behind me. It makes me look at things a little differently and suddenly I'm hoping I left it tidy this morning. I'm not sure why I care what he thinks, but for some reason I do.

As I glance around, I notice things I never have before, like the lack of personal items making it a stark space that could be a rental. Practical furniture and no objects to dust or care for. Purely functional and lacking in any personality and my heart sinks when I realise that I just described myself.

Robert, to his credit, says nothing and just hovers by the door until I snap, "It's ok, you can come in, unless you consider it beneath you."

I don't even give him a chance to reply and say roughly, "Sit down and wait. I won't be long."

As I head into my bedroom, I shut the door and lean against it, closing my eyes for a moment to reassess the situation. For some reason, my heart is racing, and I am discombobulated. It's as if nothing is the same anymore. My routine has been cast aside on a whim and I am heading off to pastures unknown with a man who I am really trying to hate but somehow just can't. As I stare around my sterile room, I wonder what he's thinking right now.

Reflecting on the story of his childhood, I can't help picturing it. On the one hand, it sounded idyllic. How I would have loved a start in life like that. My own was so different, and I've had to work extra hard to get where I am now. My past is the antithesis to Robert's. I had to beg and plead with my parents to take me to museums and exhibitions. I had to fight my sister to watch anything but the childhood trash she favoured so I could catch the latest documentary on crime and failing that Midsomer murders. I was obsessed with all things murder most foul and my sister was not. Where she had pictures of the latest pop band on her walls, I had Poirot. My own room resembled a prison cell to ensure my mind was clear. Clutter is a distracting force that I have never been able to comprehend, and why waste time doing something that doesn't lead you closer to your goals? I never understood that.

Now I've met somebody who had everything I desired, and he speaks of it as if he missed out on something. I will never understand men and definitely not this one, so with a sigh, I reach for my holdall and begin precision packing with attention to detail, adding minimum items to achieve maximum results.

By the time I zip the bag with a flourish, a strange sense of excitement is building inside me. I'm doing something completely different, and it's connected to my job. I am finally doing what I dreamed of and that's why it's so important to make this work. To solve the crime and bring the postman, whoever they are, to justice. I actually can't wait and so with a renewed spring to my step, I head outside and experience a strange flutter in my heart when Robert glances up from the sofa and smiles.

Just for a moment, a second perhaps, I stare back with an alien emotion inside. I'm momentarily dazzled by that smile because, unlike the hard businessman I have heard he is, this man almost looks human. If you take away the fact he obviously *isn't* human, given the film star good looks and wealth dripping from every part of him, there is something so vulnerable about him sitting in my small flat off Wimbledon Broadway.

"Ready?"

I arch my brow and he nods, uncurling his limbs from my Habitat sofa and reaching for my bag like a gentleman. Ignoring it, I snatch it close to my chest and growl, "I can carry my own bag. I'm not incompetent."

"You are many things, Jessica, but I agree, incompetency is not one of them."

He laughs softly as I glower at him and as I follow him out and lock my door, I wonder what will happen next.

As it happens, we head to the nearest bistro and are soon seated at a table by the window in a place that makes my stomach growl as I spy the plates of food already making their way from the kitchen to the eager diners who made it here before us.

"This is nice." Robert looks around and for once, I must agree with him. "It is."

"Do you come here often?" He winks, making my face flush a little in the light of the flickering candle that rests in a bottle between us.

"Don't ever use that line again. It's tragic."

He raises his eyes, causing me to giggle a little and the shock on his face turns it into a full-blown belly laugh. "You're laughing." He says incredulously, making me laugh even more, and it's only the waiter arriving that stops me before the tears run down my face.

We make our selections and Robert orders a bottle of red wine, causing me to frown.

"What?"

"You're driving, you can't drink."

"I can have one at least."

"Can you though?" I arch my brow and he says with a sigh. "Last time I checked."

"If you say so, but alcohol affects people differently. One glass to some people takes them over the limit because they can't deal with it. I'm guessing you're one of them."

"What makes you say that?" He rolls his eyes as I grin. "Intuition."

"If you say so." The waiter reappears and fills our glasses, and he raises his to mine in a toast and whispers, "Here's to proving you wrong in everything."

"Good luck with that." I clink my glass against his and as I sip the potent mix of berries, alcohol and spice, we hold each other's gaze for a little longer than is polite and for some reason I can't tear my eyes away. It's as if the mood has shifted a little and the cosy atmosphere and warmth from the roaring fire nearby is lulling me into a false sense of happiness. I am sipping good quality wine with a billionaire that makes Richard Gere in Pretty Woman look like a tramp and I'm guessing things don't get much better than this. I could almost believe we're on a date because the scorching gaze he is throwing me is melting the ice in my heart and so I reluctantly tear my attention away and say in a voice that is a little higher than usual, "You never answered my question. How did you make your money?"

He sets the glass down and appears a little angry and I wonder if I'm prying unnecessarily.

"The internet."

"That's a sweeping statement. You will have to be a little more precise."

"Will I? I doubt it."

For some reason, he seems cagey and the detective in me sits up and takes notice.

"I'm sensing a story here. What happened? Did it all go wrong?"

"And leave me a billionaire." He laughs, but it seems hollow now, unlike before.

"Do you want to talk about it?"

"What are you, a therapist now?"

The mood has soured, and I wonder why and just sip the wine and stare at him, willing him to speak on his own terms. It's a little trick I learned on the job that sometimes it's better to say nothing at all, causing the person opposite you to fill in the awkward silence and once again it works in my favour as he huffs.

"If you must know, I made billions but lost my best friend in the process."

The tormented gleam in his eyes makes my breath hitch and as his mask slips, I see a damaged, broken man behind it trying desperately to hold it together and I wonder if the reason I'm here now has nothing to do with the store at all and has a lot to do with what happened in his past.

Robert appears to be fighting off demons and as we both sit quietly sipping our wine, I wait patiently for the flood gates to open and let me into a world he appears desperate to hide

CHAPTER 12

ROBERT

I'm not sure why I suddenly feel so angry. I try not to think about my money and how I got it. It's a memory I have fought hard to keep hidden in a box in my mind that would blow up in my face if I ever let it out. As Jessica's words linger on the binding that keeps it hidden, I try desperately to focus on something else. It was a simple question, but one that reminded me why I don't have friends or share my life with anyone. I suppose it's because I don't want to open this box and allow it to blow my world apart.

Luckily, the food arrives to distract her from the question, and I find it almost impossible to concentrate as a small moan wafts from across the table. "Hm, this is delicious."

I stare at her, my mind dazzled by the beauty she radiates despite how much she tries to disguise it. I'm not sure why she is so defensive all the time and decide to delve a little deeper into her life while her defences are distracted by the food.

"Tell me about yourself. Are you close to your family?"

"God no." she laughs out loud. "They are very different from me."

"In what way?" I'm curious and she shrugs, heaping more pasta onto her fork and taking a big bite.

As she chews, she appears to be considering her response and I like that about her. Jessica doesn't speak without every word being appraised before spoken and I understand a lot about that.

"My parents had no ambition."

"That's not a bad thing."

"If you say so." She rolls her eyes. "My sister Sally takes after them. All she wanted in life was the standard husband and two kids. A house in suburbia, working a part-time job while the kids are at school."

"And that's a bad thing?"

"Yes, it is, actually." Her eyes flash as she leans forward, and I am momentarily distracted by how much I crave this wild beauty.

"They have nothing. A stale marriage and a couple of kids who are out of control. Money is tight and they load more debt onto credit cards that they can only afford to pay off the interest every month. Subsequently, they gamble on the lottery in the hope all their prayers will be answered, and they will become millionaires overnight. They never will."

"How can you be so sure? It happens."

"Does it though. Name one person you heard of who got rich from a scratch card."

"I don't know anyone who buys scratch cards, so no, I can't."

"That's my problem."

"I don't understand."

"People like you don't live in the world the rest of us inhabit. You don't understand what it's like to tie yourself in knots and your only way out is hoping that lady luck deals you a fresh card."

She leans back and for the first time since I met her, Jessica looks defeated, and I don't like it at all. Wishing I could help, in fact, she only needs to ask, and I would solve her sister's problems in a heartbeat, which once again surprises me. I don't do charity, only when it benefits me on a tax front, that is. I'm not even sure I like the way my thoughts are heading and so say rather abruptly, "You can't fight your sister's battles. She's made her own mess."

Jessica nods, which surprises me again, and her voice sounds hard as she agrees with me. "It's sad though, don't you think?"

"Not really." I shrug. "From what you've told me, she could pity you more."

"Why?" Rather than look angry, she merely looks interested, and I lean back, fixing her with a blank expression.

"You have a good job, admittedly, but what else? By your own admission, you have nothing else apart from a sterile space to return home to every night. You say you have no friends, aren't connected to your family, and prefer to work."

"What's wrong with that? It works for you, too."

She raises her glass, and it makes me laugh out loud and raise mine to hers in a toast. "To meeting your match."

"I'm not cheering that." Her eyes flash. "You're not my match. We're nothing like one another."

"If you say so."

To be honest, in my opinion we're more alike than anyone I've ever met. I understand how her mind works and I admire her. I don't believe I've ever met a woman who isn't giggling and wildly flirting with me by now, intent on only one thing. My money. I'm not delusional. I realise they see the successful businessman with more money than they can ever spend, and I don't blame them for wanting some of it for themselves.

However, I'm not the sharing kind and so I enjoy a few

dates that always lead to my bedroom and then I ignore their calls and instruct Sylvia to tell them to stop calling me. I've never met a woman I wanted to discover more about until now. It's not because I am insanely attracted to her either. I find her interesting, which is a first for me. She is an enigma, a challenge, and a beautiful woman. What's not to like? Even her smart mouth and barbed comments don't put me off. I like her, which is a first for me and now I have her in my sights, I'm going to do everything possible to keep her there.

* * *

As I PULL up outside my mansion, I can sense the disapproval radiating from Jessica and my heart sinks.

"You're such a stereotype." Her cutting remark rolls off me like water on a window and I shrug. "It's just a house."

"That is too big for one man. Honestly, Robert, I haven't even been inside yet and I'm already angry."

"I will not apologise for my home, Jessica. That's your problem, so deal with it."

Setting the alarm on my car, I unlock the door and enter the security code into the alarm system and say wearily, "I'll show you to your room. It's late, we can catch up in the morning."

"Sounds good to me."

Her voice is curt and full of business, and any warmth she showed me in the bistro has disappeared in the chill of winter.

I understand my home is extreme, and it's way too big for one person. She's right about that but I didn't buy it to be homely. I bought it as an investment. It's a way to make more money and I don't care what she thinks, at least that's what I'm telling myself but deep down inside, I do. Rather a lot as it happens, and I curse my bad judgement in bringing her here and not my apartment by the river. In fact, I really should relocate there because it's closer to the office and more than adequate for my needs. This house is like my soul, dark, empty and full of shadows.

We head up the grand staircase and Jessica is silent for once, which I'm enjoying. Now I'm home, my mind has switched off and I want nothing more than to shower, change and slump in front of the game in my cinema room. Just imagining what Jessica would have to say about that exhausts me and I'm not in the mood for another lecture about my living standards, so I'm a little abrupt when I swing open the door to my prettiest guest room and say wearily, "You should find everything you need in here. There's a bathroom attached and a dressing room. It has a lock that works from the inside and last time I looked, there wasn't anyone lurking behind the curtains. If you need a coffee or anything to eat, the kitchen is at the bottom of the stairs, third door to your right. Help yourself, and don't worry, I'll keep out of your way."

"Good." She moves past me into the room and then hesitates before closing the door.

"Well, um, thank you for the meal. I really would have preferred to pay half, though."

When I cast my mind back to the almost fist fight we had when the bill came, I disguise the ghost of a smile that threatens to lift my dour mood.

"It's fine. Just consider it expenses."

"If you say so."

I turn and she says quickly, "Oh and Robert…"

"Yes." I sigh inside and prepare myself for another verbal battering.

"Thank you."

"For what?"

"The lift the other day, the meal and, well, the company."

I hold my breath as her lashes dust her cheeks and she

blushes a little before a soft smile transforms her face into something breath-taking. "Goodnight."

"Goodnight, Jessica."

The door closes, but it's some time before I turn away because for the first time in my life, I felt something shift inside me where other people have a heart.

CHAPTER 13

JESSICA

I take it all back with interest.

As I stare around a room dripping with luxury, I can now understand the attraction. Who wouldn't want this?

It's magnificent and, to be honest, so is the man who brought me here. I have tried so hard to ignore my growing attraction to him, but for some reason my usual cool detachment is deserting me this time. Money, power and movie star looks are a heady combination, and I am reeling under the pressure.

My room is ten-star luxury. It suits me and my tastes perfectly. There are no fancy frills, just a cool, modern space designed for decadence. The bed is bigger than my entire bedroom at home and the sheets appear to be the finest Egyptian cotton. The scatter cushions alone appear to be spun with silk thread, and the huge, padded headboard is a designer touch I definitely approve of. The soft white carpet is both impractical yet decadent and I quickly remove my shoes to preserve its cleanliness. As my toes scrunch into the soft pile, a wave of happiness washes over me.

This place is amazing, and I haven't even begun to explore it properly. As soon as we pulled up in front of the mansion, I knew I was going to love it. It's like a white doll's house and even thought I hate and detest Christmas with a passion, even I imagined a big floral wreath on the front door, with potted Christmas trees, decorated with fairy lights on either side of the portico. In fact, this house was made for Christmas and yet you wouldn't know it was the Christmas season at all. Although it's clean and welcoming, it's also sterile and stark and it makes me wonder about the man who owns it.

Why is this man single? It just doesn't make sense because on paper, he has everything most women are looking for. There must be something seriously freaky about him, and I can't wait to discover it and throw it in his face.

As I wander deeper into the room, I can't resist touching the heavy silk curtains and running my fingers over the gleaming mirrored surfaces. I catch a glimpse of a remote control on one of them that appears to be labelled with different things to what I'm used to.

I press the one marked 'lights' and the room is cast in a warm glow that appears to be coming from the walls. I press the music on and soft classical tunes wafts through hidden speakers, bringing life to the room.

Now I've started, I can't stop and as I work through the controls, I can't believe my eyes. Curtains part revealing a floor to ceiling window and I'm guessing the view outside is as perfect as the rest of the house. All I can make out is the trees that are lit up by soft lighting, and now I understand why the other half live this way. It's addictive, enthralling and desirable and I am sinking fast into the madness that goes with it.

I head through a door that leads into another small room that is decked out with floor to ceiling cupboards and shelves. They all stand empty, but I can only imagine the amazing dresses and designer shoes and handbags that could crowd the space if a person actually called this room home.

However, nothing compares to the bathroom and if the remote revealed amazing things in the bedroom, it has nothing on what's in here. At the press of a button, the bath starts to fill and the steam from the water is even scented with lavender. Once again, the lighting is warm and subdued, but on further investigation I can change it to my preferred colour choice. A television sparks into life on the wall by the huge bathtub and once again there is a music option. As I press another button, the wall slides back and there is storage to die for. White fluffy towels, luxurious bathrobes and every designer potion and cream that graces a perfumery floor.

Part of me should hate this and be disgusted by the sheer waste of money, but the woman in me is clapping her hands with delight and willing me to behave myself so she can drown in designer decadence.

It's all too much and I spend the next hour relaxing in the bubble spa bath, watching the news and indulging in my newfound luxury. When I drag myself out, it's to wrap a warm fluffy towel around my body and liberally smear my skin with the lotions that smell like a dream.

If this is a dream, then leave me to sleep because I haven't had so much fun in years.

By the time I've wasted two hours wallowing in wealth, I turn to my holdall and pull out my loungewear that I prefer to wear in the house.

Despite how tempting the bed is right now, I could really murder a cup of coffee, so I head out to explore and search for the hub of the house, otherwise known as the kitchen.

The house does not disappoint me either, because as I head through the hallway, every step reveals even more luxury. Lighting illuminates my steps as if by magic and it must be the result of pressure pads or something because it goes out as I pass. I am so impressed with that because at least Robert doesn't waste electricity. I'm pretty certain he must have every gadget ever invented, and that impresses me more than the luxury I've enjoyed.

I edge down the grand staircase and remember the directions to the kitchen, even though I am tempted to explore what lies behind the doors that I pass.

However, the kitchen does not disappoint and as I head inside, the lights illuminate a space Mary Berry would never leave.

In keeping with the rest of the house, this space is a designer's dream and I blink in astonishment at the gleaming surfaces and walls of cabinetry that must hide everything ever required to whip up a feast for a king.

My main purpose is to make a coffee, but the scary looking barista station is a step too far, so I seize the remote lying on the marble-topped counter and press the button marked 'beverage'.

I'm amazed when a door slides open, revealing a beverage station like no other. Shelves of teas, coffees, hot chocolate and every refreshment invented shine like a beacon from their impressive home. My heart lifts when I spy a kettle and as I fill it, I wonder how much this must have all cost. It's a good job Robert has billions because I'm positive he needs them and once again I hate that I'm impressed with this standard of living when my flat has always been adequate for my needs.

A movement by the door alerts me and I spin around, and my jaw drops when I regard the man himself entering the room. Gone is the corporate suit and in its place is a tight t-shirt and shorts. He has a towel slung around his neck that he is using to wipe the sweat from his face, and I swear all my lady parts stand up and cheer as they focus on only one thing. Him.

"Glad to see you found the kettle."

"Um, yes, um, thank you."

I can't even speak properly, and I hate myself for that which causes the crazy in me to speak up to hide my confusion.

"Don't you have a shower? Honestly, that's so unhygienic."

He shrugs and grabs a bottle of water from the fridge and chugs it down.

"I have twelve showers, to be exact, but I heard you in here and thought I'd check on you."

"Twelve showers, what the…"

"One for every bedroom of which there are ten. One in the pool house and one in my gym that is currently being refurbished, otherwise I would have used it."

I'm speechless and he sighs, stretching his shoulders, causing me to focus on the rippling abs that appear to be moulded to his sweat ridden t-shirt.

"I'll clean up and then I'm catching the game. Help yourself to anything you need. Breakfast is at seven am."

He turns, effectively dismissing me, and from out of nowhere, that hussy inside me calls out, "The Christmas cards."

He turns slowly. "What about them?"

"Have you got them? I would like to take a look."

"What now?"

"Why not? In case it escaped your notice, I'm working and am currently on a job right now. Now is the perfect time."

"If you insist."

He nods towards the door.

"They're in my study. It's this way."

Despite being desperate for a cup of coffee, it appears that I'm even more desperate for another lustful gaze at my roomie and I scamper after him like a kid following the pied piper, checking out his physique as I go. I'm definitely dreaming of him tonight. He'll never find out, though. This infatuation that's developing is being given a one-night pass before I shut it down completely.

He strides off, making conversation difficult, so I say nothing and follow him to discover what all the fuss is about.

As he opens the door, I'm not surprised to see a man cave

that I would have expected from him. Panelled walls and subdued lighting surround a walnut desk and a leather chair. A fireplace kicks into life as we enter and the warm scent of brandy wafts towards me, accompanied by a wave of heady cologne. The shelves in the far corner hold leather-bound books and a few black and white photographs in silver frames. They all appear to be of dogs and for some reason it makes me a little sad that the only friends he appears to have is of the four legged variety.

"I see you're a dog lover."

I nod towards the picture and as he smiles, my heart skips a beat.

"My only love."

"He, or she?"

"She. Her name was Willow."

"Was?" My heart sinks and I hate that the light in his eyes dim.

"She was fourteen when she died. I was at university and my mother called to tell me she had her put down."

"That's terrible."

"It was for the best. She had cancer and was in a lot of pain. Part of me is glad I never witnessed her suffering and yet part of me wishes I was there to say goodbye."

I don't know what to say because I'm not the best in these situations and so I say softly, "I always wanted a dog."

"You never have?"

He looks interested. "No. My parents wouldn't let me because my sister is allergic."

"I'm sorry."

"Don't be. It was probably for the best, anyway. No attachments, no pain."

He stares at me with curiosity. "Is that what you think?"

"It's what I know, Robert. If you don't develop any feelings in the first place, they won't be hurt."

"That's sad."

"Not really." I pull myself up and say firmly, "Anyway, the cards."

"Yes. The cards."

He reaches out to a stack on the side of the desk and hands them to me, and I'm surprised how many there are.

"Thirteen." He answers my question as if he can read minds, and I shake my head. "Wow, somebody really does want you to notice them."

He points to the seat by the fire and as I sit, he says, "They are sent to the house by Royal Mail. There is no indication where they are posted from, just the London sorting office, which gives nothing away."

As I open the top one, I see the bold print revealing the worst kind of greeting.

This will be your last Christmas. Enjoy life while you can.

As I flick through the rest, the messages are similar, and I'm not surprised he reported them. For the first time since learning of this job, I understand the seriousness of the situation and despite how much I disapprove of him and his lifestyle, I experience a surge of sympathy for the man sitting silently beside me.

"Do you have any idea who it could be?"

"None."

A clock chimes on the wall and I say with a sigh. "It's getting late. We'll talk tomorrow. I'll look through them and compile a list of questions. Whoever is sending these will be caught. You have my word on that."

"That's good to hear."

I'm not sure he's taking this as seriously as he should, judging from the smirk on his face, but pushing my barbed retort aside, I say quickly, "What are your security measures for this house?"

"An alarm on every window and door, that is deactivated when they are opened from the inside. When I leave, I set the master alarm that is connected to the security company I use. The approach to the house is littered with sensors and alerts the security company to anyone coming and going and they are paid to keep it under surveillance 24/7."

"Impressive." Not that I'm surprised, and my attention returns to the cards in my hand.

"I can see now why they are sent through the post. It tells me that whoever it is, knows of your security in place."

"You think it's someone I know?"

He seems shocked at that, and I laugh out loud. "I definitely think it's someone you know. I'm pretty sure you have many enemies out there, Robert, but it takes a very misguided person to actually take it this far."

"Well, that's your job, I suppose. I should leave you to it."

He stands and says over his shoulder, "Seven am, Jessica, good night."

As the door closes on an abrupt exit, it leaves me with more questions than answers and, feeling a surge of enthusiasm for my task, I head back to the kitchen to study these over an extremely desirable cup of coffee.

CHAPTER 14

ROBERT

I had to get out of there for my own sanity. I should never have ventured into the kitchen, but the minute I saw her through the door looking so desirable it stopped me in my tracks. I could smell the shampoo and fancy lotions she obviously used and the sight of her long blonde hair cascading down her back made me long to run my fingers through it and pull her lips to mine. The soft fabric of her lounge pants hugged her curves, revealing a shapely body beneath and just seeing a woman who is so naturally beautiful standing in my kitchen did something to me I wasn't expecting.

I liked it.

I liked seeing her in my space, providing life to a place that always seems so cold. The way she scrunched up her nose as she studied the beverages made me long to draw my finger across the lines and smooth them away. The more time I spend with her the more I want and when we headed to the study, and I saw her looking so small and fragile wrapped inside my leather seat, it sparked an animal instinct that surprised me.

The concern in her eyes as she read the cards hit me square in the heart and when she lifted those gorgeous brown eyes in my direction, it took every ounce of self-control I have to stop myself from pouncing.

I want her.

I want the abrasive, hard edges of a woman who lights the spark to my life. She is everything I look for in a woman and yet she is the most disinterested I have ever met. Women usually want me. They want what I can give them, but for the first time I've met someone who doesn't appear affected by any of it and it's a humbling experience.

So, I walked away for my own self-preservation because distance is what I need right now, and I must remind myself that this is purely business, and she is here to do a job.

I head to the shower, and she follows me there. As the water rains down from the oversized shower head, I close my eyes and she is behind them. As I soap my body, she is telling me I'm doing it wrong and as I wash the sweat from my hair, she is running her fingers through it. Every single move I make, she is in my thoughts and I'm coming to the conclusion I'm going slightly crazy. Is this what happens when a man finds the woman he was always meant to? I'm certain of that, but it's obviously one sided, which is a huge blow to my ego.

Even the game doesn't banish her from my thoughts. I sense her beside me, her head resting on my shoulder, asking me what it all means. I picture her feet resting on my lap as she asks questions, causing me to growl irritably, my peace forever shattered.

I try so hard to picture the pitfalls of having a woman in my life, but when I head off to bed, the space feels so empty without her warm body to mould around mine. Imagining her tiny fingers trailing my body and her soft kisses pressed against my skin has me heading for the shower again and if I thought this would be hell sharing my space with a woman like that, I was right on the nail.

* * *

BREAKFAST ARRIVES after a tortured night where Jessica starred in every dream I had. I'm embarrassed to face her this morning after what happened in them and I'm not surprised to find her already in the kitchen, the strong aroma of coffee brewing telling me she's made herself at home already.

"Hi." Her voice is soft, and I nod abruptly, trying not to stare at the woman who is wearing a skirt that falls just above her knees and a silk blouse unbuttoned low enough to be sexy yet practical. Her hair is tied in a loose ponytail and her make up accentuates a pretty face that she tries to hide behind her usual hard stare.

"I'm not sure what you like for breakfast, but I've made scrambled eggs on brown toast."

"You don't have to cook for me."

I'm being rude, but this situation is disturbing me more than I thought it would, and I try not to register the hurt that lights those soulful eyes.

"I know." Her voice is tight and with an irritated huff, she slides the plate across the breakfast bar towards me.

"I was making some for myself and made enough for two. No big deal."

She pours two mugs of coffee and pushes one my way with a tense, "I'm guessing you hate this coffee too. Just deal with it and stop acting like an idiot."

Despite her words, it makes me smile, and she rolls her eyes. "You're so weird."

As I tuck into the unexpected treat, I hate how good it tastes. If she burned the toast, or overcooked the eggs, I'd be happier because then I would have reason to find fault with her. But like everything she does, Jessica strives for excellence, which also extends to the kitchen, it seems.

"So," She chews on her toast, making it difficult to look away from the sight of her luscious lips.

"I studied the cards and made some notes. Do you want to hear what I discovered?"

"Of course." I take a sip of coffee and feel myself relax as the caffeine hits my bloodstream.

"The words are similar on all of them, as if the postman doesn't have much else to say. It's all very basic and is designed to alarm more than anything. It's almost as if they don't know how to move past the threat that this will be your last Christmas, which tells me one of two things."

"Which are?"

"Firstly, I don't believe they actually intend on carrying through with their threats and secondly, I'm guessing they are doing this just to put you on edge."

"You can't know that for sure."

"I can't, but I've seen threatening letters before and by the thirteenth one they've evolved a little. Either the person sending these is unsure how to progress, or they are just playing a game with your emotions."

"So, you think I'm overreacting?"

I fix her with a hard expression, and she shrugs. "No. You did the right thing and, of course, you must always be on your guard. There are some seriously weird people out there and your money is like a red flag to those who have none."

"So, it's my money they hate."

"Doubtful."

"Why?"

"Because you're not exactly the friendliest guy on the planet, and I'm guessing you make more enemies than friends."

"So, what's the plan?"

She scrunches up her nose again, which delivers a powerful blow to my unguarded heart and says thoughtfully, "I will resume my search of your personnel files. I need to learn who you dismissed, reprimanded, and hired. I must discover who holds a grudge against you and eliminate them one by one from the list."

"Good luck with that. It's a long one."

She shrugs and then fixes those gorgeous eyes on mine, and I'm suddenly very hot.

"Girlfriends. I need to know who they are, were and their addresses. Friends too. It could be someone close to you, it usually is, and I need to hear of any acrimonious splits or erratic behaviour that you have witnessed."

Now I'm extremely uncomfortable because the list of casual hook ups is long and I'm already picturing the disapproval heading my way when she learns what a player I am.

Suddenly, I've lost my appetite and, pushing my plate away, I say irritably, "We should go."

"Not until you've washed the dishes. It's only fair as I made breakfast."

"Then it's a good job I have a housekeeper who does that for me. Shall we go?"

I stand before she can tell me what a waste of air I am and head for the door on a mission. This is not working out well for me at all because the only thing I want to do with my day is Detective Constable Jessica Taylor.

CHAPTER 15

JESSICA

*H*e was silent on the journey, and I wonder if I've irritated him. I wouldn't be surprised. I have a habit of doing that and as we head through the security entrance, I don't miss the surprised glances of the people we pass. I'm not sure this was such a good idea because I know how things work in places like this and I'm guessing we will be breaking news by morning coffee.

To make matters worse, Robert stops at the entrance to the store where we will part company for the day and says loud enough for anyone nearby to hear, "Have a good day, darling. Come and find me at one for lunch. There's a great little bistro nearby you will love."

To my horror, he stops and before I know what's happening, he reaches out and pulls me towards him and drops a soft kiss on my lips and whispers, "That should do it."

He winks as he pulls away and heads through the door to the shop floor, leaving me speechless behind him.

I turn to see if anyone was looking and my heart sinks when I catch the eye of a group of women hovering nearby. The envy on their faces annoys me more than it should, causing me to glare at them before spinning on my heels and heading to personnel where I intend to hide for most of the day.

To be honest, I am fuming at a public display of affection that most certainly wasn't required. Why did he do that and if he thinks I'm meeting him for a bistro lunch, he's got another thing coming?

I am beyond angry that he has made us the subject of gossip, unnecessarily in my opinion, and as I stomp to personnel, the guarded expression of Mrs Armstrong doesn't improve my mood.

"Jessica." She says it with fear in her voice and I say irritably, "Good morning, Mrs Armstrong, I need to resume my investigations. Please don't disturb me."

She nods as if in shock and as I sit at the nearby desk, I try to empty my mind of the unfortunate incident that just occurred.

* * *

As MORNINGS GO, this is one of the dullest and as I trawl through the computer records, it becomes obvious that probably every single one of Robert's employees could be a suspect.

To her credit, Mrs Armstrong keeps me wallowing in coffee for which I am most grateful and only a call from my Inspector breaks the tedium of the day.

"How are things going?"

Mrs Armstrong has taken a natural break, so I'm free to speak and I say in a low voice, "It's a laborious task, but I'll get there."

"Any ideas?"

"Not yet."

He sighs. *"Do your best, Jessie, because there's a shed load of files heading our way and I need someone to organise them."*

My heart sinks. Great, me again. Every file that passes through our office starts with me, and I'm beginning to wonder if I'm only viewed as a secretary. None of the guys are tasked with filing, and I'm getting fed up with it.

Feeling antsy, I growl, "I'll do my best, but this situation is one that needs resolution. Mr Harvey is a man with many enemies, and I intend on unmasking the postman if it's the last thing I do."

"The postman?"

Detective Inspector Ranauld sounds amused, and I say tightly, "My codename for the perpetrator."

The silence is surprising, but then his amused voice says abruptly, *"Just hurry up. I need you here."*

He cuts the call, leaving me bristling with anger. So much for my glorious promotion when I'm successful. Knowing him, I'll be back to making the coffee and filing before my feet hit the stained carpet in his office.

With a sigh, I resume my task, wondering how long I can string this out because at least here I'm important and doing something that will make a difference. I like to think so at least.

* * *

I CAN TELL that Mrs Armstrong has something on her mind when she returns because she can't stop staring at me and is shifting awkwardly on her seat and after an hour of it, I snap.

"Do you have something you wish to say to me, Mrs Armstrong?"

"No."

I fix her with an imperious stare, and she squirms a little. "I, um, well…"

"Spit it out." My impatience obviously shows because she flushes bright red. "It's just, well…" She laughs nervously, "Word on the shop floor, gossip I'm sure, is that you and um, Mr Harvey…"

"Are lovers?" I raise my eyes and she blushes so red it's quite an astonishing sight.

Before I can answer her, a low laugh heads our way and we glance up to see Robert leaning against the door frame looking so edible I openly stare. He winks at Mrs Armstrong, causing her mouth to drop and says flirtatiously, "Hey, babe, ready for lunch."

I'm pretty certain my face is as red as my companions and with an angry glare, I say briskly, "Of course."

I grab my bag and stride towards him, directing my hardest glare in his direction.

As I pass, he drops his hand to my waist and follows me out and I am burning with mortification as he publicly declares something that isn't even real and I hiss, "What are you thinking? Are you crazy?"

"I thought this was what we agreed. Our cover story."

"If anyone asks, you idiot. Honestly, you could have said nothing, and nobody would have suspected a thing. Way to go. You have just made me public enemy number one."

"In what way?"

We step inside the lift, and I say with anger, "Now nobody will like me by default."

He grins. "I'm sure you're used to that already. It may have escaped your notice, but we're worryingly alike and I'm guessing you haven't made many friends here, anyway."

"I have." I bristle with indignation.

"Who?" He smirks and I snap. "There's Rory and Adam."

"Who are they?" I notice a sharp gleam in his eye that tells me I've hit a nerve, making me say smugly, "Rory, from men's gifts and Adam from accounts. Oh yes, they wasted no time in befriending me and inviting me for drinks to their exclusive club."

"What club?" Luckily, the door opens, giving me the escape I need, and I stride out, saying over my shoulder, "Hurry up, babe, we only get one hour, remember?"

The expression on the woman's face who is waiting outside makes me laugh inside as she openly stares at our CEO who is almost running to keep up and a surge of power shoots through me as I understand the benefits of being in my position.

In fact, despite appearances, I experienced a warm fuzzy glow that shocked me more than anything when he stood in the doorway and gazed at me with those soul shattering eyes, the endearment dripping from his lips as if it belonged there.

Maybe I should bask in the glory this ruse brings with it. Perhaps I should enjoy a hot man's attention with no strings attached. It could make this job bearable and what's so bad about it, anyway?

* * *

RATHER THAN HEAD to the car, Robert falls into step beside me, and we brace ourselves for the short chilling walk to the bistro nearby. I've seen it as I stride past to reach the delicatessen on the corner and often wondered who could afford the luxury of a proper meal at lunchtime. Now I'm one of them and as we head into the warm, calm atmosphere of a place that is definitely out of my league, I am strangely looking forward to spending the next hour with the gentleman who has grown uncharacteristically quiet beside me.

"Sir, madam, your table is ready."

The maitre d almost bows, causing me to blink in astonishment. It's almost as if he's expecting us and I glance at Robert who appears to have recovered his arrogance, judging from the self-satisfied smirk on his face as he reaches out and slips his arm around my waist and whispers, "After you, darling."

I notice the expressions of a couple of women who are definitely not snatching a quick lunch, judging from the bottle of champagne in an ice bucket and the glazed appearance of two ladies who do this often.

However, the envy on their faces causes an inner glow to spread like rapid fire inside me and the reason for it is standing right here and so I smile flirtatiously, loving the surprise in Robert's eyes as I purr, "Oh darling, you do spoil me."

It almost makes me laugh out loud at the expression on his face and as I glide through the restaurant, I lap up the attention like a famous actress on the red carpet.

I could get used to this, which worries me. Luxury appears to be my new best friend and as the maitre d and his staff fawn over us, I hate that I love every second of it.

Robert is attentive and gazing at me as if I'm his one true love causing me to constantly remind myself that it's all an act. Although I'm a little surprised we're here at all because surely the postman doesn't dine in five-star luxury but then again, he could be anyone.

As we sit and eat a risotto unlike anything I have ever tasted before, I discover that Robert is easy company, despite what I first thought. He is attentive, funny and loaded with good conversation and the hour flashes past so quickly, I'm surprised when he stands and says ruefully, "We should get back. I have a meeting at two and I expect they are already waiting."

"Yes, of course."

I scramble to my feet and realise that for the first time in what seems like forever, I completely forgot about work for just the briefest amount of time.

As we walk to the door, I'm surprised to hear a loud, "Darling, what a coincidence."

"What the…" Robert spins around, and I follow his gaze to see a man and woman sitting in the alcove, staring at us with beaming smiles.

Robert sighs heavily and whispers, "I'm sorry about this."

"Sorry about what?"

I'm confused as he grips my hand hard and pulls me across to stand beside their table and the way they both assess me with curious glances makes me wonder just who they are.

My question is soon answered as Robert says wearily, "Jessica, meet my parents, Sable and David."

I stare in surprise at the rather glamorous woman beaming at me and then her husband, who appears to be enjoying a private joke.

"Darling, I'm so pleased to meet you. Robert never said he was dating anyone."

She throws him an amused look as Robert, to my surprise, pulls me closer and drops a light kiss on the side of my face before saying sweetly, "Its early days but going well."

The astonishment on his mother's face tells me this is unusual, and his father says in a booming voice, "Why don't you join us so we can learn more about your beautiful girlfriend?"

Strangely, I feel myself blushing and I'm angry about that, but before I can react, Robert says quickly, "I'm sorry we must get back to the store."

"Oh, you work together." Sable is obviously digging, and I nod. "Yes, ma'am, it's where we met."

"Interesting." She glances at her husband who stares at us

with surprise. "That's not like you, son. Mixing business with pleasure."

Robert has obviously decided to end this conversation and shrugs. "It happens. Anyway, sorry to rush off, but we have work to do."

I just catch a look on his father's face that is gone as quickly as it came but there is something telling me he is not as amiable as I first thought and I wonder if it has anything to do with the story I heard of Robert replacing him and yet as I glance a little closer, he just winks as his wife says quickly, "You must bring Jessica to dinner tonight. I insist."

"We…" Robert begins to say but she holds up her hand to silence him. "Non-negotiable. It's been too long already, and you are becoming a stranger, Robert and I won't allow it."

I have a new respect for Sable Harvey because she is definitely a woman after my own heart as she cuts him down and gives him no room to manoeuvre and Robert says wearily, "What time?"

"Seven, and don't be late."

Robert nods and almost drags me away from the table and it's only when we're outside that he groans and says angrily, "I'm sorry, Jessica. Prepare yourself for a night of pure and utter hell."

Before I can ask why, he pushes through the crowd with an urgency that has me running to keep up and as I follow him, I detect a story waiting to be told and despite his reluctance, tonight can't come soon enough for me.

CHAPTER 16

ROBERT

*D*espite the pleasure of Jessica's company over lunch, I'm in a terrible mood when I return to the office. My parents always have a habit of doing that to me and now we must face an evening in their company when I would rather pull out my own teeth slowly and painfully. I know what they're doing, and I'm almost tempted to call with an excuse.

For some reason, my parents have sought to control my entire life, and this will be no exception. It's why I keep away; why I *moved* away as soon as I could. The fact I earned so much money making me independent of them gave me my way out and they've never forgiven me for that. Then my grandfather replaced my father with the son he appears to resent and I'm guessing he's playing a waiting game for it all to blow up in my face.

Part of me wondered if the Christmas card thing was his doing. I never took it seriously at first, thinking he was just being petty. The trouble is, I don't believe he is, not really, and so when the tenth one arrived, I decided to report it. There are so many people it could be and I'm not proud of that. Although it did bring with it a very silver lining because now I have

Jessica and despite what she thinks, I'm not letting her go anytime soon.

I like her and could even be falling in love with her, which surprises me more than anything.

I love the way she tries to be cool and efficient and yet in unguarded moments, the mask slips and I see a vulnerable woman trying to disguise it. I'm protective over her, which is amusing considering she is meant to be protecting me, but there is something so fascinating about my bombshell detective and part of me hopes we never find the identity of the postman as she calls them.

The afternoon is spent taking care of business, which is luckily on the upward trend, which in turn makes the share-holders and directors extremely happy. I will be hosting an important board meeting, a few days before Christmas, where I will unveil the figures and explain my plans for development for the coming year. My grandfather always likes to attend them as is his right as the Chairman of the company. My father is also on the board of directors, but it was made clear he was to be a silent investor due to his mismanagement during the period he was in charge.

Sometimes I wonder how he feels about that. All I know is he plays a lot of golf and shepherds my mother around town, shopping and enjoying lavish lunches. Half of their time is spent in Florida where they have a villa and to everyone else, they appear to be living the dream.

However, there are the unguarded moments when I see behind the smile and note he is struggling. Part of me is sorry about that, but the businessman in me pushes it aside with scorn. He never measured up against the force to be reckoned with, otherwise known as my grandfather, and perhaps that's why he was so hard on me because it was obvious from a very young age that his own father preferred my company to his.

Sylvia enters my office and I note the shadows under her

eyes and wonder how she does this every day. She works long hours here before heading home to care for her family which appears to be taking its toll and despite my abrasive attitude, I'm worried about her.

"Take a seat, Sylvia."

She looks startled as my voice appears to come out of nowhere and she sits nervously before me, probably fearing the worst.

I don't do kindness and I'm not one for conversation, but this time I will make an exception for her.

"Is everything ok?"

"Yes, sir." She seems anxious and I repeat my question.

"I mean, is everything ok with you and your family?"

"Of course, sir."

The fact she looks down tells me she's lying, and I say in a stern voice, "I don't believe you."

"I'm sorry."

She glances up and I note the tears glistening in her eyes and say kindly, "Tell me what it is. I don't bite and who knows, maybe I can help."

I can sense she's uncomfortable about telling me whatever's troubling her and then she almost crumbles before my eyes, tears sliding down her face unchecked as she sobs, "I'm sorry, sir, it's well, I had some bad news last week and it's difficult to deal with."

If anything, I'm annoyed at myself that it's taken me a week to notice and I hand her a tissue from the box in my drawer and say gently, "Tell me."

She blows her nose and says sadly, "My mum's ill. She needs an operation, and it's fifty-fifty if she'll survive."

I say nothing and she sighs. "It's cancer, sir. She never even mentioned she was ill and the first thing I knew about it was when she called to say she'd arranged the power of attorney over her affairs and if anything happened to her, it was all in my hands."

She wipes her eyes. "I feel so helpless. I can't be with her when she needs me the most, and it's tearing me apart."

"Why not?" I'm surprised at that, and she looks worried. "My job. It's a busy time of year and, well, I can't afford to let you down, sir."

If anything, I'm ashamed of myself. The fact she couldn't even come to me tells me how much of an ogre I am. I never really considered that my staff have real lives outside of these walls and now I'm peering through the window on one, I don't like how it makes me feel.

"Sylvia." She glances up in fear at the anger in my voice and I say irritably, "Take the rest of the year off."

"Excuse me."

She looks worried and I say firmly, "On full pay. Go to your mother, do what you can to help, and I don't want to see you back until, well, the matter's resolved. In the meantime, if there is anything I can do to help, just ask."

"But..." She appears lost for words, and I smile kindly. "You are a good assistant, and I don't want to have to search for another. If you're happy, your work won't suffer. I need you to be fighting fit and firing on all cylinders. You cannot possibly work while this is going on, so leave now and get your affairs in order."

The tears that streak down her face remain unchecked as her eyes glisten, and the relief on her face tells me I've done the right thing.

"I can't thank you enough, sir."

"Don't thank me for doing what's right. All I ask is that you send your mother my regards and my wishes for a speedy recovery."

She stands and I say kindly, "Now go. I expect you have a lot to arrange and, Sylvia..."

She peers at me nervously and I smile. "If I don't see you before, happy Christmas. I hope your prayers are answered."

"Happy Christmas, sir, I wish that for you too."

For a split second, we share the same wish. Neither of us wish for material things but life changing ones. She wishes her mother pulls through and me, well, I'm wishing for something that I never thought I wanted. An end to loneliness, somebody to share my life with and, dare I even hope, happiness.

As my assistant leaves the office, I waste no time in picking up my phone and as soon as I hear her irritated greeting, I smile.

"Jessica." My voice is firm and rather abrupt, and it amuses me to picture her rolling her eyes as she huffs, "What?"

"Change of plan. I need an assistant, and you're the only one in line for the job. Be here in five minutes."

I cut the call and laugh to myself, picturing her outrage at being summoned to my office like the hired help. This should be interesting.

CHAPTER 17

JESSICA

*H*ow bloody dare he speak to me like that! Who does he think he is? I'm not his employee to summon like the hired help. I'm a professional brought in to help him stay alive and I demand respect, not orders.

Mrs Armstrong watches me warily as I grab my bag and growl, "It appears I'm needed elsewhere. I'll be in touch."

Without another word, I stride from her office with a scowl firmly etched on my face as I prepare to tell Robert blooming Harvey exactly what I think of him.

His assistant, he says. Does this mean he's fired yet another undeserving soul, who will be cast out on the bitter streets of winter, denying yet another family a very merry Christmas? I wouldn't put it past him, and I am beyond angry on their behalf.

If I wanted to be an assistant, I'd wrap up this case and head back to the station to the pile of filing I'm guessing is reaching critical levels by now.

I'm so incensed it takes me a moment to realise my phone is vibrating angrily in my pocket and with a sigh, I pull it out to see a caller who dampens my mood even further.

"What now?" I bark into the phone, not caring that I'm blunt and to the point as always, expecting my sister to admonish me like she usually does, but instead I'm a little stunned when she says tearfully, "Thank God you answered. I need your help, Jess."

"What's happened?"

This isn't like Sally, and my heart lurches when I picture one of the kids hurt, or in pain.

"I've been arrested."

What the…

"Excuse me. For a moment there, I thought you said you'd been arrested."

"You heard right." She sniffs. "I'm allowed one call and you were my best option."

Stopping in my tracks, I lean against the wall and try to make sense of what she's telling me.

"Where are you?"

"Sutton police station." She lowers her voice. "They put me in a cell and only let me out to call you."

"The cell! What on earth is going on, Sally? Why were you arrested?"

I can't even begin to comprehend any reason in the world why she would be and I'm so angry that she would involve me in something obviously illegal. What if it got out that I was related to a criminal? I could lose my job, or worse, go back on the beat.

"Burglary." She sobs and my head is spinning with disbelief.

"Burglary!" I peer around in the vain hope that nobody heard me and just see a surprised expression on one of the cleaner's faces.

Turning away, I whisper, "Tell me what happened."

"I feel so ashamed."

"It's not about you now, Sally. Tell me what you did because if I am incriminated in any way."

"Shut up, Jess. This has nothing to do with you. God, I wish I'd called Dad. He would have spared me the lecture and actually asked if I was ok."

She sounds hurt and I check myself, because of course I'm being insensitive, but now we have a criminal in the family, I'm struggling to understand what that will mean.

"Start at the beginning." I keep my voice measured, but inside I'm all over the place and she says with a quiver to her voice. "It's all a mistake."

Now we're getting somewhere, and I sigh with relief.

"Good. Then it won't take a court case to release you."

"Can you do me a favour, Jess?"

"What?"

"I need you to pick the kids up from school and, well, stay with them until I get this sorted."

She could have asked for anything, but I wasn't expecting that, and I say in horror, "You're joking, right?"

"I have no one else to ask."

"What about mum?"

"She's not answering her phone and school finishes soon."

"Dad then."

"I can't ask him; you know how unsteady he is on his feet and so impatient with the kids. It would be carnage."

As I picture my father, I'm inclined to agree with her because our father is a little on the angry side and even I wouldn't inflict him on my sister's children.

"What about Anton? He is their father."

A fresh bout of sobs heads my way and I wonder what is going on, because it definitely involves him.

"I can't ask him, he's well…"

"Well, what?"

"He's um, indisposed."

"Indisposed!"

I'm sure I'm getting a migraine as my head spins, and I wonder if there is more to this arrest than she's letting on.

"Please, Jess. Just this once, I promise you. I'll arrange something long term, it's just, well, I can't ask anyone else because it would be all around the playground like lightning."

She does have a point because even I know how vile the playground mum's can be, so I say with a sigh, "Fine. Just this once. Remind me where they go to school."

As she rattles off the address, I check my watch and note I have exactly one hour to get there and so I start walking fast as I talk.

"Listen Sally, have you got a solicitor?"

"They are getting me one."

When I picture the usual ones drafted in for these cases, I huff, "Well, beggars can't be choosers, I suppose. Leave it with me and I'll try to call in a few favours."

"You would do that?"

Sally sounds aghast, and I feel bad that she obviously has such a low opinion of me.

"Yes, I can think of a few who may be up for it, but in the meantime go with the one they offer you and I'll see what I can do."

I cut the call, and it takes me a few moments to get my mind back. I never expected that for one minute and as I head to Robert's office, there is only one thing on my mind. How on earth can I get out of this?

I'm not good with children. I don't even like them and Sally's are unruly, spoilt and, well, children. Just picturing their noise and boisterous behaviour is making me ill already, and I now realise why my mum never answers her phone. Self-preservation is a powerful weapon and mum knows it's close to that school bell ringing time. I am so cross with her because she is no doubt enjoying a session at the hairdressers or lunching with friends and isn't there when I need her.

I quickly call incase she picks up and am connected to her voice message that makes her sound like a member of the royal family.

Please leave a message and I will add you to my to do list.

I'll give her a to do list alright. I mean, what on earth is on it? Shopping for clothes, a little ironing perhaps. Flicking through a recipe book or trying to win at bowls for once down at the village centre. Some of us have actual jobs to do, which reminds me I need to tell Robert that I'm leaving and may be some time.

As I head to his office on the executive floor, I wonder if I should invent some great mystery that I am needed back at the station to solve. It would sound a lot better because I can only imagine the horror on his face when he learns of my criminal connections.

CHAPTER 18

ROBERT

*H*ow long does it take to scale a few floors in this building? It's been fifteen minutes already and I'm in dire need of a coffee that I have decided will be Jessica's first task. I'm rather smug about how things have worked out and as I check some emails and sign a few letters, I am looking forward to a very pleasant working environment this side of Christmas.

When she finally storms through the door, I glance up with a blank expression and note the flush to her cheeks and the wild expression in her eye and momentarily feel a little afraid for my safety.

"I'm leaving." She huffs out and I shrug. "Wow, you really don't like taking orders."

"What are you talking about?" She seems on edge, and I point to the seat before my desk.

"Sit."

"I'm not your dog and I already told you I'm leaving."

"Because I asked you to be my assistant? That's ridiculous."

She looks momentarily surprised and then shakes her head

and rasps, "It has nothing to do with that, you self-obsessed nincompoop."

"What did you call me?"

She growls, "Never mind. Anyway, if you let me get a word in edgeways, I'm leaving for the day. Family emergency."

"Can I help?"

"No."

She makes to stand, and I say quickly, "I'll come with you."

"You will not."

"I will if you don't tell me what it is."

I fix her with a frown, and she sighs. "If you must know, my sister called and is indisposed and needs her offspring picking up from school. I'm sure you will consider that a P45 situation but as you don't actually employ me, tough."

"But you don't drive."

"There are things called trains you know, cabs too and even a bus if it comes down to it."

She makes for the door and grabbing my jacket, I say hurriedly, "I won't take no for an answer. I'll drive you."

She makes to argue, and I add slyly, "I mean, all the time I'm with you, you are technically still at work. This way you can't be considered as failing on the job and who knows, the postman could be stalking me as we speak. It's your duty and you know it."

For a second, she stares at me with an expression I can't place before nodding in defeat. "Fine, but don't say I didn't warn you, OK?"

As we head out of the store to my underground garage, it strikes me that I can't remember the last time I left early. It seems wrong somehow and slightly misguided, but there is something about Jessica Taylor that has me doing things I wouldn't have dreamed of even last week.

Giving lifts to strangers, inviting someone to my home to

stay and lunches at bistros in the middle of day and now this. Knocking off early to do the school run.

Jessica appears caught up in her own thoughts and I wonder what has happened to divert her attention so easily and as I ease the car into the London traffic, I say quickly, "I'll leave it to you to program the sat nav."

"Oh, yes, fine." Once again, she is distracted and as soon as she punches in the location, she falls on her phone and quickly dashes off a couple of texts.

"Anything you can use help with." I'm a tad concerned because Jessica isn't normally this quiet, and she looks up and I hate the worry lines appearing around her eyes as she says, "I'm sorry. What did you say?"

"I said, can you use my help?"

"No, of course not, but well…" She sighs and then a flicker of a grateful smile ghosts her lips as she says gently, "Just thank you. The lift is more than enough."

As I steer through the traffic, I note we are forty minutes away from our destination and I say conversationally, "So, how old are your sister's children?"

"Five and seven."

"They're young then."

"Unfortunately, yes."

"What are their names?"

I swear she winces as she mumbles, "Angelina and Brad."

"Are you serious?" I laugh out loud, and she rewards me with a scowl. "Listen, my sister was a huge fan and wanted to honour that fact by naming her children after them. She believed having successful names would give them a good start in life and she must be applauded for that."

"I suppose. I mean, it could have been a lot worse. What if she was a fan of the Teletubbies? I wouldn't wish those names on my worst enemy, even though they were a very successful brand making millions and adored by all."

"You make a valid point." She sighs. "Do you want children, Robert?"

"I never really gave it much thought."

"Me neither."

I'm surprised because I thought all women wanted children. Mind you, Jessica is different to most and she shrugs. "I never decided *not* to have them. I just never envisioned I'd reach that point."

"What do you mean?"

I'm a little confused, and she says briskly, "I couldn't see myself married with two kids and a mortgage, I suppose. It didn't tick any of my boxes, and all I wanted was to be a detective. I saw nothing past that and when Sally had her own family, I wanted it even less."

She laughs softly, which makes me smile because I am fast realising I love it when she does.

"You say, saw." I nudge gently and she shrugs again. "Did I?"

She offers no more explanation and settles back in her seat and gazes out of the window at the landscape flashing past.

"Do you have any sisters or brothers, Robert?"

Her question comes from nowhere and I say ruefully, "No. I wish I had, though."

"It's not that great, trust me."

"Don't you get on with your sister, then?"

"We're different people. To be honest, we're only in each other's lives because of our parents. Sally is nothing like me, way more dramatic and content to drift along in life. Me, well, I always wanted more."

"And you achieved that. You should be proud of yourself."

"If you say so."

"I do." I'm surprised that she is so down on herself because I would have thought becoming a detective at a young age was an amazing step up and she says sadly, "When I got my badge, I considered I'd made it. To be honest, I'm still waiting."

"Are you saying this job isn't good enough?" I gently tease, and a small smile flickers across her lips.

"It will do."

As I turn onto the road where the school is, I stare in disbelief at the lines of traffic all jostling for space on the side of the road. "What's happening?"

She grins. "You're about to discover the joys of the playground mafia. Don't worry, you have the best protection there is."

Before she even draws breath, she shrieks, "Indicate."

Without waiting for me to react, she does it for me and I can see why as a delivery van drives out of a space opening like a desert mirage before us.

A honking horn on the other side of the road reveals a furious woman who is gesticulating in a rather shocking manner, and, to my surprise, Jessica merely raises her middle finger and grins at me with triumph. "That showed her."

The woman screeches past, and I say with amusement, "You may have forgotten she could be in the same playground as you. Aren't you afraid of anyone?"

"No." She shrugs and unfastens her seatbelt. "I can disarm a criminal, knock an assailant out — from behind me and restrain a grown man. I'm not afraid of a mother driving a Volvo estate. The children inside that school, though, they scare the pants off me."

With a wicked twist to her lips, she slams the door leaving me to catch up and as I step outside the car, I must have grown two heads on the journey because it's as if every woman here turns to stare in my direction.

CHAPTER 19

JESSICA

*W*e head into the playground, and we may as well be wearing fancy dress because it's obvious we are the focus of rather a lot of attention. I say 'we' but it's obviously Robert and I'm guessing they don't see many successful men in suits around here, driving a brand-new range rover. I would stare too if I was one of them and I feel rather smug as we stride to the front of the pack.

For a moment I wonder if I should make myself known to one of the teachers inside because I'm sure there are rules about strangers collecting children and I can only hope to Santa that Sally did the right thing and put me down as a guardian or something.

As the school bell rings, I observe with interest as the doors open and screaming children hurtle towards us, causing me a moment's panic because why are they not trained yet?

Robert also appears a little afraid for his life right now and I can only imagine this sort of unruly behaviour is down to the fact it's a state school. Surely, the pupils in private one's walk out in a crocodile line or something, with decorum and good manners. Breeding certainly helps and I vow that if I ever have children, I will sell my body to make sure they get the best start in life if this is the example they have.

I scan the fresh-faced exuberance of youth for familiar ones because now I think of it, I can't remember what they look like. I'm ashamed to admit that I'm hardly auntie of the year and it's unlikely they will even remember me.

However, I notice a smiling teacher leading two children by the hand who seem vaguely familiar towards us, and Robert says in a low voice, "Is that them?"

"Oh, yes, it is." I lie through my teeth because he doesn't need to know that I couldn't formally identify them in an identity parade if my life depended on it.

"Miss Taylor." The teacher smiles and I don't miss her eyes dragging the length of Robert, causing her cheeks to blush a little as she gives him a very different smile from the one she offered me. I'm astounded that teachers are allowed to flirt with the parents, but this one obviously tossed the rule book in the wastepaper basket because she is staring at him coyly and fluttering her lashes.

"Where's mummy?" The little girl, who must be Angelina, whines and the teacher smiles with embarrassment. "I told you darling, she called to say she was held up and your auntie Jessie was going to come in her place."

Angelina looks at me with curiosity and luckily Brad saves the day and throws his bag down to the ground with a groan, "I'm hungry."

The teacher makes to speak, but I say sternly, "You must carry your own bag, Brad and if you're good, we can stop for food on the way home."

"Can we?" Two pairs of surprised eyes stare at me with interest and Brad shouts "Cool. There's a MacDonalds on the way."

Angelina jumps up and down. "I want a happy meal. They have a fairy in it this month, and Sindy has one."

I stare at Robert in horror, who merely shrugs and offers a blinding smile to the teacher, who appears to be hyperventilating at his attention.

"I'm sure that can be arranged." He winks at Brad and even Angelina turns to him with a smile, and I wonder how he does this. Command attention just by being here and I may well not be for all the attention the teacher is giving me as she gazes at Robert in wonder, causing me to snap, "Yes, well, thank you, um, is there anything we should know before we leave?"

"I'm cold."

"I'm bored."

The children whine and I roll my eyes. "I meant regarding your schoolwork."

The teacher nods. "Well, tomorrow is obviously the nativity play, so please may I ask you to remind Mrs Stevens that Brad is a shepherd and Angelina a fairy."

"Wait what." I stare at her in horror, and she shrugs. "Mrs Stevens knows all about it. We have been preparing for it for several weeks and I'm sure she will have the costumes ready. Hopefully she can spare the time to attend, despite the Christmas rush."

I'm not sure if it's my own paranoia, but it's as if she already knows given the disapproval in her voice and I say defensively, "One of us will be there. You can rely on that."

Hoping like hell it won't be me, I fix my attention on the two bored looking children and flash them what I hope is my most nurturing smile.

"Come on, let's go and eat."

Their cheers are my triumph and as Robert bends down and retrieves their bags, a little of the ice melts in my heart as Angelina smiles at him and Brad appears to be hero worshipping him almost as much as the teacher.

He grins and ruffles Brad's hair and reaches for Angelina's hand and I swear I couldn't look away if I tried. A soft sigh distracts me, and I can tell I am on the same line of thought as the teacher and so, rather smugly, I say, "Thank you. Have a good night, Mrs…"

"It's Miss, actually." She stares longingly at Robert as she whispers, "Miss Travers."

He flashes her a blinding smile which astonishes me because who on earth is this man who usually scowls at anyone watching and has the personality of a troll? Here in the fresh air of the playground, he has undergone a character transplant and become every woman's dream, including mine. It's a little disconcerting and I drag myself back to the job at hand and say briskly, "Ok, we should, um, go."

As we begin the commute to the car, I'm conscious of many hovering mothers all craning their necks towards Robert and I wonder if he has thrown magic dust in the air because surely one man doesn't hold this amount of power over women who should know better. I am so surprised I'm rendered speechless and am just content for him to take charge of a situation I wouldn't wish on either of us in my worst nightmare.

* * *

THROUGHOUT THE ENTIRE journey to MacDonalds, I'm on high alert because two small children and cream leather in a super car should never be a thing. I am so worried that they will mark it or put their dirty feet on the leather, and I hate that the only words I speak are, 'stop fidgeting' and 'perhaps you should take your shoes off.'

After a while Robert whispers, "It's fine, Jessica, relax. They can't hurt anything."

Brad calls out, "This car is cool."

Angelina calls out, "I need a wee."

I call out, "Nearly there. Can you hold on?"

Robert calls out, "Two minutes."

Brad shouts, "I'm hungry. Are we there yet?"

Angelina whines, "I want mummy," and then begins to cry.

Luckily, the glorious, illuminated 'M' swings into view and I yell with relief, "Here we are!"

It has the desired effect, and the children shout with delight and I'm almost considering joining them as Robert swings the car into the nearest available parking space.

Like the children, I can't get out of the car quickly enough and as we tumble through the doors of a place I usually avoid like the plague, I now understand the need for it in society as it makes all our dreams come true.

CHAPTER 20

ROBERT

*I*f anybody told me, I would be sitting at a plastic table on a plastic chair, eating a plastic burger with two small children, I would say they were on drugs. But it appears I will do anything for the slightly hysterical woman sitting beside me, looking as if she wants to die right now. It amuses me to witness her world spinning out of control because of two small humans and it's obvious Jessica wasn't cut out for this life, judging by her startled facial expressions and total anxiety as she struggles to do the right thing. It makes me wonder what the real story is because she appears to be dancing on a tightrope, fearful of saying the wrong thing and her continuous glances to her phone and the way she is biting her bottom lip, is concerning me — a lot.

The children appear happy with their aptly named, 'happy meal' and I'm quite enjoying my Big Mac meal deal and when the children head off to the ball pit, I fix her with a hard stare and growl, "Ok, time to come clean. What's going on?"

"I don't know what you mean. We're just doing the school run."

"So why are you on edge?"

A loud scream from the ball pit makes us both jump and almost immediately, she scrapes her chair back and starts running. I watch with amazement as she dives into the ball pit and separates two wrestling children who appear to be knocking the living daylights out of one another. A woman rushes forward, shouting, "Don't you touch my kid or I'll…"

"Or you'll what, madam?" A furious Jessica drags two children out, who appear red faced and angry, and I can see one of them is Brad. Angelina is screaming behind him, and Jessica says furiously, "I watched the entire thing and if you are happy to let your child bully a small girl, then it appears her brother has a much better sense of protection than you have."

"They're only kids playing." The woman frowns and Jessica growls, "Tell that to yourself when your child grows up and is expelled for bullying. Tell yourself he was only messing around when you're visiting him in Pentonville for assault and battery and remember this day when you should have stepped up as a parent and taught him right from wrong."

I jump up and step between the women with a gentle, "I think she's got the point."

Pushing the rather alarmed looking little boy towards his disbelieving mother, I say firmly, "Jessica's right, never defend a bully no matter how old he is and…"

I turn to the furious woman beside me, who is holding a screaming child in her arms. "Perhaps we should leave."

Brad pokes his tongue out at the other boy, causing me to grab his hand and pull him away for all our safety and as we exit the happy place, I wonder if scenes like this are standard practice for parents these days.

As Jessica thrusts the coveted fairy into Angelina's hands, she stops sobbing and as we strap them into the seats, Jessica says with a worried frown, "I'm not sure we should be doing this."

"What?"

I'm confused, and she points to Angelina's small body in the seat. "She needs a car seat. It's against the law for her to travel without one. Perhaps I should get the bus and leave you to return to work."

The collective "No" makes me smile as the children appear worried. Brad shouts, "I don't want to get the bus."

Angelia starts crying again, and I shake my head. "We'll stop off and get them. We passed a retail park when we came in. I'm sure there was a Halfords there."

"But…"

"But nothing. Come on."

I was right and in no time, we have purchased two car seats, much to Brad's disgust as he complains that he's not a baby, but he soon stops as his aunt glares at him and says tightly, "Be quiet, Brad. It's the law and I will be forced to arrest Robert if he drives out of here without you in this seat."

Brad looks impressed. "Will he go to prison?"

"Yes." Jessica nods and immediately backtracks as Angelina begins to cry and says adorably, "I don't want wobert to go to prison."

"It's ok, we've got the seats now, nobody's going to prison."

As we set off, she whispers, "I'm exhausted already."

She looks it and I'm concerned about her because surely, it's no big deal being asked to pick up your niece and nephew from school. To be honest, I'm quite enjoying doing something different for once and as Jessica directs me to their home, I wonder if I would make a good dad. I like to think I would but I'm hoping it won't be as exhausting as this, and as I slide a quick glance in Jessica's direction, I would be more than happy if she was the one I made them with.

* * *

JESSICA DIRECTS me to a smart street, not far from the school, and I gaze at the tree-lined pavements with interest. It's nothing like I imagined, and I wonder what her sister's husband does for a living because these houses look new.

She directs me to a driveway, a third of the way down, and we pull up outside a white New England style house with a giant wreath on the painted door. There are a few Christmas wicker animals in the front garden that I'm positive must light up at night and I'm intrigued to see inside a home that appears well cared for.

The children scramble from their seats and Jessica sighs. "Thanks. Hopefully I'll be in tomorrow, but I may be a little late."

"Why?"

I watch the children shoving each other at the front door and Jessica says quickly, "Well, Sally may not be back tonight and until I locate my mother to relieve me from my duty, it appears that I'm stuck with playing surrogate parent."

She looks so worried, I immediately know something is up, so I unfasten my seatbelt and growl, "Let's go."

I open the door and she says in a hard whisper, "What are you doing?"

"Helping." I grin as I slam the car door and head up the driveway towards the fighting children and Jessica joins me with what can only be described as gratitude in her eyes, before fumbling in her bag and pulling out a bunch of keys.

We step inside a home that appears warm and welcoming and it's not only from the burst of warm air that greets us, taking away the chill of the wind outside.

Jessica cries out, "Take off your shoes and go and change out of your uniforms. I'll make you some drinks."

The children race upstairs and I follow Jessica into a light and airy kitchen and stare around with interest. Unlike my own, this one is warmer somehow, more lived in, I suppose.

The Christmas tree stands proudly by the patio doors that lead onto the garden and there are brightly coloured paintings attached to a giant American fridge with an assortment of magnets. A breakfast bar divides the working space from the recreational one and all around are homely touches that tell me this house is loved. Pictures on the wall are of the children on canvas, making the most personal type of art. I notice one of their family and peer with interest at the parents of the two children, noting the similarity between Jessica and the woman smiling sweetly at the man beside her.

"Is this your sister?" I point to it and Jessica nods.

"Yes, that's Sally and Anton, her husband."

"She looks a lot like you, but with curly hair."

"She had that done for the photo. To be honest, she is like me to look at, but that's where the similarity ends."

She busies herself with making us all a hot drink and I sit on one of the barstools and enjoy watching her work. I can tell she's on edge, and I lower my voice. "If there's anything bothering you, you can tell me. I'm a good listener."

"It's fine." She pastes a bright smile on her face and says in a falsely cheerful voice, "Nothing to worry about. I'm only helping my sister." Her phone rings and she almost jumps on it and says quickly, "Sorry, I won't be long."

As she hurries from the room, I can't help myself and, heading to the door, I shamelessly listen in on the conversation she is having in the hallway.

"It's fine, they're fine. We're at your house now."

There's silence as the other person speaks and then Jessica says abruptly, "It's not my fault. They are busy people and can't drop everything to help you."

She sighs as the person on the other end obviously speaks and then she says tightly, "What about Anton?"

I recognise her sister's husband's name and I hear a deep

sigh and a terse, "Are you kidding me? What the hell were you thinking of…"

Whoever is on the other end obviously hangs up because her furious expletive makes me head away from the door and as she storms in, I see the anger flashing in her eyes which makes me growl, "Close the door."

"What?" She looks up and I say with a frown, "Close the door and tell me what the hell is going on."

As she runs her fingers through her hair with an agitated grimace, I know things are bad and yet before she can enlighten me further, there's a thump of feet on the stairs and the two children burst into the room like a tornado whipping through the house and destroying it in seconds.

CHAPTER 21

JESSICA

*T*hank God for unruly children because they saved me from a grilling by barrelling into the room and distracting our attention.

As I make the drinks, Robert tries to entertain them by switching on the massive television and settling the fight that breaks out as they decide on what to watch.

In fact, the next two hours are spent in utter chaos as we attempt to do what's right and fail miserably. If I thought that children actually did what they were asked, I was ill-informed because it appears that my niece and nephew do whatever the hell they like at all times.

It's utterly exhausting, and I don't know how my sister does it and as we settle in a role neither of us has been trained for, it makes me determined to settle this nightmare once and for all.

I realise Robert has questions. He's not stupid and I wonder how much I should tell him. I wish I could confide in him, but for some reason I want him to think good of my family. If I tell him, he would be appalled and probably make his excuses and leave, and it surprises me more than anything that I really don't want that to happen.

After a while, we settle into some sort of calm and I sit at the table with Angelina colouring in a Christmas picture, while Robert entertains Brad with a computer game. There are Christmas tunes on the radio and as I listen to Angelina's excited chatter about Santa and the elves, it makes me smile at how happy that makes her.

Suddenly, Robert gets a call and everything changes.

I watch his expression alter in an instant as he says quickly, "Calm down."

I try hard not to listen, but my curiosity is getting the better of me as I try to pretend I'm not listening.

"It's not convenient. I'm well…"

I glance up as he catches my eye and I'm surprised at the desperate look in his.

He sighs heavily, "It's, well, I'm not alone."

Angelina says loudly, "When's mummy coming back?"

"Soon honey, shh."

I dismiss her quickly because I'm intrigued by Robert's conversation and, from the expression on his face, his call is as unwelcome as my earlier one.

"I know I promised, but things have changed." He sighs heavily and his voice is laden with defeat, "Ok, but be on your best behaviour."

He hangs up the phone and throws an agonised glance my way and I say quickly, "Who was that?"

"My mother."

I completely forgot we were supposed to meeting them this evening and I say with horror, "Was she checking where we are? It slipped my mind."

"Same, but no, well, she was calling for another reason."

He shakes his head and groans. "I'm sorry about this, but she's asked if we'll all head over there now."

"All!" I can't believe what I'm hearing, and he growls, "It's, well, it appears the postman has extended his round to include my parents."

"Why? What did they say?"

"They want my help; they're worried for their safety." He sighs. "I told them I wasn't alone, and they said to bring whoever I was with but to hurry. I'm guessing they know it's you. I mean, they were expecting us anyway and mum sounded well, different somehow. Frightened even, which isn't like her."

Ordinarily, I would tell Robert to leave, and I would remain here, but this could be the break I need in my own job that appears to have been conveniently pushed to one side to make room for more pressing matters, so I say with determination. "We'll all go but promise to maintain my cover. Until we understand what we're dealing with, everyone's a suspect."

Brad looks up with interest. "What's a suspect?"

I share a glance with Robert. "It's um, well, I'll tell you later."

Turning my attention to the children who are looking a little tired now, I say quickly, "Who wants to go on an adventure?"

"Me!" Four arms shoot up and I say quickly, "Ok, grab your coats and your favourite toy. We're going to visit some very important people who you must be quiet around."

"Why?" Brad looks confused and I say briskly, "Because I said so. Now, this shouldn't take long and if you're good, I will allow you both a treat."

"Can I stay up all night?"

"Can I eat chocolate in bed?"

"Can I have the day off school?"

"Can I join a circus?"

"Whoa." Robert laughs as he holds up his hand. "We will see how good you are and then decide."

He glances at me apologetically, and I note the worry in his eyes and sigh. Why is life so complicated? This morning we were both doing a job and had it all under control. At least it felt like that. Now things are spiralling fast and I'm unable to get a grip on the situation all the time I'm babysitting for my criminal sister and her husband.

As Robert helps the children back into their coats, I try my parents again in the vain hope they actually pick up and all I get is the voicemail, which I answer with a terse, "Call me the minute you get this. It's an emergency."

* * *

I LOCK up on my way out and am grateful that Robert has the kids in the car already and as we head off, Brad shouts, "Where are we going?"

"To my parents' house."

"Is it far?" He says, sounding interested and Robert shakes his head. "About thirty minutes."

"I want my mummy." Angelina whines and, turning around, I flash her my most maternal smile that I'm certain scares her because she stares at me in shock as I say lightly, "Shall we sing a Christmas song?"

Brad groans as Roberts chuckles beside me, but Angelina's eyes light up and she shouts, "I want Elsa's song from Frozen."

Brad shouts, "No way, not again, I'm sick of that song."

"Then you choose next." I say with no nonsense as I frantically search for it on Spotify. As the familiar song begins, I am grateful for the moment's respite as Angelina sings loudly along in the back, while Brad holds his hands over his ears.

Robert catches my eye, and we share a grin, and something stirs deep inside my frozen heart and perhaps, like Elsa's magic, slowly but surely, the ice is melting.

* * *

IT'S NOT that far to Robert's parent's address and I stare in awe at the grand entrance of a house in one of the more affluent areas of Weybridge. Even though I know Robert has billions, I never expected his parents to be as well off as they appear to be and I say wistfully, "Wow." The children are silent for once and I can see why, because if I thought my sister did Christmas well, it is nothing to how well Robert's parents do it.

We drive past trees lit with fairy lights, lining the route up to a house that could star in a Christmas advert. Two potted trees dazzle with beautiful twinkling lights, either side of a white front door with the biggest wreath I have ever seen in my life. Uplighter's cast the house in a magical light, picking out the windowsills that are dressed in poinsettias and some kind of projector makes it appear as if it's snowing outside. The gasps from the children make me smile and I say in awe, "Your parents' home is beautiful, Robert."

"I suppose so." He sounds gloomy and I wonder about his relationship with them. I realise his parents were hard on him growing up and yet his father was so loved by all the staff at Harvey's. I wonder how one man can be so different with strangers and not extend it to his own flesh and blood. Then again, I need to wait and judge when I have all the facts and I am eager to discover exactly what the postman has been sending them.

CHAPTER 22

ROBERT

I hate that yet again I've put everything down and raced to accommodate my parent's wishes. All my life they've controlled me, at least they tried and when we saw them today in the bistro, I recognised their need to continue when they invited us here tonight. Jessica was unaware that I texted them earlier to cancel, and I was a fool if I thought they would accept it.

However, learning they have been targeted by the same person is disconcerting and I wonder if this is more serious than I thought.

We exit the car, and the two children stare up at the snowy house in disbelief and I wonder what will run through my parent's minds when they open the huge front door. I can't picture them being happy about having two small humans dirtying their polished wooden floor and messing up their scatter cushions and, if anything, I hope that Brad and Angelina don't let me down.

We ring the front doorbell and I hear a loud, "Who is it?"

Rolling my eyes, I say irritably, "Who do you think it is?"

"Is that you, Robert?"

Mum sounds fearful, and I say with exasperation, "Of course it's me."

The door opens an inch and then a little wider and my mother stares at the sight on her doorstep with wide eyes.

"Who do we have we here?"

"Hi Mum, meet Brad and Angelina, Jessica's niece and nephew."

Mum stares at them and I'm amazed when her expression softens and her eyes light up. "Oh, how adorable. Please come in children, it's so cold out there."

If anything, the kids appear alarmed and I'm guessing I would be too because my mother is dressed in a huge brightly coloured kaftan in full makeup and dripping in jewellery and Angelina gasps, "Are you a queen?"

My mother merely laughs and extends her hand to Angelina's and winks. "If I am, you must be a princess. Come on in. I have some cookies waiting for you both."

I stare at Jessica in shock, and as we follow my mother inside her palatial home, I watch her head off to the kitchen with two extremely willing companions by her side.

Jessica makes to follow them, but I grasp her hand and pull her back and as she falls against me, I hold her tightly and whisper, "Something's not right about this."

"Why not?" The fact her lips are now close to mine makes me stop for a moment as I enjoy this unexpected outcome. She smells so good, so delicious and it's tempting to push everything aside and bury my face into her soft, sweet-smelling hair and lose myself in pure pleasure and forget what's happening right now.

"Robert." Her voice is like a breeze whispering in my ear and I hold her tighter and almost give into my urge to pull her close and kiss her sweet soft lips. Then we hear a loud, "Put her down, son, now is not the time."

We spring apart and my heart sinks when I witness the

deep frown on my father's face as he hovers in the doorway of the living room.

"Come in. We need to talk."

He glances at Jessica and nods towards the kitchen, which makes me angry that he is dismissing her, and I say tightly, "Come on Jessica, the children will be fine with mum."

"Children!" My father's face is like thunder and I know he thinks they're Jessica's. His disapproval rubs me up the wrong way and I frown, pulling her beside me with a firm grip. I glare at him to challenge me, which he obviously registers because he rolls his eyes and says roughly, "Have it your way."

The fact Jessica's hand curls around mine tells me she's a little intimidated by him and I don't blame her. I've *always* been intimidated by him and still am, to a degree. It gets worse, not better, and being here always reminds me of my childhood and the way just a look from him would have me second guessing everything I had done that day, searching for a reason for his disapproval.

As I grew older, the fact I was alive was reason enough and I never understood why he was always so hard on me. Even when I 'made it' it didn't earn me any respect from him. If anything, he scorned the way I'd earned my billions and acted as if I didn't deserve it.

Jessica is subdued beside me and I'm guessing it's this house. It always has that effect because there is never anything out of place, which makes me hope Brad and Angelina rectify that.

The huge fire roaring in the grate of a fireplace that's as intimidating as the man who stands before it provides the only warmth in this house of horrors. I note the ever-present whiskey glass on the small table by his favourite chair, and as we sit on the formal sofa, he nods towards the decanter. "Can I get you a whiskey?"

"No thank you, I'm driving."

He turns to Jessica, who also declines with a polite, "No thank you, I don't drink spirits."

My father shakes his head as if we've lost our minds and I'm guessing to him we have. He's always enjoyed a 'tipple' as he calls it and considers it's the mark of a true man. Maybe that's why he's so disappointed in me because I always preferred wine instead, something he refers to a ladies' drink, while looking scornfully in my direction.

He sits and sighs heavily, which is the only indication something is troubling him, other than everything about me it seems, and he leans forward with a hard glint in his eye. "I won't beat around the bush. We've been receiving some rather disturbing Christmas cards."

Jessica stiffens and I can tell he has her full attention. My father reaches behind him and pulls out a bundle of cards that look familiar and hands them to me with a sigh. "They don't make for enjoyable reading and at first, I put it down to a prank. A vicious greeting from a disgruntled employee perhaps, or somebody with a grudge against me."

I sift through them and hand them to Jessica who studies them with care, and I glance up into my father's eyes and note the keen interest in them as he waits for our reaction.

"Any idea who it could be?" I don't reveal my own understanding of the situation, and he shakes his head. "No, can you think of anyone?"

"No."

Jessica is silent beside me as she studies each one and my father sighs. "Your mother is going crazy about it and has insisted we hire protection."

Jessica nudges me because of course, that was exactly what I did.

He carries on. "She wants me to hire a private detective to flush them out, but I told her we will deal with it ourselves."

"But what if you can't?" I say wearily. "Just report it to the police and let them deal with it."

"The police." The tone of his voice sets me on edge immediately as Jessica stills beside me. "What good are they? They couldn't detect a rat up a drainpipe. The force today is full of wannabe superheroes who run away at the first sign of trouble. Nobody wants to work anymore and this current lot hide at the first sign of trouble, merely hoping their uniform is enough of a deterrent. No, I have no faith at all in the boys in blue with their equal opportunities and current love of hiring useless women over decent hard-working men who can actually do the job."

Jessica bristles beside me and I'm mildly interested to see if she goes off like a firework directed straight to my father's throat because knowing her, that's very likely, but to my surprise, she merely laughs softly and smiles.

"You sound like my grandfather. He never understood women's roles in the workplace. He was so stuck in the past it was like watching a live history lesson."

I glance at my father, who appears a little shocked that she spoke at all. She shakes her head. "I mean, it's a well-known fact that we dismiss everything we don't understand and prefer 'the old ways'. Nobody likes change, and I expect you were brought up to believe a woman's place is in the home unless circumstances dictate otherwise."

"There's nothing wrong with that." My father says pompously. "Ask Sable, she's made a career out of spending my money and you won't get any complaints from me."

I want to shrivel up and die as Jessica nods as if in agreement. "I wonder if she would do things differently if she was given a choice."

"I doubt it." My father scoffs. "Who wouldn't prefer to live off someone else and please themselves all day? Some say it's called living the dream."

Jessica smiles sweetly, which takes me back a little because I expected to be removing her hands from his throat about now.

"We all have our beliefs, and it takes a strong person to stick to them and go against popular ones. I admire you for that."

For the first time in my life, my father appears speechless, and Jessica takes the opening to hold the cards up and say with curiosity, "I have counted ten. Does that mean you started receiving them ten days ago, or do they come in batches?"

"Every day. Why?"

She scrunches up her face and nods. "Are they delivered here by royal mail, or hand delivered?"

"The postman brings them."

Jessica flashes me an amused look and I bite back my grin at the use of her preferred name for the vicious person responsible for this and she sighs and sets the cards down.

"Is it just the cards, or has something else happened?"

My father seems a little irritated that she's the one asking the questions and says pompously, "As you've asked, it was just the cards until earlier today."

I sit up and take note because this is different. "What happened?"

My father growls. "Somebody knocked on the door just after we returned for lunch in town. By the time your mother got there, they had gone, but there was another card on the floor."

He produces the card with a flourish and hands it to me, and I stare in disbelief at the bold handwriting.

I know where you live.

Jessica glances over my shoulder and her frown deepens as my father whispers, "It completely freaked your mother out. She went crazy and started yelling and pleading with me to call the police, a swat team even. You name it, she wanted them here."

"I can see why. May I?"

Jessica reaches for the card and turns it over in her hand and nods. "It's the same as the rest. It appears to be from one of those bumper boxes that you find in most department stores or garden centres."

Suddenly, a loud scream makes us all jump, and Jessica is up and running before I can even react.

CHAPTER 23

JESSICA

I am the worst aunt in the world. I left my sister's children with a stranger and didn't even care to check on them. Now they are hurt, or worse, and it will be all my fault.

As I push my way into the kitchen, Robert is hot on my heels, and we stare in disbelief at the scene in front of us.

Sable laughs out loud. "I told you that would work. It got their attention, just like I said it would."

Angelina is standing on the kitchen table and Brad is tucking into a plate of cookies.

"Auntie Jessie, do you want to listen to the song I'm singing in the play?"

The play! Oh, my goodness I completely forgot they are in the nativity tomorrow and I haven't even thought about their costumes.

"Come in and take a seat." Sable says with excitement. "Let our very own Christmas fairy entertain us."

We take our seats beside Sable in a trance, and she nods to Angelina. "Off you go dear."

She flicks a dimmer switch on the wall beside her, casting

the room in a warm glow that appears almost magical. The glittering tree by the window reflects its light all around the room and you could hear a pine needle drop as we wait for the show to start.

Taking a deep theatrical breath, Angelina starts to sing, Oh Little Town of Bethlehem and, to be honest, I can't tear my eyes away from her. She sings like an angel and as her little voice wafts around the room, it brings a surprising tear to my eye. There is total silence as we all watch the small person with the sweetest voice I have ever heard, sing such a beautiful, festive song that hits me hard in the heart.

Robert's hand finds mine and as I stare down at our entwined fingers, I swallow a lump in my throat. I steal a look in his direction, and he smiles softly and the expression in his eyes causes me to hitch my breath. It's as if this is the most special moment of my life as the angelic voice swirls around us like the coolest breeze. There is no music and no noise to disturb the moment and as she finishes, there is a small silence before Sable claps, causing the rest of us to join in. Even David looks at Angelina with pride and it's only Brad who obviously couldn't care less and is more interested in his cookies.

"Bravo, darling, I had every faith in you." Sable turns to us and says in a whisper, "The darling told me she was nervous about singing in front of the school. We decided to rehearse here so she wouldn't be anxious tomorrow."

If anything, I'm surprised at how much I love Sable Harvey right now. She is nothing like my first impression after meeting her earlier. To be honest, she is kinder than I thought and I stare in fascination as she brushes a tear away from the corner of her eye and says with pride, "You have a talent young lady that cannot be ignored. Your school is lucky to have you."

"The play." I hiss at Robert. "I haven't organised their costumes yet, and it's their bedtime already."

"Costumes." Sable pipes up. "What do you need?"

"I'm a fairy." Angelina shouts and Brad groans. "I'm a shepherd, but I wanted to be Aqua man."

Robert says with a grin, "We should go."

"What, now?" Sable looks alarmed. "Please stay. We haven't even had a chance to chat."

"But…" I make to protest, and she huffs, "I won't take no for an answer. I will take great delight in sorting out costumes and I made some lovely home-made soup that needs eating."

Robert appears as astonished as I am as his mother jumps up and lifts Angelina off the table and as she swings her around, Angelina giggles as if it's the best thing in the world.

"Ok, this is what will happen."

Sable decides to take charge and glances at Robert. "You entertain your father, and Jessica and I will deal with the children. When we've finished, we can all enjoy a supper of soup and crusty bread before bath time and bed."

"Excuse me." I'm a little giddy with it all and Sable says with excitement, "Everyone can stay here tonight. There's enough room, and it will be the best Christmas present I ever had, knowing this place is full of life once again."

Her husband obviously doesn't agree, but he lowers his gaze when she glares at him sharply and only Angelina's loud cheer tell me she's more than happy about this.

Robert makes to speak, and I place my hand on his arm and say loudly, "Thank you. It really is most kind of you."

"Nonsense." Sable says firmly. "It's my pleasure."

She takes Angelina's hand and says loudly, "Come on, darling, there is a wardrobe full of things upstairs that will make you the best fairy on the planet."

She smiles at Brad. "There are also plenty of options for a shepherd. Let's go and see what we can find."

I almost feel like a spare part and make to follow them but my phone rings, causing me to stop and stare at the caller ID and it's as if all my prayers have been answered when I see my mother's name on the screen.

Thank goodness for that. It's a Christmas miracle.

"I'm sorry, I need to take this." I say quickly before heading out into the hallway and back to the warm open fire.

"Is everything ok?" Mum sounds anxious and I snap.

"Not really."

"Oh no, is it the children?"

"You could say that." I exhale a breath of frustration. "Listen, I need you to come and look after them."

"Why, where's Sally?"

My mother sounds fearful and I choose my words carefully. "She's, um, away for a bit with Anton."

"Away! Where?"

Mum sounds shocked and I say tightly, "Just an, um, last minute getaway. Anyway, I work and really don't have time for this, so I need you to take charge of your grandchildren."

There's a short silence and I swear I can hear a seagull in the background.

Then my mum says, sounding guilty, *"I had hoped to avoid this."*

"What, looking after your own grandchildren?" I'm shocked and she says quickly, *"Of course not, I would love to if I were there."*

"What do you mean?" I'm confused, and she says with a hint of shade, *"I mean, in the country but unfortunately we are, well, um..."*

"What?" I'm getting impatient and she sighs heavily. *"Ok, but don't judge us, alright."*

"Judge you. For what?"

"Well, I have some good news as it happens."

"I could use some of that." I say with relief, and she replies awkwardly, *"Um, when your father and I won the lottery..."*

"I'm sorry, Mum, did I just hear you correctly? You won the lottery."

I'm shocked and then a slightly nervous laugh makes its way down the phone toward my disbelieving ears.

"Yes, well, not a lot, but enough to afford this luxury cruise for two."

"How much exactly?"

I can't believe what I'm hearing, and she says quickly, *"Twenty thousand pounds."*

"Since when?" I'm in shock, and she laughs nervously. *"A few weeks ago. It was a scratch card and as you can imagine, we couldn't believe our luck."*

"And you kept it to yourself." I shouldn't be surprised really because my parents always keep their affairs very close to their chests and mum says with enthusiasm. *"Yes, it was amazing. We didn't know what to do at first. I wanted to give some to you and Sally, but your father told me we should blow the lot on one wild extravagance and, well, I went along with it."*

"You spent twenty thousand pounds on a cruise."

I'm in shock and mum says irritably, *"What's wrong with that? To be honest, I hoped nobody would find out and yet here you are making me feel guilty about enjoying myself. It doesn't matter that we spent every penny we own on bringing the two of you up. This is our reward, and we've been making the most of it."*

She lowers her voice. *"To be honest, I wish I was single. There are so many eligible men on board all looking for a woman to spoil. I'm even considering booking one myself next year and leaving your father behind. Imagine the fun I would have."*

It gets worse because now she's even planning on cutting dad out of the picture and I'm not sure what to make of that.

"Anyway, we hoped you wouldn't discover our little subterfuge, but now you have, please don't tell your sister. I mean, you know what she's like, and she'd be angry we didn't give her or the kids any of it."

"Listen." I try to breathe and form a rational response to this and ignore the way my head is spinning and say with a measured tone. "Just have a good time, ok. It's your good fortune and of course it's up to you what you do with it. However, next time, tell us because if anything happened to you, we wouldn't have a clue."

"Of course, you would. You are down as my next of kin, and the executor of my will. You would know everything, Jessica, because you are the responsible one in the family."

Never has a truer word been spoken as I picture my parents enjoying a luxury cruise without telling anyone and my sister and her husband currently languishing at his Majesty's pleasure in a cell for burglary. I still haven't got to the bottom of that yet and to make matters worse, there is a crime to solve, that is expanding with more victims by the day. To cap it all, I must make sure two sweet little children don't suffer the effects of any of it. Then added to the mix, I am struggling to ignore the very real feelings that are growing by the second for a man I detested on sight and everything that he stands for. Christmas is merely days away and I wouldn't recognise what a festive feeling is if it hit me and yet when Angelina sang so sweetly in the kitchen, it stirred a memory that has long been forgotten.

"Mum…" I say with a sigh. "Just, well, have fun, ok?"

I don't know who is more surprised as she says with a catch to her voice, *"We will. Thank you and Jessie…"*

"Yes mum."

"If we hit an iceberg and don't make it, the key to the safe is in my knicker drawer. Well, I must go because there's a show I've been absolutely dying to watch. Good night and kiss the kids from me."

She cuts the call and as I stare into the flickering fire, for some reason, a rare smile makes it onto my face as I picture my parents living like royalty for two weeks of unexpected pleasure. How could I possibly be angry about that?

CHAPTER 24

ROBERT

I'm not sure Jessica has thought this through when she agreed to spend the night with my parents. It's the last place I want to be for sure and just being in the same room as them is bringing my childhood back with a vengeance.

Dad is obviously annoyed with my mother for issuing the invitation in the first place and yet I don't believe I have ever seen mum as happy as she is now.

She left the room holding the hand of the small girl who has melted all our hearts, with her brother trailing after them, stuffing what is close to a whole packet of cookies in his mouth.

As soon as the door closes, my father growls, "That's all I need."

"What is?" His words irritate me, and he sighs. "What if we're in danger and your mother has brought innocent children into it?"

"In danger? What from?" I roll my eyes. "You installed a better security system than me, and I went overboard."

"You can never be one hundred per cent sure of anything,

Robert, and now we must deal with a crisis on top of entertaining strangers."

"Then we'll leave." I bark, and he rolls his eyes. "And disappoint your mother, like you've always done. You really are selfish, and I'm not surprised that Samuel fell out with you in such a big way."

I can't believe he is going there, and he obviously realises his mistake because he quickly changes the subject. "Your grandfather."

"What about him?"

"He's worried about you."

"Why?" I ask the question, knowing it's merely a diversion tactic, and he shrugs, turning to the door. "We should head back to the fire. I could use a drink."

I'm guessing he's had quite a few already due to his blood-shot eyes, and it makes my heart sink. My father has always liked a drink or two and it was a habit that got worse over the years. Both of my parents like to indulge of an evening, and I'm amazed they don't fall into debt from their drinks bill alone.

We step into the room as Jessica finishes her call and as she turns to face us, I see a strange expression in her eye. She appears to be miles away and looks so vulnerable and fragile standing by the crackling fire. I immediately want to take every care she has and make them all go away.

She looks up and as her eyes find mine, it hits me like a rocket launcher. I like her. I need her in my life, and I never want to let her go. Such alien emotions for a man who vowed never to form attachments and yet here she is, the most unusual woman I have ever met who is, sadly, a lot like me.

Ignoring my father, in two strides I am by her side and leaning down, whisper, "You only have to say the word and we'll leave. Whatever's troubling you can be dealt with by me, and you have my word on that. You are not alone."

The way her eyes fill with glistening tears almost breaks me and it's only when my father says irritably, "I need a drink." That she shakes herself and her walls go up once more.

"Maybe I should help your mother. It's not right that I'm leaving her to do all the work."

The fact that leaves me with my father makes me say quickly, "I'll take you to them."

As we leave my father filling his glass from the decanter of whiskey, I fall into step beside her and fight the urge to push her against the wall and kiss the life out of her gorgeous lips. Instead, I say firmly, "Now, tell me what's bothering you and don't say it's fine because it obviously isn't."

"I'm sorry, I…"

Quickly, I tug her into the nearest room and close the door and she stares at me in surprise as I snap on the lamp and pull her down into the seat beside me. Her eyes are wide as she looks around and whispers, "Where are we?"

I glance at the William Morris papered walls and shrug. "My father's study."

"We shouldn't be in here. He'll be angry."

"Who cares?"

I certainly don't and as I slip my arm around her shoulder, I love how natural it is holding her against me.

Taking her hand, I twirl her fingers in mine and stare deep into her eyes. "Tell me everything."

She blinks against the tears and sighs. "I don't know what's happening to me. Things like this don't usually bother me, but I'm struggling a little."

"I can tell."

"Ok, you don't have to gloat." She hisses, which causes me to laugh softly. "If you must know, it awakens my protective instinct, which surprises me because I never knew I had one."

I shake my head in pretend dismay, causing her to giggle

146

and it hits me hard in the heart. Just staring at Jessica in the glow of my father's study reminds me she is the most beautiful woman I have ever met and now she is with me, I never want that to change. So, whatever is bothering her bothers me and I say carefully, "Is this about your sister? I'm guessing you're hiding where she is."

"I am."

"Why?"

She sighs. "Because I don't want you to judge my family."

"Me?"

I'm amazed, and she nods. "It's not good, Robert, and I'm struggling with it if I'm honest."

"Then tell me, I won't judge."

With a deep sigh, she says sadly, "It happened this morning after she dropped the kids to school."

"What did?"

"She was arrested."

"For dropping the kids to school?"

I'm so confused, and Jessica says angrily, "Of course not, don't be stupid."

"What then?"

"Ok, you may as well have all the facts, well, the ones I have, anyway." She says angrily, "Burglary."

For a moment there is silence, and she says fearfully, "You hate me, don't you?"

"I could never hate you. You irritate me, but I'm never angry." She grins as I tease her and from out of nowhere, I lift her face to mine and stare deeply into her eyes and whisper, "I could never hate you, Jessica because above everything, all I want is to kiss you right now." Her eyes widen and fill with longing, which is the answer I was hoping for, and she whispers, "Go on then."

It makes me smile and as our lips gently touch, it's as if all my Christmases have come at once as she parts those disapproving lips and lets me into a place I never want to leave. The fact we're in my father's study makes it seem forbidden and as I kiss the woman I crave more than anything, I hope she is experiencing a little of the emotion I am right now.

CHAPTER 25

JESSICA

How can this be happening? My emotions are all over the place and not a drop of alcohol has passed my lips. I am kissing the man of my dreams, disguised as one from my nightmares, and I'm strangely euphoric as my world shatters around me. I am so far out of my comfort zone, and I don't speak the language because what has happened to the efficient woman who controls life, not the other way around?

I should be stepping up and taking charge of everything, instead I'm snogging a man in his father's study as if I'm a teenager. I despise my own family for being selfish and putting their needs above everyone else's and now I'm doing the same thing because I couldn't stop now if I tried. It feels reckless and I can't believe I'm loving every second of it.

It would be so easy to forget the drama and see where this would lead but there is too much happening right now to carry on, so reluctantly I pull apart and say regretfully, "I'm sorry, Robert, I can't do this."

"Why?" He seems surprised.

"Because our relationship should be business. It's why I'm here, after all, and I have a job to do."

"We can do both."

"Not really." I hate the words but realise it's the right thing to do.

"Listen. I can't pretend you don't affect me because you do. If things were different, perhaps we could go out on a few dates and see where this would lead."

"Dates?" He appears bemused and I shrug. "It happens a lot, so I believe."

"I've heard." The amusement in his voice tells me he's not taking this seriously, so I harden mine a little and say with a deep breath, "So, until things have settled down and the postman is apprehended, I think we should remain as we were. It's good of you to help me with my unfortunate domestic drama, but tomorrow I will deal with this and get on with my job."

"If that's what you want."

I hate the hurt in his voice and can't look at him, especially when he says softly, "Are you sure?"

"Of course."

"Look at me, Jessica."

I know what he's doing, and it takes every ounce of self-control to face him with no emotion in my eyes at all. I need to be strong for everyone's sake and so I glance at him coolly. "It's for the best."

"For whom?"

"For everyone."

His low laugh surprises me and if I expected any anger directed at me, I'm mistaken, because he just nods with a small smile on his lips. "I understand. We'll get through this drama, as you put it, and then see what happens."

"You agree?" Part of me is happy about that, but the other part is enraged because what's wrong with me? Is he really giving up this easily? Now I'm a fraud because I suppose deep inside, I wanted him to argue with me. To tell me he wasn't giving up on us and declare his undying love for me on bended knees. Not agree with everything I just said. Wow, how to make a girl feel special.

He stands and adding insult to injury, says abruptly, "We should be going. It's getting late and the children need to be in bed."

"I know that." I bark irritably and I'm not sure if I hate myself more than I do him right now. Why did I destroy something that could have been amazing? I like Robert, despite his arrogance and I pushed him away even though it was reluctantly, and I have nobody but myself to blame for how wretched that now makes me.

* * *

SABLE HAS RISEN to the occasion in the most spectacular way. As soon as we entered her bedroom, I stopped still, and my mouth dropped at how amazing the children look. Angelina has been wrapped in layers of satin and silk, decorated with a feather boa and she is dancing around the room pretending to fly. Brad is resplendent in a shepherd's outfit that surely couldn't have been hanging in Sable's wardrobe. He is wearing with pride, brown trousers that are cut crooked at the knees. A striped shirt covered by a brown suede tunic and a headpiece worthy of an Arab prince perched on top of his head.

"Sable, you're a miracle worker."

I immediately toss aside the frostiness that has developed between Robert and me and smile at him.

"Your mother is a genie, no scrub that she's a fairy godmother." He appears as surprised as I am and Sable laughs at our expressions.

"It was nothing. I remembered we had a dressing-up box in

the attic. It was the result of many stints on the board of governors at Robert's school. Years of school plays and events, fancy dress parties and parades are stuffed in the oak chest, gathering dust in the attic."

"You were a fairy?" I can't disguise my amusement and Sable laughs out loud as Robert shakes his head irritably. She grins. "Of course not, darling. No, the fairy costume has been formed from my various scarves and lingerie."

"Lingerie?"

I steal a glance at Robert, who is now apparently concerned, and Sable waves her hand dismissively. "It's nothing more than a pair of French knickers and a camisole, made to fit with a few safety pins. Add in some silk scarves, a feather boa, and a few items of jewellery and voila, a star is born."

I stare at Angelina in shock as she pirouettes around the room, obviously loving her outfit and it's only when I peer closer that I see Sable wasn't joking. Angelina is dressed like a mini femme fatale, and I wonder if the school will be impressed when she performs the can can at the birth of Christ.

Robert coughs and appears slightly disturbed. "We should leave."

"But…" Sable makes to disagree, causing Robert to say sternly, "No mother. It was kind of you, but the children need their own home and to sleep in their own beds. It's late and they have a busy day tomorrow, and so do we."

I'm almost sorry for Sable whose earlier euphoria is squashed at his words and for some reason I want to make that right and say impulsively, "You must come to the nativity play tomorrow. It's at St Jude's, Worcester Park. Robert will text you the time."

Sable's eyes light up as the children cheer their support and she appears so grateful it makes me feel good about myself for once.

"I would love that."

I really believe she means that too, because the gratitude in her eyes cannot be fabricated.

Robert interrupts with a low, "Come on kids, say thank you and we'll get you home."

The fact I have gained a family overnight makes this a complicated situation for my heart and as we lead two small children through the festively decorated house, I can almost picture my future. Despite what I thought I wanted, I'm fast realising it's this, with Robert beside me sharing the responsibilities that life throws at you.

A gorgeous family; two children would be perfect. A beautiful home and no worries — ever. If I was given a choice, would I prefer to work or live like Sable and be a lady that lunches? The fact I'm even considering the choice tells me my world has spun on its axis and it's all because of one man. Robert Harvey.

When I find 'The Postman' and I have no doubt I will, I'm not sure whether to arrest him or hug him because without those threatening Christmas cards, I wouldn't be here now.

* * *

AFTER THANKING Sable profusely and meaning every word, we head back to my sister's house, trying to get over the fact David never even bothered to say goodbye. Apparently, he was going to bed and would catch up with us another time. I know Robert felt angry about that, but I was a little relieved if I'm honest and I wonder if I should ask Robert more about his childhood because I sense quite a story there.

However, we have two sleepy children to get to bed and I'm grateful for Robert's assistance as we park in the driveway and then each carry a sleepy child up the stairs, making sure they clean their teeth before tucking them into bed.

As I smooth away the hair from Angelina's forehead, she utters a contented sigh and, as I press a light kiss on her cheek, she whispers, "I love you, Auntie Jessie."

I am so shocked it takes me a minute to form a reply and my voice shakes as I whisper, "I love you too, Angel."

The glow from the nightlight illuminates my way to the door and as I catch a glimpse outside through the crack in the curtains, I swear I see snow falling. Then I remember Sable's projector and I smile to myself. There is something so magical about snow falling silently on a dark Christmas night. For some reason, it wraps your soul in happiness and comfort and makes everything better. As I picture Sally enjoying a different kind of night than usual, my heart goes out to her and as I close the door softly, I make a vow that tomorrow I'll do what I do best and get to the bottom of it, for everyone's sake.

I make my way to Brad's room and am astonished to see Robert perched on the end of his bed, reading what appears to be a Christmas story and for a moment I lean on the door frame, just content to watch the scene. Brad is battling to stay awake, and Robert makes me smile as he uses several accents for the characters and as he closes the book on the final page, he whispers, "Good night, Brad. You will totally rock that play tomorrow."

He makes to leave, and Brad's sleepy voice stops him as he says, "Will you come tomorrow, Robert?"

I think that time stands still as I find myself praying that he will, telling myself it's for Brad's sake, but really it's purely for selfish reasons of my own. I'm surprised about that and once again a little of the ice melts in my heart when Robert says huskily, "I wouldn't miss it for the world."

Quickly, before he sees me, I step back and move silently down the stairs towards the kitchen because my heart can't take much more of this. Everything has changed in the space of twenty-four hours, and I don't know what on earth I'm going to about it.

CHAPTER 26

ROBERT

The last thing I want to do is to leave them. However, now is the time I make my excuses and head home to my soulless mansion, where I'm happiest.

Today has confused that because this house filled with love and warmth is challenging my ideas of what I want in life.

From the moment I met Jessica's niece and nephew, I was blown away. I haven't mixed with children since I was one and turning up at their school and caring for them has opened a whole new world for me. I like it.

Then there's Jessica. We appear to be the same person and I wonder about that. Is she experiencing similar emotions right now, or is this her worst nightmare with me in the starring role?

When I kissed her, I believed we were on the same page, but the fact she pulled back and shot me down made me doubt my own mind. When we returned to her sister's house, it felt strangely like coming home and I envy them that. The house looks neat and well cared for and the tasteful decorations bring a sense of excitement to the home. Family life is so different from the one I was brought up with. This is how it should be. Love, happiness and chaos.

I head into the kitchen to find Jessica boiling the kettle and heaping coffee into two mugs and she says brightly, "Nightcap?"

Picturing my usual brandy before bed, I nod with a grateful, "Thanks, you're a lifesaver."

As I take my seat on the couch set at one end of the room, it strikes me that I haven't enjoyed a day as much as this for many years and it's all because of Jessica and her family. My mother surprised me too and I'm still trying to deal with that.

Jessica hands me a coffee and kicks off her shoes, settling beside me with her feet tucked up under her, and groans. "What a day."

"You can say that again."

She clinks her mug to mine and smiles. "Thanks for your help. You're not so bad, really."

"I'd be grateful if you kept that to yourself."

As the fairy lights in the tree beside us twinkle, I relax as the caffeine hits my system and I yawn loudly. "Sorry, now I've stopped, my body thinks it's time for bed."

I'm not sure if it's my imagination, but Jessica blushes a little and once again it hits me straight in the heart.

"You, um, don't have to go if you're tired."

She seems embarrassed and I smile. "Don't I?"

"They have four bedrooms. I could use their room and you could have the guest one. Unless you'd prefer to leave, of course. I mean, not everyone would want to sleepover in a strange house with someone else's kids. If you'd rather not, you don't have to…"

"I'd love to, but unfortunately work gets in the way." I cut her off, and she stops, the pink glow to her face illuminated by the soft lighting and in this moment, I have never seen a more beautiful woman in my life.

"OK." she whispers and I can tell she's struggling with her feelings which gives me hope at least and then she ruins my mood with a carefully worded sentence that I can't really deal with right now.

"Tell me about your friend, the one you lost?"

"I'd rather not."

"Why?"

"I said I don't want to talk about it."

"Is it because you were the one at fault?"

"Who told you that?" I stare at her in shock, and she shrugs. "Nobody. It was just a hunch that obviously panned out."

"You know nothing."

"Then tell me."

I'm not sure if it's my imagination tricking me, but she shifts a little closer and I'm caught up in the moment. The fact her knee is resting against mine and the heat of her body combined with the scent she wears is messing with my mind.

Her voice is soft and inviting and I am having a hard time resisting pouncing on her and forcing her to feel the same way, so to distract my own turbulent mind, I sigh heavily.

"Ok, but when I finish, you'll hate me even more."

"I don't hate you, Robert."

She touches my knee and whispers, "I'm just having a very hard time convincing myself that I do."

She laughs at my shocked expression and sighs. "I'm my own worst enemy. I'm sure you've learned that by now and sometimes I say things that seem the right thing at the time, but a different part of me disagrees. It's that part I'm struggling with now, so any help you can give me on hating you would be most welcome."

The fact she's grinning settles my heart because obviously we are both thinking along the same lines and I suppose she was right to apply the brakes because, as she said, she is here to do a job and

I must respect that. However, she's a detective for a reason and so I must give into her curiosity and tell her something I can't even admit to myself, about the time I chose money over friendship.

"His name was Samuel, but everyone called him Sam. We were friends at uni and shared a room."

As I cast my mind back to that time, I remember how long it took me to start liking myself again. Maybe this isn't such a good idea, but I suppose you should always face your fears, so I take a gulp of coffee and continue.

"I told you about my childhood. It was quite lonely, and I never really understood what friendship meant. It was always about the end goal. Achievement. Being the best and driving yourself to extremes to be the best you can be."

"I can relate to that." As I glance sideways, the earnest expression on Jessica's face makes me realise I'm in the company of a like-minded soul. We are the same and if anyone can understand why I did it, she will.

"We did the usual things college kids do, parties, drinking, sex."

She raises her eyes and mumbles, "Speak for yourself." Causing me to laugh softly. "Anyway, in my defence, I'd been held back and controlled for so long it was like offering candy to a baby for the first time. I couldn't get enough and I'm not just talking about sex."

"I'm glad to hear it."

"Are you?" I throw her a huge grin, causing her to back-track, "Out of concern for your sexual health, of course. Not that it bothers me if you, well…"

She sighs heavily. "Carry on with your story and you can leave out your sex life. I've got the message."

She raises her eyes and yet the smile we share makes my heart sag in relief. She understands, I'm sure she does and so I carry on in the hope this may purge a few demons.

"Samuel was into the same things I was, and I'm not talking about sex this time." She pulls a face, which makes me chuckle.

"We were studying media and IT along with a business degree. I was mainly studying for that, but I was interested in the technical side more. Anyway, one day Sam and I were talking, and we wondered why there wasn't a place to go for discussion online."

"You mean Twitter." She says with interest, and I nod. "Sort of, but something where you didn't have to sign up and form a profile."

"Like Google?"

"Similar. I thought about it some more and Sam was the person I threw my ideas at, and it began to consume me. I was like a dog chasing a cat and nothing could stop me. Sam soon got bored and began hanging out with some other guy, but I didn't care. I was so invested in the App, I spent all my spare time developing it. Sam wasn't happy, which caused many arguments because I had no time for our friendship. The only thing that mattered was achieving success with my App."

"That's not so bad. You were there to learn, anyway, not to make friends."

I knew she'd understand, but like me, she's missing the point.

"As it turned out, I hit the jackpot. I developed an algorithm along with my App. I named it 'What do you know?' and tested it on a few classmates. They used it to bypass the search engine and ask any question at all. It prompted conversation and became quite addictive."

"Like what?"

"College stuff, mainly. Where was the next party? Gossip even. Like I said, it became addictive and soon the whole campus was on it, asking questions, sharing answers and interacting in a much freer way."

"It sounds amazing, but hardly ground-breaking." She is

stating a fact, so I don't jump on the defensive and I shrug. "Yes, it was pretty basic, but it soon ran out of control. People began abusing it, using it to spread vile gossip and damaging people's reputations and lives."

"Because they were anonymous." She looks interested, and I nod. "I went back to the drawing board and tweaked the algorithm to identify hateful words and recognise malicious content. It stored the Ip address of the person responsible and issued a warning that if they continued, they would be shut down and the authorities notified. It had the desired effect, and the App started working as it was intended."

"And Sam, where does he fit into all this?"

"He didn't. He moved in with another guy who became his best friend, but I didn't even notice. I was too invested in my new business, and it became the most important thing in the world to develop its capabilities. By the time I graduated, I had attracted the interest of several big players, not to mention the Home Office."

"Wow, that's huge."

"It was. I finished college as their first billionaire. I sold my algorithm with a percentage of future profits. Although I am not involved in it now, my cut continues to make me millions on the side in royalties."

"I still don't understand the problem with Sam?"

"Because you're like me, driven by ambition and I may be wrong for saying this, but you probably don't have a huge circle of friends either."

I know I've hit the mark when she glances down and sighs heavily. "Then you'd be right. I don't."

"I tried to reconnect with Sam, but he didn't want to know. In fact, he appeared to have a huge problem with me and one night it came to blows."

"He hit you. Why?"

"Because he told me I had pushed him out. I'd cut him out

of the picture and grabbed all the praise for something that had been as much his idea as mine."

"But you developed it while he was partying. What a creep."

Right now, I really love Jessica because despite everything, she is the first person who has been on my side.

"Not long ago, he tried to sue me. He hired expensive lawyers and tried to make out I had stolen his idea. The fact I had all my notes and emails from software developers went against him and it boiled down to his word against mine. The courts threw it out, but many were on his side and considered he'd been robbed."

"How is any of this your fault?" She stares at me incredulously. "You made the decision to put business before socialising. Why does he think he can have it all ways?"

"I agree, but it doesn't excuse the fact I cut him off. It was an idea we discussed many times and if I'm honest, he did come up with some of them, but he never did anything more than that."

She falls silent and yet I know her mind is working hard and then she says firmly, "This ex-friend of yours. He knows about the software and the tracking algorithm installed on it. How many search engines and email providers currently use it, or an incarnation of it?"

"Most of them."

"I see."

"What are you thinking?" I can almost hear Jessica's mind working as she asks, "When was the last time you spoke to him?"

"I haven't, not since before the court case."

"When was that?"

"September."

"This September?"

"Yes."

"I see." She looks at me with a hint of excitement in her

eyes. "So, somebody with a grudge against you, who knows he could be tracked if he used the internet, may well consider getting even by a more old-fashioned form of intimidation."

"You believe he's the postman?"

I shake my head. "I considered that, but when I last heard of Sam, he was working in Dubai. These cards are postmarked London. It can't be him and anyway, what does it achieve?"

"Who knows how the mind of a master criminal works?"

She shrugs. "I'll need all his details. The company he works for, any contact you've had, a sworn statement telling me what you just said and details of all his friends and family. If your ex-friend Sam is the postman, he's going to be sewing mailbags in Pentonville before the Spring arrives."

CHAPTER 27

JESSICA

*F*inally, there is a breakthrough. I can't believe I passed this hot lead by, but it came to me when we were sitting side by side. It must be Sam. The story fits and…

"I think you're wrong."

Robert cuts into my thoughts, and I stare at him in surprise. "Why?"

"If it was Sam, then why involve my parents? He never met them, at least I don't think he did, and it doesn't add up."

He does have a point, but something is telling me Sam is our man, so I reach for his mug and stand.

"We should call it a night; it's been a long day. I can show you to the spare room if you like."

I hate that he shakes his head and says with a sigh, "It's fine. I should head home and catch up on some work. I'll pass by the office tomorrow morning and cancel my meetings, then I'll pick you up for the nativity if you text me the time."

"You're coming – to the play?"

I'm astonished and he runs his fingers through his hair, looking so tired I feel bad for keeping him here.

"I wouldn't miss it, and I did promise Brad. Plus…" he grins.

"You invited my mother, and I wouldn't leave you to deal with that pleasure on your own, no matter how low your opinion is of me." He makes to leave, and I say quickly, "I don't have a low opinion of you, Robert. Quite the opposite, in fact."

As he turns, a look passes between us and with a small smile, he winks before heading out into the cold night.

* * *

As I LIE in the spare bed, I wonder how I got here. Yesterday my life was all mapped out. I was doing a job that I love and my head was set on solving the mystery. I never thought I'd enjoy it though and it's all down to one man.

I am so conflicted with my emotions. The woman in me is screaming to grab him with both hands and not let go but the detective in me is trying desperately to remain professional and not become the stereotype I hear the guys joking about in the office. I want to be better than them, not to prove their misogyny right, so I'm battling with my own feelings as well as a family emergency and the realisation my parents had a secret and never even considered telling us.

I like to believe I would be happy for them and encourage them to spend the money. They won it fair and square, but I know deep inside I would have shared my good fortune with them if it was me. I suppose it's only when the situation becomes a reality that the truth comes out and perhaps I would do as they did and put myself first. It's not a bad thing and I hate myself for being disappointed in them, but then again, why would they consider me? I'm hardly the doting daughter and distanced myself from my family in the pursuit of my dream job. That's why I completely understand Robert and what he did. I would have done the same, and I also understand his guilt because nobody likes to imagine they've hurt some-one, especially a man who was his only friend.

There is so much whizzing around my mind I can't sleep, and my thoughts turn to Sable and Robert's father, David.

There is something strange about him, but Sable is completely different from what I expected. Seeing her with Brad and Angelina revealed how much she loves children, making me wonder what her relationship with Robert is like and if they are distant because of his father.

The fact Robert has gone home is also interesting because when he left, it was as if part of me was leaving with him.

Somehow, I fall asleep and it's as if my head just hit the pillow before the alarm goes off.

* * *

I HAVE a newfound respect for my sister after the morning I've had. To be honest, attempting to rise two sleepy, belligerent children from their warm and cosy beds after a late night took a superhuman effort. It took all my powers of manipulation to get them to eat the cereal I provided, and I almost forgot to pack their nativity outfits, which also gave me anxiety as I stuffed the feather boa in a unicorn rucksack. What will the teachers think when my niece dresses as a femme fatale for the Christmas story? Sally is lucky she's not here because, quite honestly, the playground mafia will dine out on this for months.

Finally, we slam the door behind us and as I open the garage, I just pray Sally's car is here because if it's not, we are going to be extremely late.

"Auntie Jess, I'm not feeling well." Angelina whines, holding her tummy and screwing up her face.

"You'll be fine." I stare at the monstrosity that is lurking in the garage and my heart sinks. Does Sally really need this all-terrain vehicle in the leafy suburbs?

The rather large and angry Cherokee jeep stands smirking

at me defiantly, almost daring me to chance my luck. This isn't a car, it's a transformer and I half expect it to morph into the giant robot and crush me to dust under its heavy boot.

Brad shouts, "I've forgotten my homework."

Tossing him the keys, I say quickly, "Go and get it while I bring the car out."

"No, I've forgotten to do it."

I spin on my heels and stare at him in dismay and he shrugs, appearing not to care less that he'll be reprimanded for this.

"Why didn't you remind me?" Once again, it's as if this is my fault and the guilt I'm wearing like a technicolour dream coat for all to see, is not easing at all as the hours tick by being a replacement mother.

"I forgot." He shrugs and I bite back, "Then you must deal with the consequences and tell your teacher that."

"But mum always does it for me."

"She does not." I gasp and Angelina nods, seemingly forgetting about her tummy ache as she senses her brother is in trouble. "She does mine too."

"Why?"

"Because she likes it." Angelina smirks and I growl, "We don't have time for this and just so you know, I'm not your mother and I will *not* be doing your homework. Understand?"

"I want mummy." Angelina begins to cry, and Brad looks a little worried. "She is coming home, isn't she?"

"Daddy too." He adds as an aside.

"Of course." I sink to my knees and pull them into my arms and say gently, "They are just enjoying a few days away. It was sudden, and they had no time to waste, but they love you very much and will be home before you know it."

"Won't mummy be coming to see me be a fairy?"

Angelina sobs and Brad's voice wobbles a little as he whispers, "Daddy promised."

It's as if they punched me in the heart as I try to reassure two children that their parents love them, despite taking off for a few days without even telling them. Subsequently missing their nativity play after landing them with the aunt from their nightmares. I'm hardly Nanny McPhee, but I am developing an attachment to the two small children who have opened my eyes to the fact that there is so much more to life than work.

"I promised to video it." I clutch them a little tighter. "So, make sure you speak up and look happy knowing they will be viewing it on live stream."

"Really." Brad sounds interested. "That's cool."

"So, they will be there." Angelina sniffs.

"Not in body, but over the internet." I hope to God he forgives my lie so close to the celebration of his son's birth, but desperate measures are needed, and I won't apologise for trying to make these children feel loved and so I pull back and glance at the angry beast waiting and say cheerfully, "Ok, jump in and let's get this show on the road."

Thankfully, they start cheering, which is better than the screams I expect when I attempt to navigate this beast through the school run traffic. I will definitely be having words with Sally when she returns about the need for a four by four in Worcester Park.

However, as soon as I turn the key and the beast roars into life, I become a different person.

For some reason, being in charge of this machine makes me feel like the most powerful woman alive. Now I am super mum sitting high up looking down on the masses and challenge anyone to get in my way. One of my favourite songs is playing on the radio, which calms my nerves and sets my mood to happy. I could get used to this and now I understand the power of the machine because as we pull out into the traffic, I am superior in every way. I can do this. I am one of them. It's not so hard and as I set off on the school run, nothing will ever faze me again.

CHAPTER 28

ROBERT

*W*aking up at home is different somehow. When I left Jessica and the kids, it seemed wrong, almost as if I was walking out on them. I wonder how their parents must be feeling because surely it's the most agonising form of separation knowing people are depending on you.

There was another card waiting for me when I got home and now, as I open it, my heart sinks.

Happy Christmas to you and your girlfriend. Enjoy her while you can because now I get two for the price of one.

It's as if a cold hand is reaching around my heart and crushing it as I let the words sink in.

The postman knows.

He is close by and watching me. My head starts to pound, and I think very hard about who it could be. Is it someone at Harvey's? It must be because I don't go anywhere else. Sure, we've been out for dinner, but they were all strangers. I'm positive the only people holding a grudge against me are Sam and my staff, but it can't be Sam. He's not even in the country.

Turning to my phone, I scroll through Facebook and type in his name. There may be some posts that tell me where he is and yet as I get to his page, I just get the message that this account is private. He blocked me.

All through the court case, he continued to allow me access, so why now? Is it because he lost, and he wants nothing to do with me, or has he got something to hide?

I try his sister's page because to my knowledge, she has no reason to block me and luckily, I was right and as I scroll through her photos, I see nothing about Sam in her feed at all. Clicking on her friends, I try to go in that way but again, it won't let me view Sam's feed. I am so frustrated because I want to prove that he isn't the one because if he is, I probably deserve this. The threats are chilling, and I wonder if they are empty ones, or does the postman intend on carrying them out? If so, Jessica is now in danger because of her involvement with me.

Sighing, I head to the office with a heavy heart and just hope things are ok there because for the first time since I took charge, I am taking the rest of the day off.

* * *

As I HEAD into the store, I question everyone I meet in my mind. The security guard at the staff entrance. The managers, who all nod courteously to me but lower their eyes as I pass. Am I really hated that much? I glance at a couple of women chatting as they make their way to their department, and they quickly stop and look at the floor. It's as if I'm the Grim Reaper as I stride through my store, causing plants to shrivel up and die and flowers to wilt. I make people nervous, and I guess rightly so, because the purge of staff that followed my appointment did not go down well.

It was never personal though, only business, and the store

has thrived under my command. Profits are up for the first time in three years and the store is undergoing a facelift that has been achieved without the need of a bank loan. The shareholders are happy and, more importantly, so is my grandfather and yet my staff are not.

I head to my office and flick on my computer, wishing like crazy I hadn't generously allowed Sylvia to take time off because I could use a coffee and someone to cancel all my meetings today. However, one email makes me smile when I see it's from the lady herself, and I experience a twinge of pride when I read what she has to say.

Morning, sir. I just wanted to say thank you again for the time off. I have managed to accompany my mother to her chemo sessions and help clean her house and make her a meal before heading home to spend time with my family. The prognosis is good, and the doctors are hoping she will only need four more sessions. I just wanted to thank you for easing my burden and allowing me to concentrate on my family when they need me most. I will be back just as soon as possible, and I hope you are coping without me (not too well, though).
Sylvia.

I dash off a quick reply.

Morning, Sylvia. Thanks for your email and I'm glad to hear your news. Send my regards to your mother and I wish her a speedy recovery. No need to rush back. It will be Christmas soon so you may as well concentrate on that. If you need anything, you know where to find me.
Robert.

It makes me laugh as I sign my name because, despite telling her on numerous occasions to use it when she talks to me, she never does. Sylvia is always respectful, which is what I like most about her. She understands this is a working relationship, and I respect her for that. However, that still leaves me without an assistant and so with a sigh, I begin to email my meetings to reschedule them, and I wonder what they would think if they knew it was to attend a nativity play of a family of strangers.

Once again, I think of my staff and wonder if the parents among them are missing their own kids' nativity plays. I never thought about that. In fact, it never occurs to me they have a life outside of Harvey's at all and if anything, I'm ashamed of that.

So, I'm more surprised than anyone when I dash off an 'all staff' email.

Morning everyone. From today I will grant two ad hoc days per employee on full pay in addition to your contracted leave entitlement to attend school plays or hospital appointments. These are two examples, but I'm aware that sometimes work can get in the way of life. Any requests must be presented to your department managers for authorisation at least a week in advance. Have a good day.

Robert Harvey

Once I press 'send', I lean back and feel good for once. Doing something nice is alien to me and I have only one woman to thank for that. Jessica, unknowingly, has shown me real life, and it's opened my eyes. How can I head off today knowing I'm doing something I'm denying my own staff? It won't matter to the running of my store. If anything, it will make my staff happier and hopefully loyal.

It's as if a veil has lifted and I see a clearer picture. Not to the extent that my father did, but I'm hoping a little leniency will go a long way to making Harvey's a much happier place to work.

CHAPTER 29

JESSICA

*S*omehow, I got those kids to school on time and was glad to see that Angelina's tummy ache appeared much better. When we got there I was grateful that her friend Alice came running up and pulled her off to play.

I didn't hang around to chat with the other parents because why on earth would I? The fact it was freezing and there is a hint of snow in the air, had me running back to the beast as quickly as my stiletto heels would let me and as I head back to Sally's, I vow to take charge of her predicament.

As soon as I return, I make myself a coffee and take out my phone, scrolling through the texts from the various lawyers I requested for help. Many came back to me with an apologetic 'no', which I expected because most of them are always busy, but one said they'd do their best and as I read her latest message, my heart sinks.

Hi Jessica. I contacted the police in Sutton and told them I would be acting for Sally Stevens and to forward me the police report. Just to inform you, she has been moved from the cells and is currently in Bronzefield prison. I will be visiting her today at 2 pm. Her husband has been sent to Wandsworth and I have a meeting scheduled in at 5 pm with him. I will brief you later.

Regards, Amanda.

Prison! I'm dizzy as I picture them in hell, and I wonder what on earth they did that was so bad they wouldn't be granted bail.

I quickly make a call to Detective Inspector Ranauld because, as a serving police officer under his command, he needs to hear I now have criminals in the family.

"Jessica, please tell me you've solved the case and are ready to resume your duties."

Biting back my irritated retort, I say calmly, "It's in hand, but that's not why I'm calling."

"I'm listening."

I take a deep breath. "Well, I must tell you that my sister Sally Stevens and her husband Anton were arrested yesterday and appear to have been remanded in custody in Bronzefield and Wandsworth."

"What are the charges?"

"Burglary." I cringe as I say the word, and his inhalation of breath doesn't make me feel any better.

"Thanks for telling me. Keep me informed, but I will need to investigate the circumstances in case you are incriminated."

"Thank you. Oh, and sir…"

"Yes, Jessica."

"I don't suppose you would tell me what you find? It's just that well, I know nothing."

"Of course. Leave it with me. Just do your job and get back here."

I cut the call, but before I can even take a sip of my coffee, the phone rings and I note an unrecognised number.

"Jessica Taylor speaking."

"Jess, thank God."

"Sally!"

"How are the kids?"

She sounds so upset it brings tears to my eye picturing her starring in an episode of Prison Break.

"They are fine. Safely at school and preparing for the nativity that I will video for you, so don't worry."

"Thank God." She sighs with relief. Then she whispers, *"What did you tell them?"*

"That you've both gone away for a few days and will be back soon."

"And they were ok with that?"

"You know children…" I laugh. "Feed them a Happy Meal and let them stay up past their bedtime and they're delirious."

"What about their costumes?"

"Sorted. Anyway, don't worry about the children, just tell me what's going on? Why are you in prison already and why haven't I been contacted to provide bail?"

I now want answers and the tone of voice is not to be messed with.

"Ok, I'll tell you, but don't judge me, OK?"

"Of course, I won't." I bark, but we both know that I will. I always have.

"Well…" she hesitates and then sighs.

"Well, Anton is an estate agent, and he's very good at it. Anyway, we like to, well, spice things up from time to time and yesterday was one of those days."

If anything, she sounds mortified and she mumbles, *"I met him at one of the properties he's selling. It's worth well over two million pounds and is state-of-the art. Anyway, occasionally we like to pretend to be having an illicit affair. We do that from time to time to keep the spark in our marriage and well, one thing led to another, and we ended up in the master bedroom, um, naked."*

I can't believe what I'm hearing, and she groans.

"Anton wasn't aware, but the owners returned early from their villa in France and caught us naked in their bed. We didn't know they had called the police already because they thought we were squatters. Well, the police stormed the room, dogs and all and we were apprehended."

"And the owners are pressing charges! It's hardly the crime of the century."

"Not on its own, I suppose not, but the woman discovered a valuable ring was missing when she did an inventory and accused us. I

told them I was naked, but they thought we swallowed it and are waiting to see if the evidence presents itself from either one of us."

"You're kidding! They remanded you for that. It's inhuman."

I am so incensed on their behalf, and she says miserably. *"I agree. At first, I was so afraid. I mean, I've watched prison dramas on the television, and I was terrified."*

I agree with that and say quickly, "Whatever you do don't tell then you're related to a detective. It won't end well."

"It's ok." she whispers. *"I told them you were a stripper."*
"Them?"
I can't even deal with her career choice right now because she's obviously not in solitary waiting for the eagle to land, which causes me concern.
"The girls." To my surprise, she giggles.
"Oh, Jessica. To be honest, everyone is so lovely in here. For instance I'm in a cell with fat Sandra; she's amazing."
"You can't call her that, it's…."
"Ironic."
"What do you mean, ironic?"
She giggles. *"She's as thin as a rake."*
"Then why do they call her fat Sandra?"
I'm getting a headache and she laughs. *"Because there is already a skinny Sandra here who, incidentally, is rather large. Like I said, it's ironic."*
Now I do have a headache, and she says with an excited giggle. *"There's also gay Gail."*
"Happy perhaps."
I'm really hoping, but Sally whispers, *"No, she's gay, and she's so lovely. Actually, she was the one who gave me my own nickname."*
"Which is?"

I can't believe I'm having this conversation.

"Sexy Sally." She says with a hint of pride in her voice. *"She's really taken me under her wing and promised to show me how it all works in the showers later on."*

Now I'm lightheaded and squeak, "Promise me you won't go into the showers with gay Gail."

"Why not? Honestly Jessica, this place is nothing like I imagined. Everyone is so kind and interested in my life. You know, there's a woman in here who has the most amazing tattoos. She said she'd do me a free one if I let her park her caravan on my driveway for one week when she gets out."

Suddenly, it's the most important thing in my life to spring my sister from this nightmare waiting to happen and I say in an urgent rush of words.

"Now listen up. Keep quiet, do your time and pray for nature to set you free because that's your only defence right now. Don't make any promises and forego the showers. Your new lawyer will be with you this afternoon and hopefully will arrange an early exit for you. Keep me informed and whatever you do, agree to nothing, and never go anywhere on your own. OK?"

"Thanks, Jessie." I detect the tears in her voice as she whispers, *"You won't tell mum, will you?"*

"Of course not because keeping secrets is something this family is good at."

"What do you mean?"

"It turns out mum and dad won the lottery and have blown the lot on a cruise. They won't be back until Christmas, no doubt with a fine tan and many excuses why they didn't give us any."

"They won the frigging lottery. Are you on drugs?"

"It feels as if I am, Sally. Sadly, no. I am under no influence at all except for insanity right now and am dealing with the fall out of my family's rash decisions and trying to keep it from the rest of the world."

"I'm sorry, Jess. I owe you big time for this."

She sounds so despondent which causes me concern and I briefly wonder if the guilt will ever diminish because there is not one thing in my life right now that I don't feel guilty about.

"It's fine. Don't worry about me."

"Oh, Jess."

"What?"

"Have you heard anything from Anton? I'm so worried about him."

"No, but I've arranged for the same lawyer as you. Hopefully, she will come up trumps and you'll be free by the end of the day."

"Here's hoping."

"Positive thoughts, Sally. We'll laugh about this over the Christmas turkey, ok."

"I hope so, and thanks, Jess. We aren't that close, but you were the only person I could turn to, which says a lot."

"I know."

I thought the same because despite everything and the fact our paths barely cross these days, I would be upset if she had called anyone else because she is my sister and I love her in a sibling rivalry kind of way.

When I cut the call, I stare at my cold cup of coffee and wonder how I've reached this place. It's as if fate has conspired and dropped me headfirst into madness to teach me the meaning of life or something. I woke up today as a very different person from who I was yesterday and now nothing is normal. However, despite it all, there is one thing that is curling around my heart and squeezing new life into it, and I really hope he honours his promise to pick me up on what could well be our first proper date. The nativity play.

CHAPTER 30

ROBERT

*J*essica texted the time of the play and I forwarded it to my mother and as I pull up on the driveway of her sister's house, I am strangely nervous. A lot happened yesterday and now, in the cold light of day, I wonder if those feelings remain. Will I still think of her in the same way? This yearning and need for someone like her in my life. For *her* in my life.

As I head to the door, I note the festive wreath and the fake snow on the window ledge. Everything is done with precision and care and as houses go, it could star in a magazine spread for the perfect Christmas. Inside was no different and I'm guessing Jessica's sister is like her a little, with her methodical approach to life with everything in its place, including her emotions.

Then again, her sister was arrested for a crime I have yet to learn the details of and part of me hopes it's all been a huge mistake. Then again, she could be a master criminal and this house was paid for from the proceeds of a life of crime. It happens, I suppose.

I ring the bell and chuckle when I hear Jingle Bells echoing back at me, and as the door swings open, my heart lurches when I see the worried expression on the woman who has captured my attention from the moment she flagged down my car.

"You came."

She seems surprised and I nod. "Of course, I never go back on my promises."

She looks confused and I grin. "Brad. I promised I would watch him."

"Oh, of course."

If anything, she looks disappointed and as I step inside, I have an incredible urge to demand she gives me a chance. If I thought differently, just seeing her was enough to realise if anything my feelings for her are even stronger. She appears so dejected, as if she's carrying the weight of the world on her shoulders and I want to be the one to lift that world into my own arms and carry it beside us so we can deal with it together.

Instead, I follow her into the warm and inviting kitchen and it's as if I've come home as I gaze around at the comfortable space that wraps you in family life, promising your own will be just as good, if not better,

"How are the kids?"

I drop onto the sofa and regard her as she flicks on the kettle and begins heaping coffee into two mugs.

"They were fine. Got to school ok, despite trying everything in their power to delay the inevitability."

She rolls her eyes and looks so gorgeous, it's taking all my inner strength not to head across and pull her into my arms because that appears to be the only reaction I have to the woman who has taken me by surprise like this.

"I heard from my sister."

"And?" This is news, but from the expression on her face, she's uncomfortable about telling me.

"It's, well, an unfortunate incident that got out of hand."

She hands me the mug and drops beside me, and I hate that my eyes immediately go to her shapely legs that she crosses, allowing her skirt to rise a little.

I'm not really listening as she relays the story because I am fighting my attraction to her with everything I've got, but when her words register, I stare up in horror.

"They did what?"

Jessica blushes and looks so embarrassed it makes me laugh out loud and she says fiercely, "It's not funny, you know. They may get a criminal record for not being able to control their carnal urges."

I know a lot about those right now and stare at her with a desperate expression, making her snap, "What?"

"It's not so bad."

"You think."

She frowns and is so like the cross fairy I first met, it makes my heart physically ache.

"Think about it. They were living in the moment. It can't be easy being parents, I guess, and I'm sure part of them as a couple gets lost in that. Most of the time they must be responsible and do the right thing, and they are exhausted at the end of the day. I was, and I only had one day of it, not even that. I expect they fall into bed at night just grateful for sleep and probably never get time for one another. This is the perfect way to keep a marriage alive because it retains the spark, which makes for a happier family life."

"I never thought of it like that." Jessica smiles and a small laugh escapes, causing my heart to lift for the second time today. I like making her happy and to see a smile on her face because of something I said and once again it strikes me how much I've changed since meeting her.

"And you. How are you today?"

She glances up and smiles, a faint tinge of red on her cheeks as the atmosphere changes in the room. I know she senses it too by the softening in her expression and the way she licks her lips nervously and, feeling a little bold, I edge closer and tip her face to mine. "I missed you."

"Stop it." She blushes and yet the happiness in her eyes tells me she feels the same.

"I hated leaving last night."

"You did what you had to do."

She appears to shake herself and pulls back a little and says with a deep breath. "Was there anymore post?"

The moment has been torn away from me as she struggles to remain in control, and I sigh. "Yes, but now they know about you."

"Me?" She looks worried.

"They called you my girlfriend and said now they had two for one. I'm sorry, Jessica, perhaps we didn't think this through."

"So, it's someone who knows we're together." Suddenly, she looks excited and grabs her phone. "We'll list the names of everyone we've met since we became an item, and our postman will be among them."

"An item?" I arch my brow and she shrugs. "I'm undercover, Robert, and sometimes that involves doing unsavoury things."

She grins, making me smile and I can't help edging a little closer and saying playfully, "So, if we were in public and were being watched, you would let me put my arm around you. Perhaps we should practise that."

She licks her lower lip and says shyly, "Probably, just so it would appear natural."

I slip my arm around her shoulder and hold her tightly against me. "Like this."

"Um, yes, perfect."

"I suppose I could whisper in your ear and people would assume it was something dirty."

"Why would they assume that?"

"Because if you were my girlfriend, it would be definitely something like that."

"Is that right?"

She rolls her eyes and I whisper in her ear, "Then I would turn your head and kiss you deeply, just to reinforce the fact, for appearances, of course."

Her breathing is fast, and she whispers, "That could work."

"Like this." I tilt her face to mine and let my lips rest against hers and whisper, "Shall we?"

"I guess it wouldn't hurt."

This time as our lips meet, it's as if I'm coming home to a familiar taste that causes my heart to thump with the knowledge that if things go my way, this kiss will lead to so much more. The pleasure of sliding my hands under her sweater and experiencing her skin flush with my own. The heat from her body and the sound of her heart beating against mine. I want more than this kiss and I want all of her, forever but I'm not about to frighten her away, so I put everything into the one thing I'm allowed and kiss her with a passion that I haven't experienced for a very long time.

Her gentle moan against my lips is enough to tell me she's loving every second of this and as her fingers wrap around my head and pull me closer, any pretence is shoved to the side. We kiss as would be lovers and if I get my way, we will be and as Jessica melts into my arms, I load everything I can into this kiss. She needs to understand my intentions and realise this isn't just a fling, for me, anyway. I am serious and won't stop trying to make her mine despite how much she is fighting this because she obviously is. Her sense of duty is holding her back, and it's up to me to prove she can have it all, if she has it with me by her side.

The kiss lasts longer than most, and yet neither of us is in any hurry to stop. I could kiss her all day and it's only when the alarm goes off on her phone that we pull apart.

"What is it?"

She says briskly, "It's time to leave for the play."

"You mean you set an alarm for the play?" I begin to laugh, and she glares at me furiously. "Of course. We can't be late, you know. The place will be packed, and I need to be in the front row because I'll be filming it for Anton and Sally. They may be missing it in person, but I will not deprive them of the magic."

"The magic?" I laugh out loud causing her to roll her eyes.

"The magic of Christmas – obviously."

She shakes her head. "Come on, we haven't got time to waste."

Chuckling, I follow her out and as I flick the lock on my car, she jumps into the passenger seat and just for one moment I wish this was real and we were heading off from our cosy home to watch our children dishing out their own brand of Christmas magic.

CHAPTER 31

JESSICA

To be honest, I was so glad of the alarm. What was I thinking? Once again, I lowered my guard and surrendered to the selfish part of me who wants it all. It would be so easy to give into the pleasure that is Robert Harvey, but I know what this is. He only wants me because he can't have me and, by his own admission, he's a player. The list of conquests and past girlfriends was so long, it took up several pages in my pocket notebook. It was embarrassing, but he didn't appear to think anything of it. He doesn't want *me* just the challenge and I am so on the edge of that it's not even funny.

It takes the entire journey to school to calm my raging libido because, unlike Robert, it's been a long time since I've let my guard down and allowed myself to be intimate with a guy. The last one was a fellow police officer and our relationship only lasted three months before he left me for a new recruit. It was a humiliating experience, but one that isn't uncommon in my life. It's easy to attract them, but not that easy to hold on to them and I have no reason to think this is any different, despite what my heart is telling me. I'm a great believer in relinquishing control to my head in matters of the heart, and it's telling me this is a job and not to look back when the case closes.

Robert is quiet, which I'm grateful for because I need to calm down and approach things as I normally do. With cold rationality because that is what's needed right now.

We make it to the school, and I'm amazed when we park next to a Bentley and the window rolls down and I see Sable dressed like a Russian in head-to-toe fur, wearing mirrored sunglasses.

"Hello darlings. I must say I am so excited to watch my angels."

Robert' expression tells me he is definitely not excited to see them and as Sable steps from the car, I stare in disbelief as her husband exits from the driver's side, dressed in a blazer and beige chinos, looking as if he's just stepped off his boat.

"Um, Mr Harvey, I didn't expect you to come too." I'm a little horrified about that and he nods, looking as if he would rather be anywhere else.

"I had nothing else to do." He shrugs and turns to his son, leaving me with Sable, who links her arm in mine.

"I must say, it's been years since I attended one of these. Who knows, the next one may be your own children with my son."

"Excuse me?" My voice is faint, and she grins, a knowing twinkle in her eye.

"I know its early days, but you are the first girlfriend we have ever met. That's how I know it's serious."

She appears so happy about that, I feel bad for deceiving her and merely smile nervously. "If you say so."

"I do and darling, let me tell you it makes me so happy. Caring for your sister's children while they enjoy a rejuvenating break tells me you are just the kind of woman I want in my son's life. Family minded, loyal and kind. A great aunt who will be an even greater mother and I can't wait to embark on this journey with you. First the wedding, oh how amazing that will be. Imagine the months of planning we will enjoy, with your own mother, of course. I can't wait to meet her. Is she here?"

She glances around and my heart sinks even further as I say brightly, "Oh, she couldn't make it; she's currently enjoying a luxury cruise."

"Wonderful, darling. She sounds like a woman after my own heart. I'm sure we will be the best of friends. Imagine the hours of pleasure we will enjoy. Family holidays, meals and helping you raise the most perfect children. So much to look forward to and it begins today."

It's as if my life is crashing down around me as she sets out a future I want more than anything. That alone surprises me, because how have I fallen so quickly for a man who irritates me most of the time? I really hope he never overheard this conversation because he would be bolting for the car never to be seen again.

I don't miss the startled looks on the faces of the few parents that have made it here before us and as we take our seats in the second row, I conclude I should have allowed more time. Now I'll have somebody else's head in my video and I'm annoyed about that.

Robert sits beside me, and Sable is on my other side and it's as if I'm caught between a rock and a hard place because my emotions are scrambled. I want this. I want what Sable wants and I even what Robert wants. I doubt his mind is set on anything other than me in his bed, and I want that, too. But I'm not stupid and it would draw an end to whatever this is that's growing between us and I would be cast aside, dreaming of what could have been if Sable had got her wish. I must be strong and resist at all costs, but it's hard when he is fast becoming everything I want in a man.

* * *

As the hall fills up, I turn my attention to the reason I'm here and as I peer around, I take in the slightly shabby interior of a school that needs a makeover. We are sitting on black plastic chairs set in rows and the stage has been decorated with colourful scenery and enough sparkle to resemble a fairy grotto. It reminds me of my own stint in one and I shiver when I remember the humiliation it brought with it.

Robert leans in and whispers, "Are you cold? Perhaps we should do what we practised earlier."

"Are you kidding?" I whisper shout. "We're in a school, for God's sake."

He shrugs, apparently unconcerned. "Just the arm part, unless you think it appropriate to indulge in a full-blown snog before the play starts."

He starts to laugh and Sable leans across. "What's the joke, darling? I must say it's lovely seeing you so happy. That's what the love of a good woman does for you, dear."

I giggle at the expression on Robert's face but am saved from answering, or demonstrating what we rehearsed, as the children start filing in from the door at the back of the room.

I search eagerly for Brad and Angelina and my heart melts when I spy Brad looking amazing in his shepherd's costume while the other two beside him are like the poor relations.

Sable claps her hands. "There he is. That's my boy." She beams as she turns to the woman behind her and points to Brad. "He's such an angel."

I cringe in embarrassment at the slightly startled expression on the woman's face, and yet I experience a warm glow when Brad offers Robert a beaming smile as he passes. My hands shake as I record the moment and I experience a lump in my throat when Angelina pirouettes in like a star in the Moulin

Rouge, swinging her feather boa like any good stripper and flashing her French knickers as she goes.

"My God." The woman behind us exclaims as she passes and Sable turns and says loudly, "Isn't she a darling? You would never know she was wearing my finest lingerie."

Once again, the woman looks astonished and I'm guessing she will need a lie down after this and I may well join her. Then as I catch Robert's heated look thrown in my direction, I can only think of one person I would rather be lying down with, and I cross my legs and count to ten and hope this is over soon because I may combust before too long.

The play begins and I'm struggling to see any similarities to the real nativity at all. It appears that every avenue has been covered as Mary is renamed 'M' not to be confused with James Bond's superior and she is referred to as 'They'. Joseph rides in on a motorbike wearing a dress and I'm beginning to understand why Jesus's creation was considered an immaculate conception. The wise men are suddenly wise women who storm in with swords like Boadicea. The manger is plastered with a certificate stating it has been sanitised for Covid and the Angel Gabriel is wearing a face mask.

I am now deeply disturbed by the whole thing and the slightly cringy way the teacher is acting out all the parts and mouthing the words in an exaggerated way, makes me want to stand up and object that the birth of Christ is being misrepresented in the most politically correct of ways.

"Wow, things have changed since I was at school." Robert nudges me, looking a little bemused by the whole thing and his father leans across his mother and says loudly, "What the hell is this?"

I shrivel in my seat as Sable slaps him away and says fiercely, "Don't make a scene, David. You promised."

He sits back wearily in his chair and closes his eyes as his wife beams with pride when Angelica steps forward to sing the song they were practicing last night.

The spotlight falls on her and I grip the phone hard, determined to record this moment for her doting parents who, sadly, can't be with us on this occasion.

As she starts to sing, it restores my faith in the magic of Christmas because the lights dim, and the projector makes it appear that the snow is falling on the manger. She sings Oh Little Town of Bethlehem and I'm certain there isn't a dry eye in the house as everyone stares at her in trance like amazement. She stares into my phone as if she's singing directly to her parents, causing a lone tear to escape from my right eye that I whisk briskly away.

Robert edges a little closer and his knee touches mine and then his hand and as I glance down at it resting on my leg, I am awash with emotion. Why is fighting him so hard? It's becoming a full-time occupation because I'm battling myself more than him because I want this. I want him and the sooner I discover the identity of his would-be murderer, the better because I am teetering on the edge of surrender and preparing to wave my white flag.

CHAPTER 32

※

ROBERT

A shocked silence stays with us all as we exit the school hall and I feel the stares follow us as we go. My mother appears to have been silenced for once and my father's face is like thunder. Jessica has apparently lost the power of speech and I almost considered carrying her over my shoulder because who saw that coming?

As soon as Angelina finished her song, she burst out crying and pointed to Jessica, shouting, "I miss you mummy, please don't leave us. I promise to be good."

Brad then rugby tackled his sister, shouting, "Shut up! They're on holiday, stupid, they're coming back."

The teachers dived in like a rugby scrum and all around us were the murmurs of 'disgusting', and 'who abandons their children at Christmas' and 'I heard they're in prison'. I had to physically restrain Jessica from punching the entire lot of them and it was only when the children were forcibly removed from the room that Jessica was called to calm them down and explain what was happening for safeguarding reasons.

We were left with reassuring smiles on our faces, wondering how long to leave it before making a dignified exit.

The fact Angelina's lingerie escaped the safety pin that was supposed to be holding it in place was a cringe worthy moment, when her French knickers fell to the floor, but luckily the camisole was long enough to prevent her eternal embarrassment. Mum didn't help much by nudging my father and yelling loudly, "That wouldn't be the first time they came down, would it David?"

In fact, she appeared to find the whole scene hilarious, but that hilarity soon died when the comments started and she glared at me fiercely, whispering, "Is this true, did they abandon their children and why did Angelina believe it was because of them?"

"Were they really arrested?" My father added, and I tried to blank the whole thing out and pretended to take a call on my phone instead.

* * *

THE TEACHERS DECIDED it would be best if Brad and Angelina returned with us and as we all head back to the happy house, we do so in silence.

As soon as we head inside, Jessica sends the children off to change and throws me a despairing look.

"That was awful. Whatever must your parents think?"

My parents certainly left fast enough and yet I couldn't care less what they think. It's what Jessica's thinking now that's my main concern.

She seems so beaten, almost on the verge of giving up and nothing like the woman I first met, and I surprise myself more than her when I open my arms and smile. "Come here."

The slight pink tinge to her cheeks makes me doubt myself, but as she moves closer and my arms wrap around her, I nuzzle the top of her head and whisper, "Everything will be OK. Your sister and her husband will no doubt be released tonight, and we can return to scoring points off each other by morning."

Her low giggle makes me smile and then she whispers, "But what if they don't? Those poor children will be without their mother and father for Christmas."

"I doubt they could hold out that long." I laugh softly. "As soon as the evidence of their innocence presents itself, they will be free to go."

"I wish I shared your view on that."

She sighs. "I mean, the children need stability. It's Christmas next week and they break up tomorrow. They need this Christmas to be extra magical to compensate them for being without their parents. What if they wake up on Christmas morning and have no presents? I couldn't live with myself if I didn't make sure every avenue was covered." She sags a little in my arms. "I will never forget the expresssion on Angelina's face when she stared into the phone camera and pleaded with Sally, who she thought was watching her 'live'. It really broke my heart."

I hug her a little tighter and say firmly, "Then it's up to us to put a smile on her face. It's time for someone else to help ease the burden, and I know just the man for the job."

"You do?" She pulls back a little and stares at me in surprise and I grin, not in any hurry to release her from my close protection.

"Once the kids are dressed, we're heading out."

"Where to?"

"Well, what's the point in owning a store at Christmas if you don't use it?"

"Harvey's?"

"Of course. First, we head to fairyland, and you can revisit old friends." I chuckle as she rolls her eyes.

"Then we'll head to the Winter Wonderland restaurant and feed them with enough food they will sleep soundly tonight before ending the evening at a show in the West End."

"How? Those tickets are like gold dust this time of year."

"Leave it with me." I wink as I release her from my arms and say with a groan, "I don't suppose I could make us a coffee. My caffeine levels need stocking up to cope with the day ahead."

"I'll make it." I pull her back and say firmly, "I'll make the coffee while you check that Angelina isn't wearing the contents of her mother's lingerie drawer."

I love the soft laugh she rewards me with and the gratitude on her face makes me feel good about myself.

As she leaves the room, it strikes me how much I've changed since meeting Jessica, and I like it — a lot.

* * *

WE HEAD INSIDE HARVEY'S, and I don't miss the surprise on the doorman's face as we walk through the main entrance. He almost bows as we pass and Brad whistles, "Cool."

Angelina is gripping Jessica's hand, and she looks around in wonder at the bright lights and the huge store displays of red poinsettias, gold bows and magical fairy lights. It strikes me that if she is this impressed with the decorations on the ground floor, she will be beyond excited when she gets to fairyland.

My display team win awards for a reason and many people just come to Harvey's to have their photographs taken beside amazing automatons, fairies, giant Santas and elves. There is a small train called Santa's Express that offers children rides around Toyland and the fairy grotto is every girl's dream deco-rated in pink and silver glitter with white fluffy animals and frozen lakes.

It is a very magical place to be and planning always begins on January 2nd every year. My buyers trawl the globe for exciting temptations, and we are now the number one store in the country that is always featured in magazines and on news segments.

We reach fairyland and I love watching the children's reactions to my staff's hard work and Jessica smiles happily and whispers, "Thank you, Robert. This is so kind of you. You know…" Suddenly she looks anxious and stutters, "You really don't have to hang around if you'd rather head to the office. I mean, you must have zillions of things to do and…"

"Stop." She looks surprised. "I wouldn't want to miss out on all the fun now, would I?"

She blinks in disbelief and as I see Mr Bennett, the floor manager, bearing down on us with haste, I whisper urgently in her ear, "I would run if I were you. Take the children to the grotto. I'll meet you there."

She turns and, seeing the rather pompous department manager heading at speed our way, she gathers the children close and says loudly, "Who wants to meet Santa?"

Their loud cheers make me smile and as they head off, I set my mood to business as soon as he reaches me.

"Sir, what an honour. How may I help you?"

I absolutely hate the way he fawns over me and say brusquely, "See those children over there."

"Yes sir." He appears confused and peers at Jessica a little more closely. "I want your staff to follow them and anything they pick up or express an interest in, I want added to my account."

"Everything, sir?"

He looks as if his Christmases have all come at once as he senses an avalanche of sales heading his way because we both know kids will pick up everything they see and, to be honest, I really hope they don't prove me wrong."

He nods with his usual reverence, and I say quickly, "When we leave this department, I want you to arrange for a personal shopper to follow us discreetly, and if she sees my girlfriend look at anything with interest, the same applies."

"Your girlfriend, sir." He blinks and narrows his eyes as he peers at Jessica again and as the penny drops, it takes his mouth with him. "But that's…"

"Do we have a problem, Mr Bennett?"

"No, sir." He recovers quickly and I say dismissively, "Good. Make sure they are all gift-wrapped and labelled accordingly and delivered to my home by the end of the week."

"Consider it done, sir."

As I head off, it amuses me to be inflating my own store's takings personally. I've never been a fan of Christmas and never saw the point of it, but since meeting Jessica and her family, everything changed. I want to make them smile. To drop a little of my own magic into their lives and what's the point of having billions if I can't spoil the people I love?

CHAPTER 33

JESSICA

I'm a little overwhelmed by everything that's happened today. It started off badly with the telephone conversation with my sister, followed by the alternative nativity play that ended in utter chaos, and now this. Propelling two excited children around every child's paradise, all the time trying to manage their expectations, while lusting after the man who made it happen.

I am almost considering waving the white flag of surrender because I'm growing more interested in him by the hour, not shutting my emotions away. He is turning out to be the perfect man, and I'm waiting for the mask to slip and reveal his true identity.

He meets us as we are next in line for Santa and slips his arm around my waist, pulling me close whispering, "Now relax. We deserve an afternoon of fun for once, and all our problems can wait until the morning."

"That would be good." I smile up at him and the smouldering look in his eye almost makes me blush, because his intentions are written all over his face. It's a lot to take in, especially when they are reciprocated, and I am dazzled by the magic dust he has thrown into my eyes.

He is good. I'll give him that and for once I won't fight against it and just give in. And why not? I deserve a bit of fun and it is Christmas, after all.

As we enter Santa's grotto, I encourage Angelina to approach Santa with her hand in Brad's and watch like a proud mother from the doorway as they tell Santa what they want for Christmas. My heart sinks when I hear Angelina asking for the same doll I broke up a fight for when I was a fairy in this very department and hiss, "Great, now she'll be disappointed."

"Why?"

Robert seems confused, and I sigh. "We sold the last one of those a few days ago. Let's hope Sally planned ahead and there is one wrapped up in their hiding place because that poor child has already been through enough."

I concentrate on Brad, who asks in a loud voice for the latest games console and my heart sinks. Why is everything so expensive these days? What's wrong with a chocolate orange and a barbie or toy train? They all want increasingly compli-cated toys that require a degree to set up and I am already buckling under the pressure of making kids happy. Now I understand what the fight was about, I sympathise because as sure as I'm having second thoughts about Robert, I would have laid my opponent out to get my hands on that doll.

When they finish, I lead the children out while Robert stays behind to thank Santa and as we step out of Santa's workshop, I walk around the department with the children, loving their youthful enthusiasm for just about everything.

It's a little strange that a woman with a shopping trolley appears to be following us and everything they touch she throws into it, and I'm frankly disgusted by her obvious lack of planning in making a list, rather than relying on strangers to choose for her.

Robert soon follows us and swings Angelina high in the air, making her squeal before sitting her on the back of a giant pony that apparently does everything but gallop.

"What shall we call him?" He says laughing and Angelina cries, "Donkey, of course."

"The one from Shrek." I laugh. "Sally told me they are obsessed with it."

"Would you like to watch the show tonight?"

Robert asks them and my heart sinks when I remember Sally moaning you couldn't get tickets for all the money in the world.

The children's joyful screams echo around fairyland and Robert grins. "I'll see what I can do."

As he pulls out his phone, I take him to one side and say tightly, "You can't promise them the impossible. Honestly, Robert, you really need to get a grip. This is ruining their childhood."

"What is?"

"You can't make sweeping statements when vulnerable children are involved. Who knows what trauma the last two days will do to their mental health and if they can't see Shrek, it will keep them in therapy for years."

"You're so melodramatic." He rolls his eyes and holds up his hand as the person answers the call. "Yes, this is Mr Harvey from Harvey's department store."

He pauses before nodding. "Yes, well, anyway, I was hoping you had room for four people tonight. Usual seats."

He taps his foot while there's another pause and then sighs. "Fine. No problem."

I shake my head and glower at him for raising their hopes only to be dashed so cruelly and as he places his phone back in his pocket, he appears annoyed. "Unfortunately, my usual seats aren't available, so we'll have to slum it in the dress circle instead."

"Are you kidding me?"

I'm astonished and he sighs heavily. "I'm sorry. It was the best they could do."

"Not the seats, you idiot." Despite myself, I laugh incredulously. "You actually have usual seats. What are you, a closet Shrek fan?"

He grins. "No, I have seats reserved at most theatres in London. Usually for corporate purposes, and I reserve the best box. They keep them available for me, but tonight they are expecting Royalty so I must concede them." I stare at him in shock as Angelina races over, carrying a huge, white, fluffy dog. "I love him. This is Snowy."

Brad charges over with a light sabre and pretends to lance off Snowy's head, causing Angelina to scream and burst out crying and by the time we have placated them and repositioned the toys on the shelves, I am emotionally drained.

To distract them, we head to the top floor and Robert arranges a table for us inside Cinderella's carriage in the storybook themed restaurant, much to Brad's disgust. He wanted to captain The Black Pearl instead, but there was already a family of five occupying that particular vessel.

As we order burgers, fries, and fizzy drinks, I vaguely wonder where my principles went. I always maintained that I would raise my own children on a vegan diet with strictly no e numbers allowed. Now I'm positively throwing them at these poor children in the vain hope of bringing a little pleasure to their lives and as I bite into my own godmother burger, I can definitely see the attraction.

In fact, I hate to admit it, but I am having the most wonderful time and it's all down to one man, who is sitting beside Brad, deep in conversation about the intricacies of Star Wars, leaving me to talk Cinderella with Angelina.

* * *

AFTER WE'VE EATEN, we waft around the store on a cloud of contentment as the harmonious hymns filter through our ears with the sounds of bells jingling, reminding us that Santa is on his way. The air is laced with Christmas scents of cinnamon, pine and orange segments. The perfumery is almost toxic as we glide through the rows and spray ourselves with designer luxury and as we head through womenswear, I longingly consider the finest cashmere, softest silk and designer leather bags, wishing I could afford just one of them.

Luckily, it's late-night shopping and so we have just enough time to walk the brightly lit streets of London towards the theatre district, admiring the festive windows that we pass and dodging the hordes of shoppers ticking items off their lists as they scurry past us.

It strikes me that I have never enjoyed the build up to Christmas before. To be honest, I've never even noticed it, but this is so addictive. It's making me want more and I say impulsively, "I wish I could decorate a tree and go carolling. Wouldn't it be fun to involve the kids in that?"

"It would." Robert appears thoughtful. "I've never been a fan of Christmas, as you know, but that's probably because I've always been on my own."

"What, you don't go to your parents' house on Christmas Day?"

"Do you?"

"Of course, if I'm not working." I shrug. "Most of the time, I volunteer to escape the false merriment and endless unwrapping. However, with children around, I imagine it's a lot more fun."

"Don't you see your sister, then?" He appears amazed at that, and I sigh. "Only if they're visiting Mum and Dad. It's tradition we pop round there for drinks on Christmas Eve. I know they go to Sally's for Christmas dinner, but I always make my excuses because I can't be bothered with it."

"What do you think will happen this year? I mean, your parents are away and, well, um, so are your sister and brother-in-law."

"I'm sure they'll all be back by then and normal business will be resumed." I say confidently but for some reason I'm not looking forward to that and to distract myself, ask, "What about you? What are your Christmases like?"

"I head over to my Grandparent's house on Christmas Eve. Have a formal dinner with them and then drive home. The next day my parents host Christmas lunch and then I return home to work, mainly."

"Do you have any other visitors?" I'm a little shocked at how cold it all sounds, and he shakes his head. "No. It's just family, not that we get along, but we go through the motions."

Suddenly, my own family seems more appealing but before I can delve a little deeper, we reach the theatre and even I experience a stirring of excitement as we step through its hallowed doors.

CHAPTER 34

ROBERT

I have attended many shows in the West End, usually in my capacity as CEO of Harvey's, while I wine and dine valuable customers and business associates. However, I can say, hands down, this is the best one I have ever seen, and it's all because of who's sitting beside me.

The children are ecstatic and laugh at even the smallest joke and their enraptured expressions make me smile. Their aunt is no different as she laughs and giggles along with them and casts many amused glances in my direction as she tries to share the joke with me. Occasionally, her hand finds mine at a particularly good point and I love how relaxed she is with me now. It's almost as if we're a proper family and it's becoming the most important thing in my world to make them happy.

But I know this is a fleeting moment that will soon be gone because undoubtedly their parents will soon be home and Jessica will revert to doing her job in the hope of solving the case and returning to the station.

My heart is heavy just thinking about it and yet I push it aside because they're here now and I must make the most of that.

* * *

MUCH LATER, we carry a child each from the car and tuck them into bed and I briefly wonder if we should have thought this through. It's their last day of school tomorrow before they break up for Christmas and I'm guessing they will be sleepy and irritable due to the lack of sleep and amount of sugar they consumed this afternoon and evening.

As we close the doors and tiptoe back downstairs, the thought of returning home is the last thing I want and, almost as if she reads minds, Jessica says shyly, "Please stay."

I glance up and see her heightened colour and shallow breathing, and the message is loud and clear. She is interested; more than interested perhaps and in two steps, I pull her into my arms and whisper, "I'm not going anywhere."

As we enjoy a long and leisurely kiss, I can feel her heart beating against mine and wonder if this is the moment my dream becomes reality and as she presses in and groans softly, there is only one thing on my mind right now. Her.

It appears she is of the same mind because she says in a low, urgent voice, "Just don't break my heart, Robert."

She pushes off my jacket and her fingers reach for my belt and suddenly all self-control has left the building and returning the favour, I push up her sweater and with a feral groan, run my hands under her shirt, loving how soft her skin is against my fingers. Her muffled moans of longing are all the encouragement I need and as we fall onto the sofa, my hand pushes up her skirt as I settle between her legs and then like a bucket of cold water, we hear the front door slam and as we pull apart like guilty teenagers, I stare in astonishment as two people almost fall into the room and Jessica says in disbelief, "Sally!"

The fact her sister was caught in a compromising position obviously doesn't deter her from saying with some relief, "Oh

Jess, thank goodness we're home. That was a horrific nightmare."

She races across and pulls her dishevelled sister into her arms and it's a little awkward as she sobs on her shoulder and hiccups, "I never thought I'd see my home again."

I make myself respectable while they are otherwise occupied and as her husband ventures deeper into the room, I note his pale face and weary expression as he stares at the scene anxiously.

He catches my eye and I stand, offering him my hand.

"You must be Anton. I'm Robert."

At the sound of my voice, the two women pull apart and Sally stares at me in surprise and then glances back to her sister.

"What's going on?"

Jessica fluffs her hair and tries not to look as if she was two kisses away from the very crime her sister was arrested for and says in a bright voice, "Meet Robert my…"

"Boyfriend." Ignoring her startled expression, I step forward and offer her sister my hand and pull Jessica close by my side. "It's good to meet you both. You have a lovely family."

"Are they ok?" Sally's anxious expression makes me a little emotional as Jessica nods reassuringly.

"They're fine. Exhausted but fine."

"Have they asked about me?"

As I picture the outburst at the nativity, I wonder if Jessica will fill her in on events, but she is obviously as shocked as I am and merely smiles. "All is good. I'm afraid we wore them out with a visit to London. They may be a little tired in the morning."

"On a school night?"

Sally appears shocked at that, and Jessica shrugs. "It was a distraction."

Anton steps forward and runs his fingers through his hair

and I can tell he's been through a lot, judging by his tired eyes and pale expression and Jessica obviously comes to the same conclusion and says briskly, "Well, it's late and I'm guessing you both want to shower and get some sleep. We'll catch up in the morning."

She turns to me and says with a slight hesitation. "We should go and leave them in peace."

"Of course."

Sally peers at me a little closer before glancing at her sister and it amuses me to witness the astonishment in her eyes.

"Wow, it appears I'm not the only one who has some explaining to do."

"But not now." Anton steps forward and places his arm around his wife's shoulders and sighs.

"Let's all catch up tomorrow."

He smiles and I note the gratitude in his eyes as he says wearily, "We can't thank you enough for everything."

Jessica squeezes my hand a little tighter. "It really was a pleasure; for us, anyway."

I detect a touch of amusement in her voice and say quickly, "OK. We'll be heading off to give you some space."

Suddenly, it dawns on me that we are leaving the two children sleeping upstairs and, for some strange reason, it makes me sad, which surprises me.

As I reach for my keys and head off to retrieve our coats, I hear her sister whisper, "Wow, we really need to talk."

CHAPTER 35

JESSICA

What on earth was I thinking? I just threw myself at Robert with no regard for playing it cool and making him work for it. He must think I'm one of those loose women and he'd be right. I don't know what came over me and being caught in a compromising position by my sister, who was arrested for the very same thing, didn't make me feel any better about the whole incident. Not to mention that I've now lost all the moral high ground I was going to torture her with.

I'm quiet on the journey back to Robert's oversized home and the fact he turns on the radio tells me he's regretting our 'moment' as much as I am. Then again, I'm not sure if I am. If anything, I'm more irritated that Sally and Anton came home.

I must be the worst kind of human because I wish they had spent a few more nights in the cells because I was enjoying playing house. It was addictive, making the children smile and the fact Robert was beside me was the icing on the cake.

"What are you thinking?" Robert's voice comes out of the darkness, and I sigh. "That I'm a despicable human being who wished her sister had spent a few more days at his Majesty's pleasure."

To my surprise, Robert's low chuckle is my answer, followed by a soft, "Me too."

"What?"

"I was thinking the same thing. It was fun, wasn't it?" His hand reaches mine and squeezes it gently, and as I gaze down at our entwined fingers, it causes my heart to shake a little. "Jessica." His voice sounds hesitant, unsure even, and I sense a conversation that could go either way. On the one hand, he may be about to say what I'm longing to hear and on the other, he may be applying the brakes. However, as he opens his mouth to speak, I yell, "Fox!"

He jams on the brakes, and we lurch forward in our seats and as we come to a stop, I see the fox's tail disappearing into the hedgerow.

"Sorry." He huffs his apology and I exhale sharply. "Well, at least he'll live to tell the tale."

Robert turns, and I watch, mesmerised, as his eyes sparkle in the darkness and he says with a slight hesitation.

"It doesn't have to end?"

"What doesn't?"

I'm not sure if I understand what he's talking about and he leans forward, a hint of excitement lighting up his eyes.

"Let's spend Christmas together. Decorate the house, shop for food, go carolling. What do you say? I've acquired a taste for it, and I want more."

"OK." I stare at him, his excitement contagious and I say with enthusiasm, "We could go to one of those places where you can chop your own. I'm sure it would go on the roof of your car like they do on the Christmas channel."

"We could make mince pies and eggnog."

"Do you even know what that is?" I've heard of it, but I'm not sure I've even had it before and he nods. "We'll google it."

"No, we won't." I frown. "We'll post a question on, what do you know?"

As we break out into peals of laughter, it doesn't strike me as odd that we are in the middle of the road in the dead of night, discussing our Christmas arrangements and when Robert stops laughing and I see that spark change in his eye to a different one, I swallow hard. "What are we doing?" My voice sounds husky and unlike me and he reaches out and strokes my face lightly, whispering, "We're falling in love."

My breath hitches as my head spins and I stare at him with a mixture of lust, desperation and disbelief, all wrapped up in happily ever after.

"We are."

I nod because I can't deny this anymore. I can't deny *us* anymore and as our lips meet, this time there are no doubts at all. This is right, and only a fool would disagree.

A loud tap on the window makes us jump apart and my heart sinks when I see a police officer peering into the car with a flashlight.

"Step outside the car, please, sir."

He jerks his thumb and Robert groans. "This is just great."

"Don't upset him, Robert. He's only doing his job."

I jump out too and the officer says sternly, "Stay in the car please, ma'am."

"I'm sorry, officer, it's just, well, um, may I have a word?"

He glares at Robert and nods to the car behind him and I watch his crew-mate heading our way to deal with Robert while I have my word.

I nod to the rear of the car and as we move out of sight, I whisper, "I'm sorry, officer, but you need to hear this before you progress."

"I'm listening." He rolls his eyes and I say slowly, "Now, in my purse is my warrant card and if you would like to take a look, you will see that I'm genuine."

"You're a copper?"

He raises his eyes as if he doubts every word and I nod,

pasting on the fiercest, most stern expression that I own. "Detective Constable Jessica Taylor, currently working under-cover under Detective Inspective Ranauld of Scotland Yard." He blinks in disbelief and nods to my purse and as I present him with the evidence, he lowers his voice.

"Are you undercover now?"

"Yes." I whisper more softly.

"I was about to learn some interesting information and then you interrupted." I wave my hand. "It's ok, I understand you were just doing your job but, well, the timing was a little incon-venient and I'm not sure if I'll get the moment back if I'm honest."

"Is it drugs?" The officer looks excited, and I shake my head. "Way more damaging than drugs. I'm sorry, I have my orders and I'm afraid this is top secret. Need to know basis, secret oaths. You know the drill."

"Of course, ma'am. I understand."

He glances around the car at Robert and his colleague, and it appears that Robert is blowing into a breathalyser and he shakes his head. "I'm sorry, leave it with me."

He smiles apologetically and holds his radio up to his ear and walks around the car.

"Dave, we'll have to let this lucky bugger go. Something more urgent has come up."

Dave glares at Robert and growls, "This is your lucky day, mate. Keep your dick in your trousers and take your sexual activities to the bedroom in the future. People like you are a public decency hazard."

He shakes his head and throws me a stern gaze. "Same goes for you."

His crew mate says quickly, "We've really got to go."

As they race off, Robert stares after them in confusion.

"What the hell was that all about? Anyone would think we were dogging on the A3 or something."

I shrug as I get into the warm interior of the car and sigh with pleasure as it melts the ice that my brief encounter with the night air provided.

"Beats me. Anyway, we have a Christmas to plan, so let's go and Robert…"

"Yes, honey." Resisting the urge to sigh like a besotted teenager at his choice of endearment, I say sternly, "Keep to the speed limit unless you want to replace Anton in his cell."

"Yes ma'am." He winks and as we head off with a roar and two large smiles on our faces, it strikes me that for the first time in my adult life, I am really looking forward to Christmas.

CHAPTER 36

ROBERT

I wake the next morning with Jessica wrapped around my body and I can't contain the huge smile that accompanies it. If I was in the line for Santa, I'm certain this is what I would have asked for and all my Christmases came at once last night as soon as we got home.

As soon as we stepped foot inside the door, we were tearing one another's clothes off and barely made it to my bedroom before we fell into bed and spent most the night falling in love as I cringingly put it. In fact, when I look back on the things I've said and done since meeting Jessica, I wouldn't believe it if I saw it myself and I am a completely different man than the one I was just a week ago. She has made me feel emotion for once in my life and, like Scrooge, my eyes are now open to the wonder of meeting that special person and letting the light in. I want to make her happy. I want to make her family happy and, most surprising of all, I want to make my own family happy and proud of me for once.

As Jessica stirs in my arms and snuggles against me, I resist the urge to pick up where we left off last night and instead, I inch from the bed with one aim in mind, making her happy.

I leave her to sleep and head downstairs after pulling on some sweatpants and a t-shirt and go straight to the kitchen to fire up the coffee machine. I'm even considering making us scrambled eggs and toast and taking it back to bed, but my phone flashes with several messages and the one from my grandfather is one I can't ignore.

He answers on the second ring with a loud, *"What's going on?"*

"In relation to…"

"The fact you took the day off yesterday. Were you sick? Are you sick? I mean, it's nine already and I'm standing in your office."

I glance at the clock in surprise because I could have sworn it was only seven am. As the hands on the clock back up the fact my grandfather is telling the truth, my heart sinks.

"I'm not sick and I'll be there within the hour."

His gruff voice radiates disapproval as he barks, *"I expected better of you, Robert, especially as it's the annual board meeting in less than an hour. I hoped we would have time to discuss things before it progressed, but obviously not. We'll discuss this later. Get your arse over here and don't spare the horses."*

Despite being a self-made man in my own right, my grandfather has always been in charge and defy him at your peril, so I forego the coffee and head back upstairs, loving that Jessica is smiling and obviously enjoying a contented dream. As I dress quickly, I feel a pang of regret that we don't get to enjoy our first official morning as a couple.

I dash off a quick note and leave it on the pillow and hate that I'm already proving I'm putting work first as I head out of the door to make the commute to the store.

* * *

On the way, I try to make it up to her and call the head of my display team to discuss transforming my mansion into a Christmas grotto. With only a few days to go until Christmas, there is no time to waste and as I make the arrangements, I congratulate myself on planning ahead and smile when I picture Jessica's excited expression when she sees it.

I know she intends to touch base with her sister and will be out for most of the day, but we had plans to meet up for lunch at the store and discuss the pressing matter of the postman, who is still at large. It annoys me that our plans are changing so quickly, but it was my fault I guess because I completely forgot about the board meeting, which reminds to never give my assistant any time off ever again because being nice gets you in trouble.

* * *

True to my word, I reach Harvey's within the hour and as I head through the main entrance, I barely glance at the doorman, who once again almost bows as I pass. I completely disregard the staff who attempt to catch my eye as I head in the lift to the top floor.

The Christmas carols that serenade me as I go, reminds me of Jessica's wish to go carolling and I dash off a quick text to my housekeeper in the hope she can persuade the local choir to sing at our door tonight. Time is of the essence because I don't have any and if Jessica wants the perfect Christmas, she is getting it.

As I enter my office, my heart sinks at the glower on my grandfather's face as he sits in my chair, going through the post. He points to the seat in front of my desk, and I don't even question falling into it, a little nervous about what he has on his mind.

"Your assistant is missing and on further investigation, I understand you authorised extended leave. Why is that?"

"Her mother's sick and she was struggling."

"I see." He strokes his chin and the icy glare in his eyes makes my heart sink.

"There is also the matter of the email that was sent from your computer giving the entire staff two extra days' paid leave to attend. what was it, nativity plays or hospital appointments?"

"I did." I face him with a hard expression, and he hisses. "And you didn't consider it prudent to run this reckless use of the company's profits by the Board. It does concern them, after all."

"It was my decision as CEO."

I return his glare and he laughs out loud. "So, you make all the decisions now like your father did and look where that got him."

He doesn't even give me a moment to reply and slams his fist down on the desk and bellows, "He almost ruined this company, and you know that. We are hard for a reason because what good would it be to anyone if we closed? Your lenient ways could cost these people their livelihood and you must be cruel to be kind. I thought you knew that."

I can't even disagree because he's right. My father put the staff's happiness over the profits of the store, and it nearly cost them everything. I make to speak, and he says wearily, "I don't want to hear your excuses. We'll consider that a lesson learned. Now I want to hear about the woman you've been racing around town with. Your father tells me her sister's in prison and she's got you by the balls."

"Then my father is wrong." I growl, rising to Jessica's defence immediately.

"Jessica's sister is home with her children and my balls are just fine, thank you. Yes, I've met a woman and yes, she makes me happy. What's so bad about that?"

To my surprise, he smirks and then his expression changes. "Good."

"What do you mean, good?"

"It means I approve. Bring her to dinner on Christmas Eve. We would like to meet her."

"You would." I'm surprised by the sudden change of atmosphere and my grandfather sighs heavily. "It's not good to be alone. Your grandmother is beside herself. She was even thinking of inviting Patricia's granddaughter over and locking you in a room until you proposed to her."

He chuckles at the horrified expression on my face because Patricia's granddaughter is ten years older than me and a vicar.

"As if that's a good idea." I shake my head as he laughs out loud. "It would be entertaining to watch, though. I'm almost disappointed."

Now the tense atmosphere has gone, I relax a little and as our conversation turns to business and the healthy profits the store is enjoying in the run up to Christmas, I focus on my work and what I thrive at doing. Making money.

CHAPTER 37

JESSICA

The first thing I do when I open my eyes is stare at a ceiling that isn't my own. It takes me a moment to remember where I am and as the memory hits me of what went on here last night, my cheeks burn. Tentatively, I slide my eyes sideways and spy a note placed on the pillow, and my heart sinks.

I knew it.

Bleary-eyed, I sit up and snatch the note and for some strange reason my heart performs a happy dance of joy.

Morning gorgeous, I'm missing you already. I've been summoned to the office by my grandfather and that's the only reason I've left. I can't wait to see you for lunch as we arranged. FYI, I regret nothing and can't wait to carry on where we left off. xxx

The door slams downstairs, which makes me sprint from Robert's bed like a gazelle and grabbing his dressing gown, I head outside the room and lean over the bannisters to try to steal a glimpse below. I see an older woman carrying a basket, and my heart sags in relief when I remember that Robert employs a housekeeper.

"Hello."

I call out so I don't scare her, and she looks up in surprise as I shout, "It's ok, I'm Jessica, um, Robert's well, um, girlfriend."

She waves and calls back. "Pleased to meet you. I'm Mrs Grant. I'll get the kettle on."

By the time I've thrown on some clothes and dragged a brush through my hair and teeth, she has two mugs of steaming coffee ready and a huge smile on her face.

"I must say, I'm surprised. You are the first person I've ever met here, except for Mr Harvey, of course, and I've only met him once."

"How long have you worked here?" I slide onto the bar stool and grasp the coffee as if I'm an addict.

"Five years."

"Say what?" I stare at her with wide eyes, and she laughs. "I met him at the interview and after that our paths never crossed. He is out when I work, and we communicate through WhatsApp."

"That's…"

"Perfect." She smiles. "It suits us, and we get along, virtually, anyway."

"So, you don't really know anything about him."

"I wouldn't say that, dear." She winks. "When you are responsible for a man's washing, cleaning and shopping, you quickly form an opinion."

"I suppose."

I take a swig of my coffee and hate asking the next question. "Does Robert entertain here much?"

I realise I'm going to hate the answer when she fidgets on the spot.

"There have been a few occasions when there's evidence of an overnight guest."

My heart sinks because I'm guessing that's all I am.

"But they have never stayed before." She quickly recovers. "When Mr Harvey told me to make up the spare room for a houseguest, I just assumed it was a relative, or a friend of his. I was pleased to learn it was for his girlfriend. I mean, nobody should live their life on their own. It's not right."

"I suppose."

I wish I hadn't asked because now all I can picture is how many women were here before me and yet I always knew he was a player. I don't have to like it though.

Sighing, I drain the cup and say apologetically, "I'm so sorry, I really need to get ready. I have some errands to run and, well, it's almost mid-morning already."

"Of course." I try to ignore the knowing twinkle in her eye and as I break the record for getting ready, I head outside and begin the short walk to the station.

* * *

"You've got a lot of explaining to do, my lady."

Sally's death stare cuts me down as soon as I step foot inside the home we vacated so quickly last night.

"Says you." I shrug as she heads to the kettle and says over her shoulder, "First, I must thank you for the rather emotional, belligerent, and exhausted children that I deposited at school with the promise that you and Robert will come for Christmas."

"Say that again." I blink as the words sink in and she sighs. "Apparently, they love him. You too, strangely. They were more upset that you weren't here, than happy to see me and Anton. All they talked about was the shopping, the visit to Santa, and eating dinner in Cinderella's carriage. Then they wouldn't shut up about Shrek the musical and I am beyond annoyed that you got tickets when I offered to sell my own body for some and was rejected."

I grab the mug of coffee she slides my way and shrug. "Robert has connections."

"So, who is he?" She cuts straight to it and stares at me eagerly as she prepares to absorb the gossip.

"My boyfriend. We told you last night. I met him at work, and we fell for one another."

"At work. Is he a detective, or a criminal?"

Her eyes are wide, and I laugh out loud. "He's a shopkeeper. The owner of Harvey's if you must know."

"What!" she almost spits out her coffee. "The Harvey's. The impossibly expensive, designer, wet dream of a store Harvey's that I can't even afford to shop the sale Harvey's?"

"Yes, it's no big deal."

"No big deal, you say. That man's the most eligible bachelor in London. I read in the gossip columns he's a billionaire, for goodness' sake. I can't believe it."

"As I said, it's no big deal. Anyway…"

I fix her with a stern look. "Enough about me and my rather amazing, interesting sex life." I grin, causing her to giggle and suddenly it's as if we're teenagers again, obsessing over a hot guy from class and fantasising about catching his eye.

"Anyway…" I clear my throat. "What happened? I never heard you were being released. I would have come and got you."

"It was so sudden." She leans back and sighs heavily. "That lawyer you arranged was seriously hot and not in a gay Gail's understanding of the word. She was a demon and even I was afraid of her, and I face the playground mafia every day. Anyway, she arranged a meeting with the police and tore them to ribbons before my eyes. She demanded my release, and it's only because of staff sickness that it took so long to get me out. She was waiting at the gates and drove me to collect Anton, who had a similar day to mine, and then she dropped us off last night."

"I knew she was good." I am so happy that something I did made a difference and helped my family and yet above everything, I miss my niece and nephew and feel slightly miffed that I didn't get to take them to school on their last day.

Remembering the whispered stories in the school hall, I say anxiously, "What did you tell the other mums? I heard someone mention that you were arrested."

"I bet that was Angela Price. She's such a stirrer. Just because her husband's always doing time, she expects the rest of us to do the same."

"I couldn't say."

Sally looks angry. "I saw the looks the minute we stepped out of the car and as soon as I got the opportunity, I told everyone Anton had surprised me with a few nights away in complete luxury. That shut Angela Price up, I can tell you, and the envy on their faces was worth its weight in gold."

"So, what now? Is the case over? Has it been dropped?"

"It has." She smiles with relief. "The owners have decided not to press charges, on one condition."

"Which is?" I'm staggered by this news and so relieved I didn't even realise how anxious I was.

"That we call by one night for dinner and, well…"

"What?"

She seems a little embarrassed and says quickly, "It appears they thought the whole thing was such fun when it had time to sink in. They couldn't believe we had the audacity to go through with it and apparently, they are not averse to a few fun and games themselves and they decided it may be fun to swap."

"I can't believe what I'm hearing, and say weakly, "Swap! You don't mean…"

"Yes, I do." She takes a swig of her coffee and grins. "They said we should pool our ideas and swap stories. It will be such a fun evening, especially when I relay my prison diaries."

"Your what? All two days of it, you mean."

She shrugs. "Two days may as well be a month when you're in prison. The stories I could tell you, my dear sister, but I won't."

"Why not?"

"Because what happens in Bronzefield stays in Bronzefield. It's the code."

"The code? What are you, a pirate now?"

I stare at her in incredulous disbelief, and she pretends to zip her mouth shut and mumbles, "I will never tell."

"But you just said you were telling the people who put you there in the first place."

"Because they're *involved*." She rolls her eyes. "Anyway, I don't suppose you are up for a bit of babysitting duty on Christmas Eve. We had to promise them we'd spare them a few hours then."

"Christmas Eve! Couldn't you say no? After all, you do have children."

"It was either that or spend Christmas in prison. I think you'll agree we made the right choice."

"Fine. But don't go doing more than conversation. I know what these people can be like."

"Of course." She turns away and I note the sudden flush spreading around her neck and my heart sinks. Great, my sister has now officially fallen down the rabbit hole and I'm the idiot left to pick up the pieces again.

CHAPTER 38

ROBERT

*D*espite my grandfather's anger, the board meeting was a great success, largely because of the vintage champagne I ordered and the healthy dividend they can expect in their bank by the morning.

My grandfather went off to lunch with his close friend Albert Grimes, leaving me to wait for Jessica like a teenage boy with his first crush.

On the dot of one, she strides into my office with a grave look on her face and my heart sinks.

"Is everything ok?"

"I'm not sure."

She shrugs out of her padded coat and tosses it on the chair beside her and fixes me with a worried stare.

"I took a call from my superior on the way over."

"You're needed back at the station?"

My heart sinks and I feel the depression circling.

"Not yet."

I breathe out and she chews her lip as she prepares to deliver whatever news she has.

"He tracked Samuel Masters and apparently, he returned to

London from Dubai at the beginning of December. Do you remember when you received the first Christmas card from the postman?"

"It was around the sixth or seventh, then the rest began arriving."

"I see." She appears thoughtful and I interrupt her thoughts. "It can't be Sam. He may hold a grudge against me, but this really isn't his style."

"You don't know that. People change and when money is involved, all bets are off."

"It's not him."

I glare at her, and she leans forward with a stern, "With due respect, Robert, do you know that for a fact?"

"You know I don't."

"Can you vouch for every move he's made since the beginning of December?"

"Now you're being facetious."

She smirks. "Tell me, with your newfound knowledge of everything Samuel Masters, what exactly has he been doing since he returned from overseas?"

"You know I can't."

"Exactly." She nods, apparently satisfied. "Sometimes the crime is committed by the closest person to the victim. I've seen it countless times, and it explains how they know your movements and about me."

"So you're saying it's someone close to me? That's preposterous. I don't have anyone who is close to me and so unless it's you, think again, detective."

"Your parents. Your grandparents."

"Now you're being ridiculous."

"Am I?"

She fixes me with a hard gleam in her eye and says firmly, "Everybody is a suspect until the case is solved. Now this is what we'll do."

As she tells me exactly what's going to happen over the next few days, I struggle to take it all in. Now I realise why Jessica is obsessed with her job. She loves it and the passion in her voice and the sparkle in her eyes tells me she's an outstanding detective. In fact, I don't believe I've ever seen her looking as beautiful as she does now and when she finishes, I say huskily, "Ok, we'll do it your way if you agree to one thing."

"What?"

"Lock the door. I want you to take down my particulars."

The surprise in her eyes is soon replaced with lust and she says breathlessly, "You're a wicked man and as it happens, that is just my type."

Lunch can wait, work can wait, and life can wait because there is only one thing that matters now and it's showing this woman just how obsessed I am with her.

* * *

"This isn't going to work."

After a very enjoyable working lunch, we left the office and are now standing outside a house in Notting Hill that apparently belongs to Sam Masters.

"Of course, it's going to work, trust me. I've been over it a thousand times already."

As I stare at the determined woman beside me, I don't doubt that for a second, and as Jessica rings the doorbell, I almost consider running. The last time I saw Sam, he was yelling at me from across the courtroom that he wanted me to rot in hell, and it took three policemen to restrain him. I even considered employing bodyguards for a while because, subsequently, I spent most of my time looking over my shoulder and jumping at every shadow.

Now we're standing outside my would-be murderer's house and despite the fact Jessica assured me she was trained in disarming a man and was, in fact, top of her class, I'm still not convinced.

We hear footsteps pounding down the stairs, and I tighten my grip around my scarf as I feel the wind bite.

The door opens and a pretty woman looks out with a curious smile.

"Can I help you? It's not religion is it, it's just that I'm busy wrapping presents and attempting to make mince pies? I'm afraid I have no time for religion at Christmas."

Jessica shakes her head. "I'm sure Jesus would be happy to hear that on his birthday."

"Oh." The woman's face drops. "It is religion, and now I've offended you. I didn't mean to do that. Let me donate something to your church to compensate."

"It's not religion." Jessica withdraws her warrant card and shows it to the woman whose face pales immediately, "I'm so sorry, I should have paid it, but I forgot and then the deadline passed, so I kind of thought it didn't matter anymore."

"It's not whatever you've forgotten to pay either," Jessica says with an irritated sigh, "but whatever it is, pay it immediately before you spend Christmas wrapping a lot more than presents in prison."

"Of course; my apologies. How can I help you?"

"We are here to see Samuel Masters." Jessica says curtly.

"Sam! What's he done?" Her eyes are wide as she peers anxiously down the street.

"We are not at liberty of discussing that with you, miss…"

"Carlotta, Sam's wife."

I stare at her in surprise because I never realised he was dating, let alone married. Even during the court case a few months ago, he came alone with only his parents for company. Jessica also seems surprised and I'm guessing this is news to her too. "His wife?"

Carlotta appears a little edgy. "I get it was a stupid idea but well, one drunken night in Vegas at the work's party made for a very memorable trip and we're working out a way to deal with it."

"I see." Jessica turns to me, and I glimpse a hint of amusement in her eyes that is quickly replaced with cool disinterest.

"Is he in?"

"Who, Sam?"

"Of course, Sam."

Jessica rolls her eyes as Carlotta shakes her head. "No, he went out to deliver some letters. I must say that was hours ago, but well, the lines in the post office are murder at this time of year. Shall I give him a message?"

"We'll wait."

Jessica nods towards the house and Carlotta shakes her head. "I'm not letting you in because you are strangers, and that ID could be fake. As I really don't have time to be murdered this Christmas, you'll have to wait in the coffee shop across the road where you'll notice him coming from a mile away because he's wearing an orange jacket."

She closes the door before we have time to argue and Jessica says through gritted teeth, "Great, now she'll be straight on the phone to him, and he'll be on the run by teatime."

She glares around angrily, but I'm relieved that I never came face to face with him and I wrap my arm around her shoulder and pull her close by my side.

"It was worth a shot, but to be honest, I couldn't care less anymore."

"What do you mean?" She appears confused as I shrug. "If it's Sam, he's harmless. I'll step-up security to make sure I keep my own personal detective happy, so she'll stay with me."

"Is that right?" The pleasure in her eyes makes me smile and for a moment, the chill of the icy wind doesn't even register. We are standing in the middle of one of the busiest streets in

London at Christmas and even the promise of snow can't chill the warmth that's spreading through my heart right now.

They say you know 'the one' when you first set eyes on them. I completely agree because when I first saw Jessica hailing me down as a taxi, I took one look, and I was done. Done living alone, done trying to be single, and done living in my own personal bubble. I wanted her then and I want her now and so I draw her close and whisper against her lips. "I love you, Jessica Taylor, and I want you to move in with me."

The way her eyes sparkle and the heat from her breath hovers between us, creating warmth on the frozen streets of London, makes it even more magical. The scent of chestnuts roasting from a vendor nearby mingles with the haunting tunes of a carol playing from an open window. The passers-by rush past with their shopping bags and loud conversation as they speak into their phones and the constant traffic splashing up rain puddles does nothing to dampen the spirits of the busy people who are caught up in the last-minute rush of the festive season.

"OK." Jessica's eyes are wide and her breathing shallow as she delivers me my finest gift and as we seal the deal with a long lingering kiss, the whistles and honks of horns mark the special moment when Robert and Jessica, against all the odds, found each other during the most magical Christmas ever.

CHAPTER 39

JESSICA

*I*t's as if I'm in a movie and I'm playing the starring role. Who knew that my first undercover job would deliver my soul mate?

There was never going to be a different answer when Robert asked me to move in with him. The thought of leaving has weighed heavily on my mind for a while, and now I don't have to. We will be an official couple and who knows, even married with our own family in a few years' time. The future is promising, and I'm giddy with excitement for once in my life and as I walk on air beside him back to the car, my head is awash with plans for our future. It feels so good knowing I'm not on my own anymore and I've never met a man who I'm as comfortable with.

We talk all the way home about our new life together and as we pull into his magnificent driveway, I stare in astonishment at the lit trees in the garden and the up-lighters trained on the house itself. Either side of the grand door are two potted bay trees that are lit with fairy lights and decorated with huge poinsettias providing added colour. The door itself is proudly holding a huge red poinsettia wreath, interspersed with pine and candles flicker in lanterns on every step, which cast a magical glow that lights our path up to the door.

"What's happening?"

I stare at Robert in disbelief, and he smiles, the pleasure evident in his eyes.

"I brought Christmas home with us."

"How?"

I stare in amazement at the festive scene and hug my arms around me in joyful excitement.

He takes my hand and says lightly, "Let's go inside, away from the cold."

As he opens the door, I blink in shock at the oversized Christmas tree standing proudly in the grand entrance hall. It's the most beautiful tree I have ever seen and is decorated with tasteful gold and silver decorations from the top to the pot it stands in. Underneath there are exquisitely wrapped gifts in gold and silver and I whisper, "Are they real?"

"Of course."

"But…" I blink in disbelief as he takes my hand and leads me into the living room where another tree reflects what appear to be thousands of sparkling fairy lights in the floor to ceiling window. This one is decorated in white and green and the corresponding gifts below are decorated with holly sprigs and feathers. Candles burn on every surface, casting a magical glow in the room, and a welcoming fire is roaring in the grate. It's almost as if we've interrupted a party or something because we certainly never left it this way this morning.

"Do you like it?" He appears anxious and I clap my hands and cry, "I love it."

Laughing, he drags me into the kitchen to admire another tree decorated in more natural colours with berries and cinnamon sticks. Once again, the gifts match below, and I shake my head in wonder. "I can't believe it. Are we expecting visitors or something?"

He nods. "I wondered if we could invite your family over. I can't wait to see the children's faces when they unwrap their presents."

"What presents?" I'm confused and he says with a smile, "They are hidden in one of the bedrooms. Come and see."

We head upstairs and as he opens the door with a flourish, I stare in shock at the contents of fairyland, wrapped in pink for Angelina and navy blue and silver for Brad.

Robert says with pride. "We could arrange them by the fireplace and say that Santa delivered them."

"Delivered what exactly?"

"Everything they wanted at Harvey's. I had a personal shopper follow us and she took note of everything they liked and here it is, all wrapped up and waiting for them."

"Robert…" A huge ache is growing in my heart as I prepare to burst his bubble. "It's very kind of you, but we can't possibly give them this number of gifts. It's obscene."

"What do you mean?"

He seems a little hurt and I let him down gently.

"It's just that Sally and Anton will have already organised Santa's gifts and we would overshadow that. Then they would expect the same every year and well, they just can't afford it, not to mention it's wrong. It's too much."

"Why, I can afford it?"

"That doesn't mean it's right."

I look around me and sigh. "As lovely as is, it's just a little, well, over the top."

"What do you mean?"

I smile and say softly, "I'm guessing you had this all done for you. Unless you're Buddy the Elf in disguise."

He chuckles and I press my lips to his and whisper, "You have a good heart, Robert Harvey, and I love you for it, but when I told you I wanted to get a tree and go carolling, I meant *us*. As a couple doing normal things. Building up to Christmas like everyone else and making memories to cherish that will become our traditions."

The doorbell ringing tears my focus away and Robert seems worried.

"Um, I'll get that. Stay here."

He heads off at speed, telling me something is up and as I follow him, I stare in shock as he opens the door, and a huge burst of Silent Night fills the house.

As I race to his side, he peers at me with a sheepish expression, and I gasp when I see what appears to be twenty people all dressed in bobble hats with thick winter scarfs tied around their necks. They are wearing huge boots on their feet and are wrapped in winter coats while holding lanterns on sticks. They sing so beautifully and as Robert's arm slips around me and pulls me close, he drops a light kiss on my cheek and whispers, "Happy Christmas, darling."

My eyes mist with unshed tears as I sing along to The Holly and The Ivy and then I take pity on them and invite everyone in. They crowd into the kitchen and serenade us while I heat up some mulled wine and offer them a tray of homemade mince pies that have miraculously appeared and it's as if the Christmas fairy has waved her magic wand and instantly delivered Christmas.

As evenings go, this one will live in my heart for eternity because I don't believe I've ever been as happy as I am now and despite the sheer decadence and waste of money, I know that Robert's heart was in the right place. He just needs me to manage his expectations and cap his enthusiasm in the future, and I'm more than happy to step up and bring him in line.

CHAPTER 40

ROBERT

*B*ringing Jessica home for good was my proudest moment and we will never forget last night. However, in the cold light of day, there is a lot to do and as Jessica compiles a checklist while dressed in her pyjamas, she looks so adorable as she sips her mug of coffee across the breakfast bar.

I finally feel at peace. I have never been so happy and as we make our plans, one event I have forgotten makes me groan when she mentions we are babysitting tomorrow night.

"What is it?"

She looks concerned, and I groan. "I promised my grandfather we would go to his usual Christmas Eve dinner. Do you think your sister will be back by seven?"

"They are leaving at six, so I doubt it." Jessica looks thoughtful.

"It's fine. I'll head over there, and you go to your family meal as usual. It's the only way around it."

"Or we could take them with us."

"To your grandparent's dinner."

She appears horrified, and I shrug. "Why not? They wouldn't mind."

"Are you sure about that? I mean, they are rather loud and can't be trusted to behave."

"Who, my grandparents?" I chuckle as she rolls her eyes and I shrug, "I hope they don't."

I picture the usual stuffy, formal dinner we endure and hope that Brad and Angelina shake it up a little."

"Run it by them first." Jessica says firmly. "Then, if they agree, we'll all go. If not, we stick to the plan."

"Have you heard from your parents?" I'm interested to know, and she pulls a face.

"Only a text telling me they get back on Christmas Eve but won't arrive home until past eleven. It's alright for them. They are going to Sally's for dinner and just have to show up."

"I can't wait to meet them."

She fixes me with an agonised glare. "Just promise me you won't judge me on my family. They do what they always want and expect the rest of us to fall in with their plans. Take Sally, for instance. She's dining with strangers, and I mean that in the usual sense of the word and who knows what she learned in prison? I'm not even sure if Anton still has a job after his flouting of the rules and I guess a lot is riding on their dinner with the people they burgled, for want of a better word."

"Did they ever find the ring?" I forgot to ask about that, and Jessica nods. "It turned out the owner of the house forgot she had sent it for repair a month ago. That's where it was the entire time and if it were me, I would be boiling over with rage, but Sally just waved it away with a relieved smile and said that it was all a misunderstanding, and they were really nice people as it happened, and she hopes they will all be great friends."

"When did she tell you this?"

"When we caught up the morning after, they, well, inter-rupted us."

"Oh yes." I laugh softly, enjoying the blush staining her cheeks and loving how she tries to disguise her embarrassment with a brisk, "Anyway, none of this solves the crime I was sent here for. I'm going to head over to Sam's house again today and see if I can flush him out. Has there been any other deliveries in the last couple of days?"

Nodding, I head to my study and return with three cards, and she lays them out on the marble breakfast bar.

"Interesting." She picks up one with a robin on the front and turns it over to read the back. Then she does the same with the other two and nods. "They are the same as the others. Obviously, a box purchased from a value retailer. The card is flimsy, and the picture quality is poor. Obviously, whoever it is, doesn't like wasting money."

"Or lives near a value retailer." I shrug. "You can't pass judgement on that alone."

"Probably not."

"It could be a member of staff that I fired. There is quite a list of those."

"We ruled them out because of my involvement. I'm guessing it's someone who is close to, or has access to your movements."

I sigh and look at my watch. "I should go. I have meetings and a store to run."

"Of course. We'll meet back here later and hopefully I'll have got somewhere by then."

I hate leaving her to go to work, and I wonder if this insatiable need I have developed will ever subside. It appears that I'm only happy if she is by my side and when she isn't, I'm wondering where she is and if she's thinking about me.

As I head to the door, I'm surprised when the bell rings and without thinking, I open it wide and stare in shock at the person waiting outside.

"Sam!" He nods and I note his hands are deep in his pockets, making me wonder irrationally if he has a gun in there.

"Hi, Robert."

Jessica instantly appears by my side and her eyes narrow as she takes in the scene and then she says briskly, "Samuel Masters?"

He appears a little shocked and I'm not sure if it's the pyjamas with unicorns on, the tousled hair, or the fierce look she's giving him.

"Yes. I'm sorry, have we met before?"

"Detective Constable Taylor, please come inside. I have some questions to ask you."

I almost feel sorry for Sam as he shuffles nervously into the hallway and stares around with wide eyes.

"Wow, is this your house, Robert?"

"It is." I feel bad about that because it's obvious it was paid for with the money he believes is also his and I say guiltily, "Come into the kitchen. There's some coffee on the go."

He follows us in and I'm strangely nervous and a little emotional as I see my once best friend again. I've never had friends until him and not any since, which is sad when I think about it.

Jessica pours him a coffee and points to the Christmas cards lined up on the breakfast bar.

"Do you recognise those cards, Sam?"

He glances at them with a bemused expression. "I'm sorry, I don't understand?"

"It's perfectly simple, Sam. Did you send Robert these cards?"

Sam looks startled. "No! I've never sent Robert a card, ever. In fact, I don't send anyone cards."

"Is that right?" Jessica starts pacing the room before saying angrily, "Then why did your wife tell us you were at the post office when we called yesterday – posting some cards?"

She raises her eyes and Sam visibly pales at her fierce expression.

"They weren't mine." He appears bemused. "I was helping Carlotta out. She was inundated with preparations, and I was pleased to get out for some fresh air."

"So, you never sent threatening cards to Robert. Is that what you're saying?"

"Of course not." To his credit, Sam seems shocked, and I'm surprised to discover I'm extremely happy about that.

"I see." Jessica catches my eye and I'm not sure if she believes him and Sam obviously notices it too because he sighs heavily and says with a groan. "Look, when I returned from the post office yesterday, Carlotta told me a detective and a man were asking about me. She described you and when I showed her your picture, she confirmed it was you, Robert."

He fixes me with an apologetic smile. "I was glad you called because I've been meaning to get in touch."

Jessica is listening carefully but is thankfully silent for once and he rakes his fingers through his hair and appears upset.

"For some time now, I've wanted to clear the air between us. The court case, well, it was never my idea, and I wanted you to hear that from me."

"What do you mean? Who else would it be?"

I'm confused, and he appears almost sorry for me when he speaks. "I'm sorry, man, it was your father."

Jessica gasps out loud and my head spins as I roll the words around my tongue. "My father?"

Sam nods. "He came to me and told me you were boasting that you had made billions off an idea that wasn't all your own. He made out you were greedy, manipulative, and selfish. He told you you had even stolen his job and had him thrown out of his own company because you weren't content with what you had. That you couldn't form your own ideas and just stole from others."

"My father said that." I can't process what I'm hearing, and Sam nods miserably.

"He told me we should teach you a lesson. That people like you should be made to pay for their sins and learn that not everything in life will go their way."

I'm in shock and Jessica moves beside me and rubs my back, whispering, "Are you ok, honey?"

I'm not sure that I am, and she says to Sam, "Why are you telling us this and how do we know you're telling the truth? This could be part of the revenge plan you have against Robert."

"I don't expect you to believe me." Sam says shamefaced. "I'm not proud of what I did but I was angry. I still am if I'm honest and not for the reasons you think, either."

"What are those reasons?" Jessica asks for me and Sam sighs. "I lost my best friend, and it hurt, man."

I stare at him with regret, and he bites his lip and says angrily, "I loved our friendship, and you tossed me away with no regard for my feelings. Even when I moved out, you couldn't care less. I thought we were better than that, but you obviously didn't care and just chased the money and the fame and left me behind. It wasn't about the money for me, it never was. I'm not a fool. I understand I was just a sounding board and never contributed to the actual idea, but to shut me out completely was harsh."

His words heap a huge dose of reality onto me, and the pain it brings doesn't make me feel good about myself.

Sam carries on. "I graduated and ended up with a great job as it happens. I'm stationed in Dubai for six months of the year and the rest of the time I spend here in London or travelling. Life is good except for one thing."

"What?" Jessica sounds intrigued and Sam says in a hollow voice, "I lost my best friend, and I've never replaced him."

I don't have any words because I'm not an emotional man

but after the past few days I've discovered emotion is a very good thing and so I surprise myself, as well as the two people standing before me when I say thickly, "I'm sorry, Sam."

"I don't understand." Sam is obviously confused and stepping forward, I extend my hand and say sincerely, "I wasn't a good friend, and you were the best, if not the only one, I ever had. I became obsessed with my idea and pushed you aside. I'll admit to that. I'm not proud of it, but I want you to know it was never about you or the money. I suppose I wanted to achieve something on my own. There was this burning need inside me to prove to my family I wasn't the waste of space they thought I was."

My childhood was spent trying to live up to the person my parents wanted me to be and to be the person my grandfather demanded and I am beginning to realise I carried around a huge burden of expectation, which I suppose is why my business became so important to me.

I stare at Sam earnestly and say with a catch to my voice, "I'm sorry. If I could rewind time, I would do everything differently. Can you forgive me?"

Sam appears as emotional as I am and as he nods, for some reason we forego the handshake and hug it out instead and for a man with no emotion, I suddenly discover I have rather a lot of it and as two friends reunite, I finally enjoy an inner peace that has been absent for a very long time.

CHAPTER 41

JESSICA

I don't cry — ever, but I'm crying now because seeing Robert with Sam is the most beautiful thing ever. Friends reunited and putting the past behind them. It's a moment I will never forget, and it strikes me that in interfering in Robert's life in the cruellest of ways, his father inadvertently did him the greatest favour. It brought us together and Robert reconnected with the only friend he ever had.

The largest part of me wants to believe that this was David's plan all along, but having met him, I doubt it. What kind of father sends threatening cards to his son and tries to deflect attention away from him by sending them to himself? It doesn't make sense, and I'm certain that Robert will have a few words to say to his conniving father.

I leave the two men to talk and head to my room to change. Now I no longer need to flush Sam out, it leaves me with a sinking feeling. *It's over.* The crime has been solved and I need to inform Detective Inspector Ranauld and head back to the filing.

My heart aches when I sense change coming. My job has always been the most important thing in my life, but since meeting Robert, my priorities changed. Maybe it's because we rushed into a relationship so quickly and are operating in a haze of lust. Perhaps spending more time together will reinforce the reason why I prefer to work, but I doubt it. There is something so right about our relationship and other people may not understand and think we are rushing into things. Perhaps we are, but we are both kindred spirits and this is not normal for either of us.

With a heavy heart, I shower and change into my usual skirt and blouse for work and shrug on my jacket before tying my hair back and slipping into my stilettos.

As I grab my bag, I know what I must do, but I'll miss spending so much time with the man I found in the most unexpected of ways. When I reach the kitchen, I hear laughter and find the two men deep in conversation over a coffee and as they glance up when I head into the room, I note the pained expression in Robert's eyes when he sees what I'm wearing.

"What's happening?"

He stands and I say in an even voice. "I need to report in to work. I'll let you know what's happening when I know."

He leans down and whispers urgently, "You don't have to. We can pretend the case isn't solved and string it out for a bit."

"No, Robert." I roll my eyes. "That's not how it works. I need to close the case and return to my job. That doesn't mean I'm not returning here this evening; it just means that life will change for us during the day."

"Not today, though. Please wait until after Christmas; give us that at least."

"I can't. I'm sorry."

I peer past him and note Sam watching us with curiosity and I wave my hand and say pleasantly, "It's good to meet you, Sam. I'm so happy things worked out. I'm sorry to dash off, but you know, work gets in the way."

He smiles and waves back with a pleasant, "It's good to meet you, Jessica."

As I make to leave, Robert grabs my arm and whispers, "This changes nothing. I love you and we will make this work."

"Of course we will." I press a light kiss on his lips and smile, "Just for the record, I love you right back. Now go and build bridges and let me do my job."

* * *

IT DOESN'T TAKE LONG to reach the station and as I walk into the familiar space, I catch the eye of the desk sergeant and smile, causing him to stare back, appearing a little stunned. "Morning detective." He mumbles respectfully, and I grin.

"It's a good one, don't you think?"

He shrugs. "If you say so. I've got three in the cells, a wife nagging me to pay her attention and kids who want stuff for Christmas that cost more than the national debt. I'll be happy when I get a day off and Christmas is over."

"Scrooge." I wink as I head off, noting how different things are already. I don't pass the time of day with anyone and always studiously ignored my colleagues. Now I've learned the value of communication and friendship, I am not going to revert to my old ways.

The office hasn't changed, and I can almost taste the tension and frayed nerves that run on alcohol and adrenalin. I thrived in this atmosphere. Loved the tension, using it to fuel my hunger for solving crime and bringing down the bad guys. But if I'm honest with myself, all I ever did was step aside and allow the more senior detectives to head out into the field and grab the glory. My hard work sent them there, but it was soon forgotten when they took the credit as the arresting officer.

I never got to speak at any trial. Never got the satisfaction of seeing the results of all my hard work through to the end and now I'm heading back as one of them. The person who ticked another one off our list and caused the stamp of 'case closed' to be imprinted on the paperwork.

Nobody looks up as I pass, and I don't blame them. I never engaged with them anyway, so I may as well be invisible, and it's all my fault.

As I knock on Detective Inspector Ranauld's door, his gruff 'Enter' wraps me in familiarity and makes me smile. It's as if I'm coming home, but now there's a huge part of me that wants to change the address.

"Jessica. Please tell me it's done and you're back."

"It's done and I'm *almost* back."

I take the seat opposite him, and he raises his eyes.

"Almost back. I don't understand."

"It's simple. I solved the case and am owed leave. Now is the perfect time to take it before I'm involved in another case."

"And you think that's your decision to make?"

He regards me with a blank expression, and I nod. "I do. You see, Inspector Ranauld, I've worked every Christmas since I started. I never complained and always volunteered to cover for everyone else. I rarely take holidays and am always one of the first in and one of the last to leave at night. By my reckoning I'm due several weeks of rest days owed and annual leave that has built up, so yes, I am taking this Christmas off and will return after the New Year because I've earned that right."

I regard him coolly and for a moment he just stares before a spark of admiration lights in his eyes and he grins.

"Agreed."

"So, I can…"

"Take the rest of the year off, detective. You earned it."

A warm sensation slides through me as I get what I want. I did it. I stood up for myself and presented the facts and didn't back down. Detective Inspector Ranauld is obviously impressed too because he reaches into his filing cabinet and pulls out the bottle of whiskey he reserves for closed cases and fills two glasses.

As he hands me a glass, it's as if he's handing me a medal because this is as good as it gets. Standard procedure for the arresting officer who gets to announce to our fearless leader that we have another case to file and marked closed.

He leans back in his seat and listens as I fill him in, and then shakes his head as the tale comes to an end.

"Families." He huffs. "It's always the families. What are they teaching them these days?"

"I'm certain that's the end of our involvement." I say thoughtfully. "I mean, Mr Harvey is unlikely to press charges, and I suppose it's up to them to sort things out between them."

"Good job, detective. At least it eases our burden a little."

He stares at me closely before remarking, "You've changed."

"Have I?"

I take another sip of my drink and he nods. "You are more self-assured and more relaxed than I've ever seen you before. It appears that life in the field suits you."

"It does." I take this moment as a sign to speak up and say a little harshly, "I don't want to return as the general dogsbody, Detective Inspector."

"I see." He raises his eyes and I nod. "I want to be given a chance. Sent on some proper cases and not just to research and watch the other detectives grab all the fun."

"Be careful what you wish for, Jessica." He leans forward and smiles.

"Think about what you want over Christmas. If you decide this is it, then I have no problem in granting your wish."

"Really." A warm sensation spreads through my soul as everything I wished for comes true. A job I love and worked so hard to get, coupled with a man I couldn't have wished for if I tried. I have it all, at least I think so and it's the most amazing feeling ever.

He smiles, a rare sight that causes me to openly stare and chuckles. "Now off you go, and I'll see you in the New Year. Have a great Christmas, Jessica, you've earned it and detective…"

"Yes, sir." He nods with respect. "Good job. I'm proud of you."

As I walk away, it's with a spring in my step and then I stop in the doorway and glance back.

"Happy Christmas everyone."

I giggle at the stunned expressions of my colleagues who raise their heads from their work and for the first time since I got this job, I receive genuine smiles and hear a chorus of 'Happy Christmas' back at me.

CHAPTER 42

ROBERT

CHRISTMAS EVE

*W*e collected Brad and Angelina from Sally and Anton's and it was great to see them both. They raced straight past Jessica and jumped into my arms, and it felt so good. It surprises me how much I love these kids already and I'm in no doubt I want many children of my own with the woman who I am fast learning I can't live without. The morning she was away from me was an anxious one and yet when she returned and told me she had arranged leave until the New Year, I exhaled with relief. Now we can enjoy Christmas because the store is now closed until Boxing Day at least and I have one precious day off to spend with the people I love.

My grandfather surprised me by agreeing to the children spending the evening with us and, as we stand at their door, I wonder how I'll react when I see my father.

I still can't believe he turned out to be the postman and

despite talking at length about it with Jessica, I'm still none the wiser.

It was good to reconnect with Sam and we have already arranged to meet up for a drink after Christmas and I hope it marks the beginning of a long and happy friendship.

The door opens and my grandmother peers out to the unusual scene of me holding a small child, with another one clinging onto my arm.

Jessica is quiet beside me, and I can tell she is nervous to meet them, and I'm surprised when a warm smile breaks out across my grandmother's face as she says happily, "Welcome. Come in, it's freezing out there."

We pile inside and in the general confusion of removing our hats and scarves, I hear Jessica instruct the children to take off their boots, so they don't mark the floor. Then she stands and smiles warmly at my grandmother, who is regarding her with curiosity.

"I'm Jessica. I'm pleased to meet you. Thank you so much for inviting us."

She pulls the children beside her and says, "This is Brad and his sister, Angelina, my niece and nephew."

My grandmother casts a glance in my direction and I am happy to note the approval in her eyes before turning her attention back to the newcomers.

"Welcome. I'm so happy to meet you. Especially on Christmas Eve. It's such a magical time of the year, isn't it?"

Brad nods and Angelina calls out, "Santa's coming tonight. Do you have a chimney?"

"We have five." My grandmother smiles and I note a gleam in her eye I'm not used to being there.

"Have you remembered to make Christmas cookies and set out reindeer food?"

Angelina chatters to her as if they've known each other for years and I'm aghast when she curls her little hand in my grandmother's and says in a high voice filled with excitement, "Shall we get the tray ready?"

My grandmother's cheeks flush with delight as Brad adds, "I could show you where he is now if you like. I have an App that tracks him."

"Goodness me." My grandmother exclaims. "Whatever next."

As we follow them inside, I steal a glance at Jessica, who appears worried. "I'm sorry. I can intervene if you like."

'No." Stopping, I pull her into my arms and nuzzle my lips against her neck. "It will be good for them and perhaps it will bring a little life to a place that hasn't seen much of that lately."

"There you are darlings."

We pull apart and watch my mother and father dusting their feet on the welcome mat, and I experience a sharp pang when I catch my father's eye. It may be my imagination, but I detect a touch of animosity directed my way, which saddens me.

Why does he hate me so much? I've always sensed it and now it's been confirmed I'm not certain how I'm going to deal with it.

"Where are my angels? I simply must have my fix of them today."

Mum looks at Jessica and smiles. "Hurry up and persuade Robert to marry you and give me as many grandchildren as you can. I am starved of youthful fun, starved, I say."

She brushes past us with a cursory kiss on my cheek as she heads off to enjoy some time with the children, leaving my father standing awkwardly beside us.

He clears his throat and says gruffly, "We should find your grandfather."

As we head into the parlour as they call it, Jessica whispers, "Are you going to tell him you know?"

"I'm not sure." I shrug. "This may not be the time or the

place, but I would like an explanation. He owes me that, at least."

She nods. "I agree. Just see how things pan out. You'll know when it's the right time."

As we head into the room, I watch my grandfather stand to greet us and note how frail he is looking now. For some reason, he appears smaller, thinner even which makes me sad. We've always had such a great relationship and I will miss him greatly if anything happens to him and as he smiles at Jessica with a twinkle in his eye, I instantly know he approves.

"Welcome, my dear, you must be the woman who achieves the impossible."

"I like to think so." She shakes his hand, smiling warmly, and he chuckles. "Any woman who can drag my grandson away from his desk earns my respect and my irritation in equal measures." He winks to deflect the bite from his words. "However, one thing's certain, there's a place for work and there's a place for family. It's getting the balance right. That's the difficult part."

My father snaps. "I don't think you ever did." He says with venom, which obviously irritates my grandfather.

"Maybe not, but it doesn't mean I don't want that for Robert."

"Yes, Robert." He rolls his eyes. "The golden boy. The one true heir who can do no wrong."

I can sense the tension building and note Jessica's startled expression and I know we need to have this out before the others make it in here.

"What's your problem?" I direct my comment to my father with a low growl.

"Excuse me."

"You heard me."

"What's going on?" My grandfather interrupts and I jerk my

thumb towards my father. "Ask him. He's the one who has a problem with me."

"I don't know…"

I hold up my hand and say with a snarl, "Don't pretend. I know it was you who urged Sam to sue me."

"Sam, the man who tried to claim part of your fortune?" My grandfather appears shocked and yet my father merely turns an interesting shade of red and yells, "So what if I did?"

"And sending me threatening Christmas cards, promising to kill me and Jessica. What was that all about?"

My grandfather explodes with a loud, "What the…"

My father turns on him.

"This is all your fault."

"My fault!" My grandfather bellows. "How do you work that one out?"

"Because of him." My father points at me. "You gave him everything. All your love, respect and time. It was always Robert this and Robert that. Robert, who could do no wrong and Robert is way better than you will ever be. I could do nothing right at all. Whatever I did, you found fault with. You beat me down and crushed my spirit and humiliated me when you chose him over me."

"Because you weren't good enough!" My grandfather roars, and Jessica gasps and steps back a little at the venom in his tone.

"No." My father laughs hollowly. "I was never good enough. You told me that often enough and I started to believe it myself. But Robert was. You were so proud when he made billions. You couldn't wait to rub it in my face and tell me how much better he was than me."

"But why did you try to bring me down?"

I speak up and even I detect the hurt in my voice. "You're my father. You are supposed to want the best for me, to have my back and support me. Not threaten me and bring me down. Why?"

"Because you had it easy." He turns, and for the first time I note the weariness in his eyes. "You never had to try. It was all so straightforward for you, and you were becoming exactly like him."

He nods towards his father. "You were cold, calculating, and manipulative. You never had any friends and the only one you ever did you turned your back on. You didn't work at friendships or relationships, just business. Just. Like. Him."

He sits on the sofa with his head in his hands and stutters. "I tried so hard to be different. I wanted respect and thought the best way to earn it was to be a generous employer. I wanted people to like me. To believe in me and want to do what was right — for me. I took my position at Harvey's, vowing to make a difference. To make it a happy place to work and it would thrive. And it did for a while and then the sales dipped, and expenses grew. I was out of my depth, but I didn't want to admit that to either of you."

I share a look with my grandfather, who appears dumbfounded, and I watch as his expression softens, and he moves to sit beside his son.

"I never knew." He sounds disappointed and I know it's because of his own part in this and so I join them, sitting on the other side of my father and without knowing what to do, I pat his back with compassion and say gently, "It must have been hard."

My father turns and for a moment just stares and I see the apology in his eyes as he whispers, "Can you forgive me, son? I only wanted to shake you up a bit and make you look at things differently."

I catch Jessica's eye and note the tears in them and with a smile of encouragement, she nods, making my decision an easy one.

"Of course I forgive you. You're my father and I understand you were desperate. It must have been hard and well, I admire you for owning up to it and hope we can move on and have a more open relationship from now on."

"Me too, son." My grandfather slaps my father on the back and says gruffly, "I never realised how hurt you were. It was never personal, only business, and I never connected the two. I'm sorry too."

A movement by the door makes us look up and we see my mother and grandmother staring in amazement as they are flanked by the two small children. It's obvious they listened to every word judging from the expressions on their faces and then Angelina shakes her head and glances at Jessica, saying in a sad voice, "Are they on the naughty list, Auntie Jess?"

For some reason, it lightens the mood instantly and the laughter that breaks out chases away the shadows and lets the light in.

It's as if a fresh breeze blows the cobwebs away and lightens the mood and as we all set about the business of celebrating Christmas Eve, I have a feeling that things will be very different next year, for all of us.

CHAPTER 43

JESSICA

I don't usually get nervous, but I am now. We are hovering on Sally's doorstep armed with gifts for the whole family, and I'm glad we could fit them all into one car.

When we woke this morning, I was astonished at the number of gifts Robert had arranged. I say arranged because it's doubtful he even knew what was in the tastefully wrapped boxes because apparently the personal shopper was following me, too.

Subsequently, I had to administer a hard lesson in gift giving and we were nearly late as we stopped by the local hospital to gift the children's presents to those who are in for an unhappier Christmas than our own. My gifts were given to the nurses on duty who were overcome by the generosity of a man who had never bothered with Christmas before.

It was good to do something amazing and Robert got as much pleasure from giving strangers their gifts, than he would giving them to me.

"Jess, Robert, come in."

Sally throws open the door and we follow her inside, loving the aroma of turkey and other culinary treats.

"Robert!"

The children yell at the top of their voices and drag him into the living room to show him their presents from Santa, and Sally rolls her eyes. "Thank God for reinforcements. They were up at five and haven't stopped since."

I follow her into the kitchen where Anton is heating up some mulled wine and, as he ladles some into a glass, he smiles. "Happy Christmas, sis-in-law."

"Back at you, bro-in-law."

We clink glasses and share a grin and Sally groans. "I hope Mum and Dad aren't late. They are so selfish. I mean, who disappears off on a cruise during the run up to Christmas? They were needed, and they were off gallivanting."

"I was here." I remind her and she nods, her eyes reflecting the gratitude she has expressed a thousand times already.

She lowers her voice and says playfully, "So, Robert Harvey, you dark horse. Trust you to snag yourself a billionaire; it's not fair."

"What are you saying?" Anton slings his arm around his wife and kisses her on the cheek.

"I wouldn't swap you for all the billionaires in the world, darling." She winks at me and shows me the crossed fingers beside her, and we burst out laughing as our parents stumble into the room and shout, "There they all are! Did you miss us?"

"Nanny, Grandpa!" Two exuberant children fall into the room, followed by a smiling Robert, and as he reaches my side, I grasp his hand and say proudly, "Mum, Dad, meet my boyfriend, Robert."

"Oh, my." Mum clasps her hand to her throat as if she's seen the Angel Gabriel and stares at me in wonder. "You have a boyfriend. My prayers have been answered."

Dad rolls his eyes and shakes Robert's hand. "I'm sure I'm meant to plague you with questions about your prospects and all that nonsense, but to be honest, we are that desperate for someone to take her off our hands, all I can say is thank you."

"Dad!" I can't help laughing and Sally interrupts, "You don't need to worry about Robert's prospects, Dad, just saying."

I nudge her sharply before frowning at my parents. "Anyway, what's all this about winning the lottery?"

"Oh yes." Mum looks at Dad with a sheepish expression.

"I understand we should have come clean and shared our prize fund, but well, it has always been on our bucket list, and we were in danger of never ticking it off. Easy come easy go, as they say, and you would only squander it."

She points to Sally before directing me a short, "And you would pay some more off your mortgage rather than having fun or treating yourself, so we decided to blow the lot – except for five thousand pounds!" She shrieks and dad nods, beaming from ear to ear. "Half each for both of you. Happy Christmas, girls."

"You mean…" Sally claps her hands. "We are all lottery winners."

Robert slips his hand in mine and whispers, "I won the jackpot with you, Jessica. Meeting you was worth all the millions in the world."

"Don't you mean billions?"

I whisper against his lips and as I pull them to mine, I whisper, "My Christmas billionaire. If anyone's lucky around here, I think you'll find it's me."

* * *

DINNER IS THE USUAL CHAOS, full of arguments between Sally and Anton over timings and portions and over excitement on the part of the children and my mother. As usual, dad tells crude jokes and gets admonished by my mother and Sally drinks too much and plugs in the disco ball, wrenching anyone nearby from their seats to dance to Abba in any available space.

The crackers make Angelina shield her ears and Brad continually asks for someone to play with him and then we all slump in front of their huge television to watch the King's speech.

Sally sits beside me, and as mum plays dolls with Angelina, she whispers, "I don't know how Robert managed to get that doll. They sold out ages ago and any subsequent deliveries resulted in an all-out war."

"He called the supplier, and they sent him one of their samples. It's not what you know…"

"It's who you know." She finishes for me and lowering her voice says with a giggle, "It was so much fun last night at the Musgroves."

"The people who had you arrested."

I roll my eyes and she nods, glancing around to check that nobody is listening. "They are so free spirited, you know, and I'm ashamed to say…"

I close my eyes and wish I could close my ears too, because I definitely don't want to hear this.

"We all went skinny dipping in their hot tub and drank margaritas. I haven't had so much fun in ages, and they told us we could come and stay anytime we like. They are out of the country for six months every year and told us it would put their mind to rest knowing someone was in the house. Imagine that Jess, we will be living like millionaires for six months of the year, and they're going to pay us."

"Pay you."

"Yes." Her face radiates excitement. "They will pay us five hundred pounds for every week we stay there."

"But I thought they were selling the house." I'm confused, and Sally shakes her head.

"They changed their mind. They like the fact they have some non-stuffy friends to hang with when they're here, and to be honest, I am definitely up for that."

She turns to chat to my dad, leaving me slightly bemused and mum comes and sits beside me as Robert takes his turn to play with Angelina.

"Robert seems nice."

"He is."

"Where did you meet him?"

"Work." She raises her eyes.

"So, he's a detective."

"Not really. I was sent to discover his stalker."

"His stalker!" she looks impressed. "You know, I had a stalker once."

"You did not." I scoff, and she grins. "I married him."

We burst out laughing as dad glances across and growls, "Turn the television up, all this chatting is distracting me from the storyline."

He stuffs his hand in the quality street tub and returns his attention to the screen and mum sighs. "Such a keeper."

She turns to me and smiles softly. "Seriously though, Jess, you need a man like Robert in your life. He will be good for you and distract your attention from working all the time. You never know, maybe we will be attending a wedding in the not-so-distant future. Your dad took out an insurance policy to help pay for it, so don't let money put you off naming the date."

"He did?" I'm actually impressed because my parents are the most frivolous people I know and she nods, looking proud. "Oh yes. He did the same for Sally and we never do one without the other. So, is Robert the one? He's certainly hand-some. What does he do for a living?"

"He's the CEO of Harvey's department store in London."

Mum blinks. "Wow. He has a good job. You should defi-nitely hang onto him."

As I notice Robert laugh at something Angelina says, I experience a warm feeling growing inside me as I picture my future filled with scenes just like this one. Yes, Robert is a keeper and for a woman whose idea of love was solving crimes, I've come a long way in a very short time.

EPILOGUE

ROBERT

I can't remember when I had such a perfect Christmas, and it's all down to the woman who's glancing nervously at the clock on the wall.

"Relax."

"I can't." She turns to stare at me, and my heart misses a beat because it does every time I do. She is perfect, and tonight is no exception.

She is wearing a long, dark green, satin dress that moves as if it has a life of its own and is complemented by an emerald choker that I had to pretend was a fake before she would accept it. It isn't, but she doesn't need to know that. Her blonde hair is piled high on top of her head, held in place with emerald grips and the heightened colour on her cheeks is due to the excitement she's feeling and the heat from the roaring fire she is standing in front of. She looks incredibly beautiful in the warm lighting and, as always, my feet carry me across the room to enable me to pull her into my arms.

"Are you happy?" I whisper as she gazes up at me from under her insanely long lashes and she nods, a small smile tugging at the corner of her lips. "I am. Are you?"

"Ecstatic."

I make to kiss her perfect lips and she says shyly, "You'll get lipstick on your face."

"Then I'll wash it off." Nothing can deter me from kissing her at every opportunity and that need hasn't changed since the moment I met her standing in the street wearing a tutu.

Kissing Jessica is my most favourite pastime, and only the ringing of the doorbell can stop me. We pull apart and she smiles shyly. "So, the moment of truth. Just so you know, the minute my mother sees inside this palace, she will move in. You will need to forcibly remove her, and I don't rate your chances."

"She would be most welcome."

"Liar." She grins. "At least Sally won't be jealous now she has a mansion of her own to play with."

"Yes, interesting proposition. I hope it works out for them."

Thinking of Sally and Anton and their 'arrangement' with the Musgroves, I hope it doesn't end in tears.

The doorbell rings and Jessica groans. "We should let them in."

"We should." Raising her hand to my lips, I kiss it gallantly and then we head off hand in hand to let our visitors in.

I'm so proud as we walk to meet them and glance around me with pleasure because the house has never looked more alive. The decorations my design team installed added heart to the home, and it is perfect in every way. Most of all, though, it's the woman beside me who has given this house a beating heart, and I have discovered that sharing my life is much more rewarding than working alone.

I know we have moved fast; some may say foolishly so, but

we both know this was meant to be. Our future is bright and I'm certain of that.

Jessica is due to return to the job she loves, and that's fine by me. She is fiercely independent and adores what she does, and only a fool would try to take that from her. One day we will marry and start a family of our own, but for now we need to discover one another first and I am in no hurry to share her.

We reach the door and Jessica takes a deep breath and grins. "We should let them in. Are you ready for chaos?"

"I can't wait."

She laughs softly which hits me straight in the heart and as she opens the door with a flourish, one by one our guests head in from the cold and fill the house with warmth, laughter, and life.

Everyone is invited, including both sets of parents, my grandparents, Sally, Anton, and the kids, of course. Sam and Carlotta and various business acquaintances and a select few members of staff, including my mysterious housekeeper, Mrs Grant and her family. It's good to see Sylvia, who informs me that her mother is doing well, and she will be back to work after the bank holiday.

As the party gets started and the staff I hired hand out canapés and drinks on silver platters, we mix with our guests and enjoy their company.

As the evening progresses, we move to the large ballroom that has never been used and dance the night away to the music the DJ I hired provides. The children are beside themselves with excitement as they explore every part of the mansion and they are closely followed by Jessica's mum.

Then as we stand on the terrace to watch the firework display at midnight, Jessica snuggles into her heavy coat and holds my hand and as the clock strikes midnight and announces the new year has arrived, I take her in my arms and whisper, "Happy New Year."

The smile on her face is brighter than any firework as she whispers, "Happy New Year."

As we kiss under the starry sky with the fireworks exploding all around us, surrounded by our close friends and family, nothing else matters. I cannot wait to see what the next year brings because surely nothing can be better than the one that is barely behind us. It brought me friends, family, and hope for the future but above everything it brought me love and as we mix with the people that mean the most to us, I thank God and a little bit of fairy dust for delivering me the best Christmas I've ever had.

* * *

If you liked My Christmas Billionaire, you may want to check out My Christmas Boyfriend.

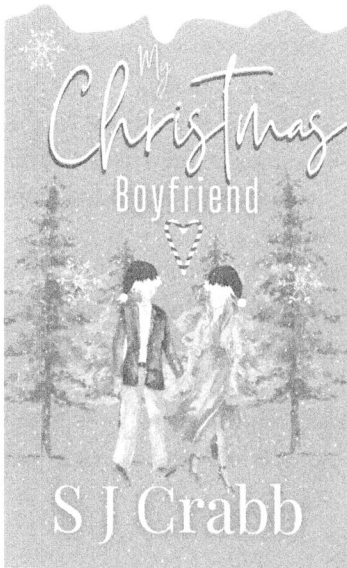

Thank you for reading My Christmas Billionaire.
If you liked it, I would love if you could leave me a review as I
must do all my own advertising.
This is the best way to encourage new readers and I appreciate
every review I can get. Please also recommend it to your
friends as word of mouth is the best form of advertising. It
won't take longer than two minutes of your time, as you only
need write one sentence if you want to.
Please note this book is written in UK English which can differ
from the US version.

*Have you checked out my website? Subscribe to keep updated with
any offers or new releases.*

sjcrabb.com

WHEN YOU VISIT MY WEBSITE, you may be surprised because I
don't just write Romantic comedy.

I also write under the pen names M J Hardy & Harper
Adams. I send out a monthly newsletter with details of all my
releases and any special offers but aside from that, you don't
hear from me very often.

If you like social media, please follow me on mine where I
am a lot more active and will always answer you if you reach
out to me.

Why not take a look and see for yourself and read Lily's
Lockdown, a little scene I wrote to remember the madness
when the world stopped and took a deep breath?

Lily's Lockdown

MORE BOOKS

More books by S J Crabb

sjcrabb.com

Printed in Great Britain
by Amazon

14925539R00154